How do you define hate?

"Do you know anything about skinheads?" She saw her parents exchange Meaningful Glances, the kind she and Dan were learning to perfect.

Patrick said, "They're losers."

Her dad laid his fork carefully across his plate. "They're anti."

"Anti-what?"

"Anti-Catholics," her mom said. "And anti-Jews, anti-blacks, anti-Asians, anti-Hispanics. They're hate-filled people."

"They shave their heads," Jonathan announced. "They're as bald as a bowling ball. They're Cone-heads."

"They're white supremacists." Mrs. Grady began brushing crumbs off the table into her hand, and Laurel noticed her lips pressed tight.

Laurel asked, "You mean plain old racists?"

"As usual," Patrick said, "you oversimplify. They're a socioeconomic violent counterculture gang menace."

"Talk English," said Jonathan.

Patrick summed up his case: "Scum."

ALSO BY LOIS RUBY

Miriam's Well

point

SKIN DEEP

LOIS RUBY

SCHOLASTIC INC.
New York Toronto London Auckland Sydney

For my top-of-the-mountain thinker
and invaluable consultant,
JEFF RUBY.
This story would be only skin deep
without you.

The excerpt from the song "Skin Deep" is used by permission of Karl Matthew Alvarez, artist; Karl Matthew Alvarez, mechanicals; and Alltudemic Music, publisher.

ISBN 0-590-47700-5

12 11 10 9 8 7 6 5 4 3 2 1 5 6 7 8 9/9 0 1/0

Printed in the U.S.A. 01

It's just skin deep
And that's as far as it goes
It's all done with mirrors
And painted smiles . . .
Reflection . . . obsession
The hype of style.

— All, from their album *Allroy for Prez*

It can hardly be argued that either students
or teachers shed their constitutional rights
to freedom of speech at the schoolhouse gate.

— Justice Abe Fortas

PROLOGUE

Dan changed.

Laurel could pinpoint exactly when that change started. It was at the Mall Crawl, the night the skinheads came. On the Saturday night closest to Halloween, the college town of Boulder, Colorado, goes completely berserk. Just about everyone shows up in costume at the outdoor Pearl Street Mall that streaks through the heart of town.

The point of the Mall Crawl is, anything goes and the more bizarre, the better. There are no prizes for Best Costume or Most Obnoxious Behavior, because picking one winner out of the ten thousand would start a riot. You could say the whole event is a riot looking for a spark to ignite it.

That year, if there had been a trophy for Most Outrageous, the skinheads would have run away with it. They ran away with Dan, didn't they? But all that came later, with his shaved head and steel-toed boots and tattoo, and that swastika on his shirt that nearly brought down Boulder High.

It happened step-by-step, and Laurel refused to

see it, because Dan was the first boy she'd ever loved. Oh, at first she caught a few subtle things, like when Dan started rolling his jeans up above his ankles and his T-shirt sleeves almost to his shoulders. He thought showing bones and biceps was *macho*, but she thought he looked like a reject from the road show of *Grease*.

And he'd get angry over the dumbest things, such as when the school janitor, who wasn't all *there*, would leave his mop pail in the middle of the hall. A thousand other kids walked around it and didn't even notice, but Dan acted as if old Mr. Bemis had left it there deliberately to trip him.

Even before those changes started showing up, Dan had come to school with a buzz cut, which made his ears stick out. Laurel's heart sank when she saw him, and she wanted to tell him how ridiculous he looked, but she reminded herself that only parents were supposed to get worked up over hair. What difference did it make, really?

Still, it was his hair — the hair on his legs — that she had noticed that last day in August, before her senior year started. Could a whole school year have passed so quickly, when so many of the days had seemed to crawl by in slow motion?

She and her brother Patrick and her friend Joy had gone to school to get their class schedules and locker assignments.

"Yes! I got into Japanese." Patrick waved his schedule around, and beads of sweat flew off his freckled nose. The school was too cheap to run air conditioning, of course.

Joy made a polite effort to look at the schedule, indulging Laurel's little brother, with whom she flirted outrageously. "Japanese *and* German? You specialize in Fascist languages?"

"Hey, I'm a man of the universe. Japanese is the language of commerce, and German is the language of philosophy."

"Yeah, but English is the language of Colorado, and it's required. I don't see it down on your schedule."

Patrick snapped the paper out of Joy's hand. "No! The computer. It does it to me every year." He bounded over to the counselor's office.

"We'll wait for you outside the office," Laurel said, because at least a cross-breeze made the hall bearable. And there *he* was, hunched over on a bench, filling in squares on his class schedule. He was using the eraser end of the pencil a lot; all Laurel could see were smudges. His elbows jutted into his knees, and that's when Laurel noticed his great legs, muscular and tan, covered with golden hair.

Joy poked her in the ribs. "A new guy," she mouthed. "Not a neuter, either. This one has testosterone."

Laurel looked him over more closely. His khaki shorts were neatly pressed, and he wore some generic T-shirt. She couldn't read it while his body was folded over that way. An incredible crop of blond hair just brushed his collar, even with his head bent forward. John Lennon glasses made the perfect statement on his face, which looked scrubbed and newly shaved.

Laurel pulled Joy behind a juice machine in the hall. "I swear, I'm going to faint. Is he a god, or just a California surfer?" They peeked around the machine, which churned and rattled. Good thing, or he'd have heard Laurel's heart pounding.

Joy whispered, "I'm trying really hard not to think of guys as meat, but he's a whole lot better-looking than your average carcass." They inched back out in full view, and he looked up.

Yanking off his glasses, he asked, "Who's better for English, Hodges or Molina? The only way I can make this schedule work out is to take either Hodges or Molina second hour."

"Hodges," Joy said.

"Definitely Molina," Laurel assured him, because that's who she had second hour.

He wrote Molina in the smudgy little box. "You guys are lucky. You got all this done last spring." A great voice, a radio DJ voice. "I'm new, so I've gotta settle for the dregs. I never actually planned to take statistics in my senior year."

"I'm in it, too," Laurel said, remembering that it was only offered sixth hour.

He looked straight at her, his grin showing perfect little cat teeth. "Then I guess stats is going to be okay."

Suddenly probability and standard deviation seemed like words from a Shakespearean love sonnet.

Coach O'Malley came barreling out of the office, all knobby-legged and flabby in his cutoff sweats and tank top. "You the new kid who's been looking for me?"

The gorgeous blond guy jumped to his feet. "Yes, sir. Dan Penner. I've been swimming for Coach Garrett in Limon."

The coach pumped his hand, then stepped back to inspect him. He spotted the glasses on the bench.

"Oh, those are just for reading. I can see fine in the water. I hardly ever wear them, anyway."

Laurel and Joy tried to listen while the two guys exchanged some cryptic information about times and distances. But a group of rowdy seniors had clustered around the lists posted on the office windows and had taken over the hall, according to their customary style.

"They musta accidentally left your name off the honor roll," Greg Gunther said, punching Mark Moore's arm.

"Yours, too," Mark replied. "Some coincidence." Then he noticed Laurel and Joy. "How was your summer?" He tossed the question their way, but didn't wait for a response, reminding them that they were lower-echelon seniors, from the slag heap.

Joy rolled her eyes, as Mark Moore and another guy, Doug Somebody, carried on the banter. "Hey, Doug, don't you think Greg's name's more likely to show up on the detention list, anyway?" to which Marlene Burke tossed her hair like a horse's tail and said, "We're seniors. We're beyond detention. I mean, I'm the head cheerleader, and you're a starter, Mark. There'd be hell to pay if they sent us to detention."

They wore their coolness like peacock feathers, and Laurel thought, It's going to be a long year. She and Joy were already plotting to nominate Bella Donna Prozac, Joy's ferret, as Homecoming queen against Marlene, who, of course, was the People's Candidate.

"Seniors rule, seniors rule," the Cool Ones chanted.

Laurel said, "Have you heard there's a new senior? Her name's Bella Donna Prozac. She's a tiny blond, with a classic long neck, and — what color eyes, Joy?"

"Pink."

"Right, dark eyes. She's really gorgeous, I hear."

"Cute little teeth," added Joy.

Marlene was already defending her territory. "Where's she from?"

"Denver."

"No, Barcelona," Joy sweetened the pot.

"With a name like Prozac? No, she's probably a Polack," Greg said.

"Who's he?" Mark asked, pointing to Dan Penner, and Marlene squinted to get a better look. She didn't have her contacts in, probably because she'd woken up too hung over to squeeze them onto her bloodshot eyeballs.

Meanwhile, Coach had also finished his scan of Dan Penner's body. Maybe he was hoping to spot fins and gills, but he apparently settled for the fact that there were no obvious gross defects, so he grudgingly said, "Well, come by tomorrow morning about six o'clock, and I'll see what you look like in the water."

"I'd like to see what he looks like in the water, too, in spandex," Joy whispered.

"I'll be there, sir."

"Me, too," Marlene said.

Coach O'Malley spun around and said, "No visitors, Miss Burke. Swimming's not a rah-rah sport."

"Hey, you're the coach," she said, with a broad, mocking gesture.

Coach rocked the swinging door nearly off its hinges and disappeared back into the office.

"Seniors rule," the Cool Ones chanted. "Right, Joy? Say it, Laurel, seniors rule!"

"Yeah, seniors drool."

The pack oozed on down the hall like a colony of amoebas. Dan watched the whole show with an above-it-all smirk that Laurel found very appealing.

And then, surprising herself, she moved closer to him and said, "A bunch of us are going to the lake tonight about five o'clock. It's really a reservoir. It's as close as we come to a lake, here. You want to come and meet some kids?"

"It'll be great," Joy added, nodding toward the motley crew. "None of *them* will be there."

Looking from one to the other, Dan handed Laurel — not Joy — the back of his class catalog. "Draw me a map."

And that was the beginning of the normal part, before the change began.

CHAPTER ONE

"Turn it down, Sudi!" Dan's mother shouted. "I can't even read the directions on this box, what with that music bouncing off the walls."

"There's no privacy in this dump," Sudi muttered, turning the volume button the wrong way.

"Sudi!"

Dan shot out of his room and turned the radio down.

"Okay, miss, then *you* fix dinner." Mrs. Penner slammed the rice box down on the stove.

"Why should I? I'm not even hungry. Anyway, I've got a test in world history tomorrow."

"You're the most self-centered creature."

"Truce," Dan yelled, waving a white dish towel. He squinted to read the instructions on the box — he had to start wearing his glasses more — and measured the rice and dumped it in a pot of water.

His mother snatched the measuring cup out of his hand. "Anybody know if Saralyn's coming home for dinner?"

"Of course she's not," Sudi said. "She lives at the law library."

"Wouldn't hurt if you studied now and then."

"Oh, Mother, come on. Saralyn has no life, none. She's got her nose in those dusty law books eighteen hours a day."

"She'll be somebody, someday."

"I know, I know, and I won't be anybody. Well, who cares about someday? This is *today*. I'm a college freshman. I'm supposed to be having a good time. Or would, if I lived in the dorm like normal people." They'd just moved to Boulder so Sudi and Saralyn could go to school without the expense of living away from home. But Sudi wanted action, freedom, space. Dan understood that, wanted the same things, and here they were, stuck in this puny duplex. As the only man in the house, he had his own room, but Sudi and Saralyn shared a room that was barely big enough for one, and their mother slept on the sofa in the living room and wedged her meager clothes into the girls' closet.

Sudi stared at the low ceiling. Dan followed her eyes. The walls and ceiling met at something less than ninety-degree angles. A cobweb hung from a corner. He'd have to attack it with a broom. Somehow he guessed things were different in Laurel's sprawling white colonial, not that he'd actually been inside the place in the month they'd been dating.

Sudi slammed her textbook shut. "This place is so — blue collar."

"Who do you think you are?" Mrs. Penner

raged. "I got news for you. Donald Trump's not looking at you for his next wife."

"I hate this duplex. When the old geezer next door turns over, my bed shakes."

"So? Dorms have thin walls."

"You just don't get it, Mother!"

"Right, I'm as dense as a melon, you've told me that plenty." She turned on the faucet full blast, and water splattered off the bowls in the sink and hit the walls in a spray that would probably leave blue spots on the cheap paint.

"Hey, girls, girls," Dan said, reaching for the water faucet. "Come on, Sudi, come study in my room." He was always the peacemaker, absorbing the blows from both sides of the war. Sudi strode triumphantly past their mother on her way to Dan's room, the only private place in the house, if you didn't count the bathroom. Dan forced up a smile for his mother, a smile without much warmth, but it was enough to tease her anger out a bit. He followed Sudi, swallowing his own anger. Lately, the peacemaker had come to realize that he didn't like either of the warring sides much.

But with Laurel, it was different. He felt this sort of *boing!* in his chest as he thought about the old sixties saying, make love, not war.

"What's the smirk for?" Sudi asked. She smoothed Dan's limp gray sheet and lay down with her brown hair hanging off the edge of the bed. "Oh, don't tell me. It's that Laurel person," Sudi said with a groan. "Even upside down I can see that sick puppy dog look in your eyes."

"What have you got against Laurel?" Dan's knees were stuck under the ridiculous desk he'd outgrown when he was eight or nine.

"Well, let's see." Sudi counted objections off on her fingers. "She's boring, she wears socks, her hair's as fuzzy as Aunt Jemima's, and she's Catholic. I thought we outgrew Catholic when Mom wised up."

"You've never even met Laurel."

"I don't have to. I can tell how she leads you around by a nose ring, like you're her show dog."

"She does not. Why don't you lay off of her for a while?"

"Oh, Dan, didn't I raise you to go after something more exciting than Mother Teresa? To hear you tell it, her halo never slips." Sudi spun around and hung her feet off the bed. She picked up a *Sports Illustrated* and held it at arm's length over her head. "How come it's always black guys on the cover?"

Dan didn't bother answering, because Laurel occupied his mind. He was recreating, for the thousandth time, that first evening at the lake.

He'd taken off his shirt and was down to his decent public swim trunks, not the Speedos he swam in with the team, and he'd heard Joy whisper, "Omigod, Laurel, he's as golden-brown as a Thanksgiving turkey!" "Shh!" Laurel had hissed, elbowing Joy, but he'd noticed that her eyes were on him, too, all through the evening.

He remembered her eyes especially on the other side of the campfire, at dusk. He liked the way her hair frizzed out in the humidity, in little fluffy spirals around her ears and forehead. She wore a two-piece suit, orange and red polka dots on black, and when the sun went down, she tied a huge orange beach towel around herself. The only thing showing were her shoulders and the black strap of the suit tied around her neck. Everything else was there, to imagine. He imagined.

Then, with fall only days away, there came a warning breeze. Some of the kids huddled closer to each other, and closer to the fire. He heard all their names — Karen and Mike and Joy and Erika and Dennis and Wayne and Pete — but he couldn't yet put names to faces. He watched Joy make a play for the guy he thought was Dennis, but Dennis (who could have been Pete) seemed more intrigued with the marshmallows on fire at the end of his coat hanger.

Dan pulled on his T-shirt and sweats, and that was a good excuse to hobble on one foot over to Laurel's side of the fire. He leaned down and said, "Want to go for a walk?"

Without a moment's pause, she jumped up and slid into her sandals.

Down the shore a bit, Dan said, "I just wanted to thank you for inviting me. Your friends are fun. I'll probably like them a lot if I ever get their names straight." Laurel just nodded, holding the towel fastened around her side. Should he take her hand? Would it cause the whole tent of the towel to collapse? Please?

He brushed her arm — just a hint — and she

tucked the flap of the towel in tighter and took his hand.

"Why me?" she asked. "Why not Joy, or Karen Gilardo?" She pointed vaguely down the beach. "Erika's got a great sense of humor." Meanwhile, she held his hand really tight.

The moon and sun were carrying on this contest for dominance, and the sun gave up in defeat and sank into the lake. The moon began her triumphant march into the darkening sky. Dan had never quite thought of the sun and moon this way before. The sun was just that thing that woke him and growled, "Get up, get to swim practice." The moon meant David Letterman. But, now . . .

"Isn't it an amazing moon?" Laurel asked. "Don't you love it when you wake up and it's daylight, but the moon's still out there?"

He nodded, pulling her close and brushing the damp coils away from her face. She closed her eyes, shuddering lightly, inviting his lips.

When they'd come up for air, he'd noticed that the moon was only a sliver, but brighter than he'd ever seen it before.

"Oh, God, listen to this, Dan." Sudi shot up on the bed. "They're actually having a Gay Olympics. I can't believe *Sports Illustrated* is giving it space. Dan? You're ignoring me."

"I'm thinking."

"About *her*, I'm sure. Oh well, at least I know you're not going to be trying out for the Gay Olympics swim team."

CHAPTER TWO

Like a well-trained animal act awaiting command, Laurel's family bowed their heads for the blessing before dinner. As soon as her dad said, "Amen," the act came to life. Laurel and her mother went to the kitchen to get the spaghetti and salad, and Patrick, the one who was specializing in Fascist languages, cornered the Parmesan. If it were possible to get hooked on grated cheese, Patrick would be the pilot case.

"No fair," Booser yelled. "He'll take it all." Booser's name was really Beau, but no one had called him that since his christening eight years earlier.

"Mom, do I hafta eat salad?" Jonathan asked.

"A small helping."

"No cucumbers," Jonathan bargained.

"Tomatoes, though."

"But nothing green."

"Except the lettuce," Mrs. Grady said patiently. "Patrick, pass the Parmesan to your brother."

"I'm not through with it, Dad." He heaved more onto his spaghetti mountain.

Gary, the middle child, asked to be excused.

"You've not eaten a bite," Mrs. Grady reminded him.

"But the Simpsons are on."

"Gary Everett Grady, sit! The Simpsons will have to get into their squalid little weekly adventure without you tonight." Mrs. Grady spooned some sauce over Kim's few straggly noodles and cut them into bite-sized pieces. "Ah-ah, finger out of nose," she scolded, and Kim yanked her finger away from her face.

Loc sat in his usual island of sullenness. He refused to eat spaghetti because it wasn't Vietnamese.

"That's all right, Loc," said Mr. Grady. "Neither is the peanut butter sandwich you may fix yourself in the kitchen. Those are the only two choices."

Loc reluctantly picked up his chopsticks.

"Pretend it's chop suey," said Gary.

"That's not even Chinese, let alone Vietnamese. So much for cultural integrity," Patrick said, tossing his spaghetti and sauce and cheese with two spoons. It was all turning orange and glutinous. If something crawled on to his plate, it would be stuck forever, like a mosquito in amber.

Why couldn't she have been an only child? Laurel wondered.

Sudi dropped the *Sports Illustrated* to the floor. "What are you reading?"

"Same book I've been struggling with since school started, *The Fixer*."

"What's it about?"

"Some Jewish guy in Russia. They turn him into a hero, or something. I can't get into it. It's on this college prep reading list."

Sudi flopped over onto her stomach. "Your bed really stinks, Danny."

"It's September. Must be time for my annual sheet change."

"Are all men gross, or is it just you? Of course, I wouldn't know, not having a father like normal people."

"You have a father," Dan said quietly.

"Oh, sure. A runaway. A lot of good he does us, up there in Maine."

"Mom's here."

"Mom's impossible. She definitely goes for the sympathy vote, soaking her poor rough knees. Really, you'd think she's the only woman who ever had to work."

"Give her a break, she's a gardener. She spends hours a day on her knees."

"Oh, she loves it. It's left over from her Catholic school days. Too bad she left the church. She'd have made a great nun."

"Yeah? Then where would we be?"

"Maybe we'd have turned up in Senegal, or Uzbekistan, as somebody else's fertilized eggs."

"You're outrageous, Sudi."

"Only when I'm at the top of my game."

* * *

Laurel looked around and wondered if other families were anything like her own: earthy, funny, squabbling, sprawling like an unweeded garden, growing helter-skelter, pumpkin vines tangled among radish sprouts. What a crop!

There was Patrick, looking like a redheaded transplant from Dublin. Jonathan and Gary were just a year apart — Irish twins, people called them — but they didn't look anything alike, or even anything like Patrick. Jonathan's blond hair was wispy and flyaway, and he was growing his second set of front teeth before the first fell out. Gary had teeth spaced across his mouth like a picket fence, as though some of Jonathan's leftovers could have fit into Gary's gaps. Beau, Booser, was supposed to have been the baby of the family, much to Laurel's disappointment when it seemed like she was doomed to live with four rascally brothers and no other girl on her side of the ledger.

Then came Kim. Laurel glanced over at the "new" baby, who was nearly five but still as small as a leprechaun. She *certainly* didn't look like the rest of them.

Kim's slanted eyes and brownish kinky hair were like road maps to her heritage. The story was that her birth mother, who was Laotian, had had a date with a black soldier. Kim's mother spoke about three words of English, and the soldier probably didn't have a flair for languages, either, so they never had a second date. By the time Kim was born, the soldier was who-knows-where?

Laurel's parents had been at a convention when

her mother, who was a nursing professor, had come upon Kim's crib during a tour of San Francisco City and County Hospital. Kim had been four, but was the size of a one-year-old, with eyes huge in her olive face, and her hair a snarly nest.

That night Laurel's mom had brought her dad back to see Kim. "I didn't say a word," she would tell people later, "but my eyes were frantically pleading with Bradley."

"But we have five children of our own," Mr. Grady had protested that first night at the hospital.

Then, as if Kim had gotten some stage cue, she'd turned her skinny body over and faced the wall, her bare buns sticking out. She had a tiny birthmark. Mr. Grady had run his thumb over that raised mark, and he was hooked.

"So," Laurel's parents would tell people who stared at their unusual family at the grocery store or at Boy Scout suppers, "that dropped the bread crumbs, and it was barely a hop, skip, and a jump until Loc found his way to us."

Now Laurel looked at Loc, who was small for eleven. He seemed so isolated from the rest of them, although he'd been in the family for months already. He just wasn't as lovable as the helpless little runt Kim had been. Loc had had two Vietnamese parents, but when he was nine, his mother had bled to death giving birth. The Catholic Social Services caseworker said that Loc's father must have been terrified at having five little ones to care for, because he broke the only window in their apartment and harvested a shard which he drove deep into his belly. All the little ones went to relatives who already had too many children, but Loc, the oldest, was left to shift for himself — until the Gradys found him.

Now he sulked over his spaghetti, sucking it in a strand at a time. "Vietnamese way," he said.

Dan's mother was subdued at dinner, as she always was after they'd had a fight. She spooned some mushy-looking reddish hamburger goop next to the rice on his plate. "Goulash," she said, which is what she called anything that didn't have distinguishable body parts.

Sudi picked at her dinner. "I'm sick of being poor."

"Even rich people don't eat roast beef every night," Mrs. Penner said. "They slum now and then."

Sudi waved her fork around, as if to encompass their entire kingdom. "Slumming is a way of life around here."

"I'm going to find a job at a Circle K or some fast-food joint," Dan announced, and his mother glanced up sharply.

"What about the swim team?"

"The final cuts aren't until Thursday and Friday."

"But when you make the team, you'll be swimming twice a day and half the weekend all through the fall. When would you have time to work?"

Or see Laurel. Or get some homework done, or finally read *The Fixer*. Or fill out college applications. Or take bike rides up into the Flatirons. Or even make friends with one or two guys. Since they'd moved to Boulder six weeks before, he'd had no guys to hang out with. Women, he was surrounded by women all the time.

"Well, don't look at me." Sudi put her hand flat over her heart. "I'm not getting a job in my freshman year. I'll flunk out, I swear. I can't handle school *and* work."

"I'll get a job, don't worry."

"Oh, Danny, it's not fair to you, either. If your father just forked out a few bucks now and then . . ." Mrs. Penner looked around the tiny kitchen of their duplex, with its elfin-size refrigerator and stove of olive-green 1970's vintage. "I could go back to hashing in a coffee shop on weekends."

"I'll find a job, okay? Let's just eat this — whatever it is."

"Goulash," his mother said.

Dan shoveled forkfuls into his mouth, wondering how people ever got ahead, ever got together enough money to pay their share of a pizza, or go to a rock concert, or get tattooed, or buy an old clunker. He felt around in his pocket, counting his money. Even a heap of junk on four tires had to cost more than . . . two dimes, a quarter, and half a dozen pennies.

Laurel's mother asked, "Honey, have you thought of inviting that boy over for dinner?"

"Dan?"

"Yes," said Dad. "The one who calls here forty times a day."

"Bradley, don't tease her."

Laurel blushed. It was a big source of pride in the family that Laurel finally had a boyfriend, but where would Dan fit into this unmanageable garden? She watched Booser wipe spaghetti sauce off his chin with the back of his hand, and Kim was picking her nose again. Jonathan sorted through the salad on his plate like a prospector with a pan of gold. Patrick's spaghetti was pasty enough that he could cut it in chunks. French bread crumbs circled Gary's chair, and Loc was making obscene sucking noises.

"Sure, invite him, Honey. We'll do lasagne," her mother said brightly.

Laurel pictured gooey cheese strings hanging from Booser's mouth, and flecks of prospected spinach dotting Jonathan's plate, and Loc attacking his lasagne with chopsticks. "Maybe at the turn of the century," she said, "when they've all grown up some."

"She's mean!" Gary yelled.

"She's a witch; burn her!" Jonathan added.

"Well, I don't know," their dad responded, "I sort of like her."

"That's because she's the oldest," Patrick muttered. "It's her birthright, and anyway, she's the only girl."

"Except me," Kim said.

"So naturally Laurel's your favorite," Patrick continued. "The rest of us are just cheap imitations."

"I love you all the same," Dad said. Loc looked

up, as though ready to challenge Dad. "All of you, the same."

The dinner ordeal was finally over, and Sudi flopped into a chair to watch *Married . . . With Children*. There was only a divider between the kitchen and living room, and Dan heard the obnoxious laugh track while he washed the dishes. He turned up the water. Damn, no more hot. Scummy family, he thought. Whose — his or the Bundys'? Well, weren't he and Sudi and Saralyn and their mom just like the Bundys, only unmarried . . . with children?

Mrs. Penner passed through the living room. "Sudi, help your brother with the dishes."

"After."

"Now!"

"On a commercial."

But by the time Dan stacked the last pot to dry on the dish rack, Sudi had gone out to ride her bike — probably so she could smoke without their mother having a fit — and Mrs. Penner was snoring in the rocking chair. Dan went to his room, which wouldn't have met government standards as a janitor's closet, to grab a jacket. He'd make another stab at finding a job.

He decided to make a circle of all the convenience stores and bike shops within a twenty-minute walk. He'd cover a few tonight, a few after school tomorrow, and by dinnertime, he'd have something in the bag, to get those women of his off his back.

* * *

Free-Wheeler was a bustling shop that smelled of rancid grease. The man in the back of the shop spun the disembodied wheel of a bike and said, "Haven't got it yet. You want something?"

"Yeah, a job," Dan said. "I'm good with bikes, and I can fix anything."

"Too late. We hired a couple of college guys before school started. Hungry guys. They're working for peanuts."

At a Circle K, the manager said, "Where were you last week when my split-shift man quit on me cold? I hired some African four, five days ago. I mean a real African. Kenyan, I think." He plunked down a handful of change for a girl who was already ripping into a Drumstick ice cream. "You're in the right place, wrong time, kid. I don't know about you, but that's the story of my life, eh? Matter-of-fact, back when I lived in Hogsbreath County . . ." Dan was out the door before he ever heard what state Hogsbreath County was in. Probably Arkansas.

Maybe it wasn't a good idea to job-hunt after dinner. Maybe this was something you had to do by sunlight. Maybe the day managers had more authority. Sure, that made sense. Maybe he'd go on home and see how long it took *The Fixer* to put him in a hypnotic state. Maybe he'd just go home and call Laurel, who always made him feel better when the rest of the world conspired to make him feel like leftover goulash.

CHAPTER THREE

The library was not a quiet place, because, as the librarian always said, "A bustling School Library Media Center is the workshop of the fertile mind grinding its way into production."

Laurel and Joy watched some new kid draw intricate designs on his arm with the precision of a draftsman. His bald head was beaded with perspiration. Laurel caught a glimpse of a swastika and several interlocked symbols that looked demonic. A girl in a wheelchair sat by the window, sketching the tree outside. A group of debaters argued in frantic whispers on the other side of a revolving rack. Two freshmen girls had a stack of books piled on the floor in front of them as they thumbed through the indexes. The librarian looked delighted to be the barker at this circus, trotting from tent to tent and chirping, "I love a bustling School Library Media Center!"

Patrick came in to renew six books for his research on Japanese culture. He stopped at the table where Laurel and Joy weren't having much luck studying. It was two away from the table which was automatically reserved for the Cool Ones.

"What?" Patrick asked. "Only three this hour? Are some of them actually in class?"

"Be careful, little brother, you're only a junior." They glanced over at the Cool Ones, Greg Gunther, Mark Moore, and Marlene Burke, who held court at their table as if it were their divine right as kings and queen. Joy and Laurel called the table The Slab.

The name always made Joy laugh. "Sounds like a place you'd do autopsies."

"It's tempting," Laurel said, and Patrick added, "And so handy if they ever drown in their own self-importance."

Laurel said, "I think it's time to start the campaign." With a withering look, she reminded Patrick that he was a lower classman and not a player in the drama, so he hung back and watched them operate. They left their books open and sauntered over to The Slab, where Greg was copying whole paragraphs from a book. Mark had found an easier method than taking all those sweaty notes. Hovering over an encyclopedia, he was surgically removing a paragraph with a razor blade.

Marlene scolded him. "At least you could have used an outdated encyclopedia, Mark. Where's your sense of responsibility?"

Patrick crept up behind Laurel. "Noblesse oblige," he muttered and was, as usual, ignored.

Laurel tapped Mark lightly on the shoulder, and he jumped and sliced meat. Now the encyclopedia page was dotted with royal blood. He stuck his finger in his mouth and muffled the obscenities.

"Oh, I'm so sorry," Laurel said, faking as much sincerity as she could muster.

"We just wondered if you'd seen her yet," Joy said.

"Who?" asked Greg, maintaining his perfect quarterback posture.

"Bella Donna Prozac," Joy announced proudly.

"A new girl? I haven't seen her," Marlene said, sounding rather smug, as if not seeing her meant she couldn't possibly exist. "Is she in any of your classes, Greg?"

"I'd have noticed a new chick. Have you seen her, Mark?"

Still sucking his finger, he said, "I don't know. What does she look like?"

Laurel could barely keep a straight face. "She's a fox." Well, didn't ferrets look sort of like foxes?

Joy casually said, "I hear she's already been nominated for Homecoming queen."

Greg, the shoo-in for king, was nodding hungrily, but Marlene was in a sweat.

"Someone new? She couldn't snag enough votes compared to — "

"Someone like you," Mark said. The finger was out of his mouth, and a bead of blood formed at its tip again.

"Oh, don't worry, Marlene," Joy assured her. "Bella Donna's cutesy little Spanish accent will really turn people off. It's practically like a bark, anyway. Don't you agree, Laurel?"

"No question."
"And what she wears!" Joy said. "Really! It's skintight. Everybody who sees her is just disgusted."
"She's really hairy, too, haven't you noticed?" Patrick couldn't resist the comment.
Joy was annoyed at the intrusion, but it gave her additional fodder. "Oh, yeah, just this mass of rich, reddish-blond hair. She really flaunts it. By the time Homecoming comes around, Bella Donna won't have a friend left in the school."
"And what a tail." Laurel summed it all up: "She's a real animal."
By now Greg was salivating, and Mark was checking his reflection in the dark wood of The Slab. "Introduce me," he commanded.
"Oh, you'll be the first," Laurel promised.

Dan left right after school, to get a head start on anybody else out job-hunting. He stopped in to pick up an application at the Corner Store closest to his house. The kid behind the counter wore a University of Colorado sweatshirt with a huge grinning buffalo on it.
"I'm looking for a job," Dan said. The guy didn't seem to get it. "Are they hiring here?" The clerk shrugged his shoulders and babbled something Dan couldn't decipher.
Dan pantomimed a pen scratching across a paper. "Job application?" The clerk smiled, obviously embarrassed by his slowness. "You don't speak any English?"

His face brightened. With considerable effort, he managed, "Paper or plastic?"

"Those my only choices? What do you speak, Spanish? Español? Italiano?" Dan signed words tumbling out of his mouth, and the guy seemed to understand.

"Farsi," he said.

"How the hell do you survive in college?" Again, the guy looked clueless. Dan pointed to the C.U. sweatshirt, poking the buffalo in the eye.

"Ah, engineering," the clerk said proudly.

"I think I'm in the twilight zone."

"Doo-doo-doo-doo, doo-doo-doo-doo," the clerk chanted, and Dan laughed. They must have had *Twilight Zone* reruns in Farsiland, or wherever it was the kid had just come off the boat from.

Well, no luck here, but there were a dozen other convenience stores around the campus. There must be somebody who spoke American English so he could at least finagle a job application.

But, after tromping from Corner Store to Quik Trip to Kwik Shop to Circle K, he discovered that every cash register was covered twenty-four hours a day, from now until the year 2000.

At the sixth one, a gentle little balding man, who had a desk of orange crates in the back of the store, told Dan, "I'm sorry, son, I'm only hiring WOG's."

"WOG's, sir?"

"Yeah, Worthy Oriental Gentlemen. They're the only ones who won't rob you blind. I'm afraid you're just too white."

A storm was moving in. Dan decided he'd tackle the fast-food restaurants tomorrow, but now he had to get a haircut. No question, he'd make the swim team. His times were consistently better than most of the guys', and Coach was already asking him about his afternoon class schedule. He was sure he'd be on the bus for the meet at Fairview next week. So he couldn't put off the regulation haircut any longer.

It was disheartening to watch the pile of summer's growth fall around him on the barber's floor. He tried not to look in the mirror as more and more head, and less and less hair, appeared. But when it was all over, he rather liked the familiar look of a serious athlete, a guy who knew his way through the water like a shark.

The next morning before school, he was waiting at Laurel's locker with the picture of Bella Donna Prozac.

Laurel saw him and dropped her books, just missing his foot. "Your hair! What happened?"

"Well, it's not like I was in an accident and it burned off or anything." He passed his hand over the bristly hedge. It was a satisfying feeling. "It's for swimming. Coach O'Malley's law. As soon as the season starts, I've gotta shave my legs, too."

"I hate it." She ran her hand up his neck, against the grain. Chills rippled through his back and shoulders, and that made him even madder. What did she think, that he grew his hair just for *her*?

She stepped back and saluted. "I hear the Marines are looking for a few good men, Sarge."

Then Joy came along. "My God, you've sold your soul to a barber. Well, it's your prerogative, as a white European male. Where's the picture?"

He pulled the five by seven out of a manila envelope.

Joy gushed, "Just look at her. She's everything we promised Greg and Marlene and Mark."

She was Tracy Maris, last year's queen of the annual James Dean Daze celebration in Limon. Dan felt a wave of pride that he'd once had a girlfriend that looked this good. Tracy Maris had liked his swim cut. She just didn't like *him* after a couple of months.

Laurel eyed Tracy suspiciously and opened the frame. She pulled out the photo and said, "I'll get a few dozen copies made and we'll put up posters all over school."

Joy fiddled with her hair, winding it into a knot that she pinned at the back of her head. A bristly tail poked over the top.

"What's the matter with *your* hair?" asked Dan.

"Nothing. I'm just putting it away. I'm late for my FemPower meeting."

"Yeah?"

"Well, I can't very well go to FemPower with hair streaming down my back like Lady Godiva, can I?" She pinned her hair back severely. "Those stray tendrils around my face make me look way too vulnerable."

Dan said, "It looks great on Bella Donna Prozac."

"Oh, sure, but she's supposed to be a sex object.

I'm more fully evolved." The knot popped loose, and Joy had to work it like stubborn dough. "Gorgeous hair can be such a curse," she moaned. "Well, I'm late."

After school, Dan hurried to the pool to check the roster for Fairview. No Dan Penner. He knocked on Coach O'Malley's window and was waved in.

"I know what you're here after, Penner," Coach said, spinning a Boulder High School baseball cap on his finger.

Dan clenched his fists. Two guys were drinking Cokes just outside the glass office, which might have been the only thing that stopped Dan from punching the coach.

"Look, bottom line is, we gotta go with what we gotta," Coach said.

"What does that mean?"

"You're a good swimmer, Penner, not champion quality, but more than passable. Problem is, I've got other guys as good as you who've paid their dues. Been working out with me to make varsity since their freshman year. Am I gonna cut them?"

"I've been working since freshman year, too, just not at this school."

"Well, and then, I've got the Uncle breathing down my neck. Principal says I've gotta save two spots for the my-norities. These days," Coach said with a chuckle, "every team's gotta look like the goddam United Nations."

"Why did you even let me try out? My times

have been great, my personal best."

"I'm telling you, Penner, talent's no problem. If you were named Washington or Ramiriz, you'd be in the water for me."

"It's not fair, Coach."

"Listen, you're good enough to make the Neptune team."

"Private swim club? Who's got the money?"

"Maybe you could work it out." Coach opened his desk and started pulling a letter out of an envelope. "I could call Coach Earhart over at Neptune. Want me to?"

"No, sir. What I want you to do is send Washington and Ramiriz over there."

Coach smiled and crumpled up the letter he was reading. "It's the times, Penner. Can you hit a tennis ball? *They* haven't discovered tennis yet."

Laurel waited for Dan outside the locker room. Why was it taking so long? Finally, he came out of the gym, and she couldn't read anything on his stony face.

"Well, are you going to be a prune?" He just slid past her without a word, so she ran ahead and walked backwards, facing him. "That was a joke, see? Shriveling up in the water like a prune?" Then it hit her. "No. He cut you from the team? Oh, Dan." She put her arms around him, but he shrugged her off.

"How could he cut me? He never let me on. It's no big deal." He strode toward the swinging doors to the main hall and didn't even hold the door for

Laurel. She stopped it before it slammed into her chest.

"What are you going to do now, Dan?"

"Live with it. Get a job."

They turned the corner to Dan's locker, but the route was blocked off by a folding fence, padlocked like a prison corridor. On the other side of the barricade, Mr. Bemis washed the floor with an obscenely thick gray mop.

"Hey, I've got to get to my locker," Dan said, almost in a growl.

The custodian flashed a mean grin. "Too late." His sparkling teeth were a contrast to his almost blue-black skin.

"Come on, man, I've got my homework in there."

"Four-fifteen this hall closes." He went on mopping, in a slow parody of industry, safe behind the locked barricade.

Dan spun around to Laurel. "Jesus Christ, they're everywhere," he shouted, his voice bounding off the walls of the cavernous corridor.

"Who, Dan? I don't understand."

"Don't you ever run out of questions? Get off my back, for once." He ran down the steps and out the side door of the school, leaving Laurel seesawing between rage and tears.

Sudi picked up the phone, and Dan waved wildly. "No, Dan isn't here," she said. "He's run off and joined a punk band. Don't panic, I'm just kidding. Yeah, I'll tell him." Sudi hung up. "It was

Goody Two-shoes, tugging at your leash."

"I don't want to talk to her, or anybody."

"No problem. Nobody else calls, anyway."

There was a light frost crunching under the wheels of his mother's rattly Jeep. Dan pulled into the parking lot of a Burger King that flashed a sign saying **HELP WANTED**. Inside, the counter girl shoved a bag of burgers at a kid in line and said to Dan, "The night manager doesn't work on Thursday nights. Come back tomorrow, but don't hold your breath."

The duty roster was full at all the McDonald's, and Mustard's Last Stand and The Sink were laying off help because this year's crop of college kids didn't seem to have much money left over for eating out. The more dignified sit-down places along Pearl Street only hired people with experience, but you couldn't get experience until you got a job.

At Arby's, Dan thought he'd finally struck it lucky. The manager asked him a few questions.

"What's your name? Penner? Are you from Yugoslavia or anything?"

"No, sir, just eastern Colorado."

The manager looked him over carefully, as though he were measuring him for a coffin. "Any handicaps?"

"No, sir, I'm strong and fit. I never get sick."

"Um-hmm. You on welfare?"

"No, but I really could use some money. That's why I need a job." Dan thought sure he was scoring major points. He pulled himself to his full height and thrust his hands in his pockets.

"Okay, son, I'll level with you. I'd like to give you a chance."

He was in!

"But this is an equal opportunity employer."

"That's all I ask for, equal opportunity."

The man sucked foam from an enormous plastic mug, while the counter attendant yelled back to the kitchen, "One reg beef!" Someone else, whose face was hidden, sliced meat into thin, pinkish-gray wafers. Dan heard a volcanic dishwasher hissing in the back of the kitchen. He could do any of those jobs.

"We're an affirmative action shop, son. Right now I'm overstocked with white, middle-class Yuppie types. Check back with me in a month or so, and we'll see how it goes."

Fury rising in his cheeks, Dan backed toward the door. "Do you know how many times I've heard this crap?"

The man looked up sharply.

"You think there's any place else in this world where it's a big disadvantage to be white? This is crazy!"

"Good luck, son," the man said quietly. "Now get out of here."

Dan drove around town and out into the country for an hour, maybe two. The tank was on empty, and he had no money to fill it up, so he went home. But he couldn't go into that claustrophobic duplex where his mother would be watching TV with hot compresses on her knees, and Sudi would be stomping around, mad at the world in general and their mother in particular. So he coaxed the car along on fumes and went to Laurel's house.

She was sitting on her porch. He could see she'd been crying, and he felt a pang of guilt. Men weren't supposed to make women cry; that's what his father used to say, while his mother would be in the back bedroom bawling her eyes out. She never cried after he left, though.

"I'm sorry," he began, tamping down his own anger. He felt a vein throb in his neck. "I shouldn't have taken it out on you."

"You're right, you shouldn't."

"I've just had a lot of disappointments this week."

"Life's tough for everyone. Bella Donna can't get her fill of rats and rabbits, either."

"Hey, it's our first fight in over a month. That's something to celebrate."

"What, our first fight, or the fact that we've had a month without one?"

He sat on the step below her, leaning against her legs. She was shivering; he felt her goose bumps. So he took off his jacket and hung it around her shoulders. It was way too cold to sit outside without a coat. His glasses felt cold in his shirt pocket. But he and Laurel sat out there anyway, barely speaking, until the night turned black. She played with his bristly hair, rubbed his neck, which felt so open. He missed the warmth of real hair that used to swing at the back of his neck.

He wanted to pull her over to the porch swing and be all over her, but he had to go slow. She was still hurting, he guessed, because if he knew anything, it was how women felt. But he also knew that no woman had a clue in the world about how he felt. Wasn't that what his father used to say? "She doesn't understand me, your mother. Women, I swear, they live off on another planet. They live in atmosphere we men can't hardly breathe in."

Finally, Laurel said, "I'm sorry, too, Danny. You must be really heartsick about the swim team."

"Hey, I'm over it already." Brave words. It was the job thing that was really stinging, anyway.

He felt her nod, as though she were trying to believe him.

They were quiet a good long while, until she said, "It's not too soon to start thinking about costumes for the Mall Crawl. It's just a few weeks until Halloween and we've got to have something really original."

"Could we go as Abbott and Costello? Antony and Cleopatra?"

She shook her head.

"Simon and Garfunkel? Green Eggs and Ham?"

"They've all been done a hundred times. Wait, you'll see, it's the craziest thing you've ever lived through." Laurel smiled sweetly and laced her fingers in his.

So, he didn't have the swim team or a job or a car or money, but he had Laurel. He wasn't about to tell her this, but she was a lot kinder and smarter than Tracy Maris could ever be. Right now he was sure he'd do anything in the world to make Laurel happy. She kissed the top of his head.

One of the few fair things about life was that hair grew back.

CHAPTER FOUR

It was October 29, Mall Crawl Night. By the time Laurel and Dan struggled out of the car in their bulky costumes, and walked about two miles to the Pearl Street Mall, the streets were like Calcutta, thick with hungry, thirsty, noisy people in funny clothes. Many were high on various known and unknown substances. There was the standard assortment of clowns, ghosts, witches, Draculas, Frankensteins, pirates, Marilyn Monroes, and ballerinas in drag. But five minutes in the throng, and Laurel and Dan knew that the only thing that really counted was a warped imagination.

Laurel yelled over her shoulder, "Don't let go of my hand, or we'll never find each other."

"It's not like there are too many people here dressed as a 3 Musketeers bar," Dan shouted back, but he hung on to her hand. They slid through the crowd, bumping and jostling jugglers, walking watermelons and bunches of grapes, assorted barnyard freaks, a half-dozen Marie Antoinettes, the

Grim Reaper, Jabba the Hutt, a tin woodsman looking very arthritic, three President Clintons, a Mad Hatter, a bottle of poison, a stunning variety of life-size condoms, and several thousand gawkers who hadn't bothered to dress up.

"Wish I'd been more original," Dan yelled as he bumped into another can of Coors.

"Brother!" The other can threw its arms around Dan, rumpling his label. "Sorry, I thought you were part of my six-pack." The can slipped back into the crowd.

Laurel yanked Dan into an alley off the mall. "Just to breathe a minute," Laurel explained. The sound of a hundred jam boxes and a dozen out-of-sync live bands was muted by the canyon of buildings. The narrow alley was a relief. It was cold enough that she could see her words in front of her, in thick puffs of air. It would have felt nice if Dan could have warmed her, but it wasn't easy for a candy bar to cuddle up to a can of beer, so she tucked her free hand into her wrapper.

At the end of the alley a crowd stood quietly facing some sort of spectacle that Laurel could only imagine. "Let's go see." She pulled Dan along. Ahead of them, spanning from building to building across the width of the alley, stretched a huge, home-painted banner, which read:

W O W!

Under the banner six scary male specimens stood on cable spools, evenly spaced across the alley. Their smooth faces grimly set, they sang a song Laurel had never heard before, low and solemn, as if they were in church:

> Put up a fence
> Close down the borders.
> They don't fit in
> In our new order.

They all had shaved heads, or hair as close to their scalps as the fuzz on a kiwi. Laurel thought she recognized a couple of them from school. They were poured into tight jeans rolled up above their ankles, and tucked-in T-shirts, except for one whose shirt was cut off about three inches above his navel. Most wore braces. Not orthodontic appliances; suspenders. A few had black jackets, but they mostly gave the impression that they were just too cool to be cold, even though it was freezing. They hulked with their feet spread, their boots planted firmly on the cable spools.

"Great costumes. Just look at them," Dan said. Laurel thought he was laughing at them, the way they sometimes poked each other and pointed behind the backs of punks with spiked purple hair and black lipstick and dog collars. "These guys have got a lot of style."

"If you like the gestapo," Laurel replied with a grim laugh.

Dan moved closer, and Laurel followed. The guy

with half a shirt stared at them, as if *they* looked funny. His shirt said SKREWDRIVER, and bragged about that rock band's world tour. Well, they'd never been to Colorado, so who cared? But what fascinated Laurel was what the guy had below the shirt. A garish tattoo of the American flag rippled across his belly in slashes of red and white. In place of the white stars on the midnight-blue square, there was a Confederate flag.

"Ouch, I'll bet that stung," Laurel muttered to Dan, who seemed locked in place, as if the Skrewdriver guy were hypnotizing Dan with his chant . . . "Put up a fence/Close down the borders./They don't fit in/In our new order. Put up a fence/Close down . . ." Dan's foot tapped in rhythm.

Of course, these guys weren't the only crazies around. The Mall Crawl brought out all the weirdos, perverts, iconoclasts, and miscellaneous misfits in Colorado. For instance, a fortyish man in a Superman costume, a man who really shouldn't have been wearing tights, passed out flyers that warned the whole crowd it was going to hell. He stood on a chair and shouted, "Drop to your knees, sinnahs, and let Jeez-uz into your craving hearts."

Not far away, a man with dusty black skin and dreadlocks made the Israeli national anthem, "Ha-Tikvah," resonate from a drum that looked like a wok.

Two C.U. football players in cheerleader drag did a cancan. They weren't wearing any underwear. The world's oldest and most leathery female hippie passed out plastic poppies with little tags on them that said NO NUKES and offered the home phone number of the director of the Nuclear Regulatory Board.

Dan barely noticed anything. He seemed transfixed by the guy with the flag tattoo, and Laurel was starting to feel uncomfortable. "Let's go eat."

"Wait." Dan moved forward and asked, "What's WOW! mean?"

"Wow, man, it's, like, Wow!"

Another one of the goons said, "You've heard of NOW?"

"You mean the National Organization for Women?" some girl shouted.

"Yeah. Well, we're WOW!"

A college sorority type said, "I don't get it."

"She doesn't get it! Tell her, K.C."

"Proudly, Scott. Okay, let's put it like this. We're antipollution."

"Environmentalists, yeah!" a bunch of kids yelled, because everyone's really into ecology in Colorado. But the sorority girl still looked puzzled.

The one they called K.C., who seemed to be the leader, crooked his finger and motioned for her to come closer.

If he'd signaled to Laurel, she'd have been much too inhibited to go up, but she sensed something magnetic about this K.C. person, and she instinctively moved forward a bit in the crowd.

Now the sorority girl's friends pushed her toward K.C., until she stepped up on the cable spool beside him, pretending to be embarrassed. Her dangly earrings bobbed, and her curly hair flew all over the place. She cracked gum.

K.C. yelled across the banner to the guy at the far end. "Okay, Dolby, tell these nice folks about WOW!" Somehow, the whole crowd fell silent.

The one named Dolby handed his end of the banner to another shaved-head guy and traded places with K.C., beside the girl. Dolby's T-shirt said JEWS AND FAGOTS RUN THE GOOD OLD U.S. OF A. He took the girl's hand and placed it over the word FAGOTS. "Nothing to worry about here," he assured her. She was dressed as a melodrama vamp, with a slinky dress and a feather boa. Dolby put his arm around her as if she were his little sister. "This is a white woman," he shouted. She giggled and strutted, her perky little chest just darting into the night. "A white woman. Now, see that ape over there? You want him messing with this white woman?" The crowd turned to look at the guy in the dreads. His drum was silent. "WOW! WHITE ON WHITE. We don't want nobody on this white woman but a white man, right?"

"Right," yelled a few drunken college students.

"That's not only racist, it's sexist!" someone else yelled.

"Hey, it's plain and simple antipollution," K.C. yelled back. "Case closed." With a flick of his arm, he ordered Dolby back to his post at the end of the banner.

Now K.C. spread his arms out, as if he were

offering a benediction. The crowd quieted again. He was practically whispering, and every word was clear. "Do you love your country? Don't answer. I know you do. So let me ask you another question." His voice began to rise. "Do you want to live in a country where fags cut your hair?"

Now the crowd stirred uneasily.

"Do you want to live under a Zionist Occupied Government, where Jews decide what school you can send your kids to?"

"You guys are full of it," someone shouted, and people began to pull away from the skinheads. After all, this was supposed to be a night for fun.

Something turned in Laurel's stomach. She felt a chill run through her, a sudden breeze off the Flatirons, or a cold slash of fear up her back, like a skunk's stripe. People just don't come out and say racist, hateful things in front of a whole crowd, not even in Boulder, where anyone was likely to say anything, no matter how outrageous. Private thoughts, private prejudices, she reminded herself. Wasn't that the American way?

She watched the Rastafarian gather up his drum and his money can.

"Where ya going?" K.C. shouted. The drummer froze in place, his steel drum a shield out in front of him. A group of Asian students made a circle around him, and for a minute, Laurel thought they were going to jump him.

"Hey," K.C. yelled over the crowd, "looks like the nigger needs Chinamen to protect him."

Then a swarm of cops appeared out of nowhere,

and somebody huddling in a doorway tuned up a trombone, and a monkey on a leash began to leap from one person's shoulder to another, lugging his master behind him, and the crowd quickly slid away from the WOW! banner.

Dan and Laurel melted back into the mob on Pearl Street. Outside the Moon–Sun Emporium, they spotted Joy by her distinctive costume. Joy was the executioner, and her date had no head. She led him, stumbling through the crowd, with her plastic axe slung over her shoulder.

"That is you, isn't it, Joy?" Laurel peered under the executioner's hood.

"It's me!" She waved her axe, and the headless one mumbled from under his cape, "Who's that, Joy?"

"Laurel and Dan."

"Who's under there?" asked Dan.

"Jack the Ripper, or Ted Bundy, or some sort of serial killer. Anyway, he got what he deserved," Joy said, chopping the air with her axe. People around her made a wide berth.

"I can't breathe in here," came the cape-voice.

"Oh, all right." Joy pulled the snaps on the black cape, and out popped a rumpled head. "Kyle, this is Dan Penner, and you met Laurel last year at the football game. Kyle's imported from Aurora," she said proudly, as if he were a valuable French art treasure.

Laurel said, "Dan and I were just going to get something to eat. It's way too crowded here. Dan?" He'd moved away from her and was standing on a large rock in the center of the mall, gazing back down the alley where the baldies, marching with their banner, were just coming onto the mall.

"Danny!" Laurel yanked him off the rock, and motioned with her head toward Joy and Kyle. He pulled his hand away, and immediately she wished she hadn't acted like a snarly wife. "Let's go over to Luigi's, want to?" she said more softly. "It's way off the mall, and nobody will be there tonight."

The four of them cut through parking lots and backyards and went into Luigi's through his kitchen entrance. No one was in the cramped dining room except two middle-aged couples crowded into a booth, loud and obnoxious and definitely not acting their age. Kyle picked the table farthest away from them.

Dan and Laurel each slipped out of their cumbersome costumes, since they had on jeans and sweatshirts underneath. Laurel pulled the rubber band off her hair and let the curly brown stuff just drop to her shoulders in its usual frizzy bush. Dan lifted her hair off her neck; a thrill/chill ran through her. *How much longer until we can be alone?*

The executioner and her victim, re-headed, stayed in character. Laurel noticed that Joy was a natural in her role. Her eyes, so much darker and more intense than Laurel's, needed no macabre makeup to give them a menacing look. What a way to think about your best friend since fourth grade. She'd always been scared of Joy just a little, she realized, then quickly dismissed the idea.

The menu was on the wall, and they decided

on a deep-dish, Chicago-style, black olive-and-hamburger, the largest one Luigi made, which was about the size of a trash can lid.

While they waited for their pizza, Joy said, "Okay, what's *the* weirdest thing you saw tonight at the Mall Crawl? Kyle, you go first, because you're from Aurora, which is like suburban vanilla land."

Kyle twiddled the ties on his cape. "I don't know. Maybe the girl who came as a lawn chair?"

"Oh, you can do better. Dan?"

"I'd have to say the two-headed aardvark. Every step they took, they clunked noses, or beaks, or whatever you call those things that suck up ants."

"Snouts, I think," Joy said. "Laurel?"

"I'm thinking."

"Okay, I'll go. I'd have to give the prize to Snow White and the Seven Dorks. Freud would have been impressed with such an imaginative variety of phallic symbols. Laurel, your turn."

"The weirdest thing I saw were those skinhead guys. They seemed so — "

"Sure of themselves," Dan said.

"Hostile," she corrected him.

The pizza came, delivered by someone whose acne was in a particularly ripe stage.

"Oh, please," Joy said, turning away, but the boy didn't notice. Kyle had no trouble stuffing his newly attached face. Dan finished a wedge of pizza in four or five bites, but the cheese was still too hot for Laurel to put to her lips.

"Yeah, we saw those guys, or at least I did," Joy

said. "Kyle was still getting *ahead*. I couldn't believe the one with the tattoo across his gut. The guy must be a lunatic to endure that much pain to make his belly colorful."

"Pretty brave," said Dan.

"Oh, Daniel, Daniel, where is your mind?" Joy asked.

Kyle said, "Those skinheads are really hot in Denver. They show up at every punk club and every concert, and they're always marching around looking like Hitler's cheerleaders."

"Well, they give me the shivers. Let's not talk about them." Laurel frowned and picked an olive off the pizza, but had no more appetite.

Joy ignored her, as she always did when she had a hotter audience. "Everybody wears those clunky Doc Martens, but I'm betting the boots those guys were wearing have steel toes. Don't you wonder where they get steel-toed boots? I mean, you don't just walk into Sears and ask for Nazi-type boots, do you?"

"Personally, I don't care." Laurel picked up the greasy bill and studied it intensely.

Dan said. "Their whole look is amazing."

"Their faces come with permanent sneers." Joy imitated the look perfectly.

"Very attractive," Laurel said. "Let's pay and get out of here." They started dividing up the bill, but all Dan could scare up was seventy-nine cents.

"Big spender," said Joy, while Kyle stared at the sad pile of coins in front of Dan and muttered, "You ate about twenty dollars worth."

"It's all I've got."

Laurel quickly made up the rest of their half of the bill and slid her hand into Dan's under the table.

Joy and Kyle decided to go back to the Mall Crawl, but Laurel whispered, "Let's go home, Danny." She didn't mean "home," exactly, because her house was always swarming with children and parents and toys and bikes and TV's and dogs and gerbils and unfinished projects.

The evening hadn't turned out the way Laurel expected, but later, parked in front of the house, things turned mellow again. Dan left her in the car for a second and magically produced a red rose from behind a shrub in Laurel's yard.

"Happy monthiversary," he whispered. "It's our second."

"Oh, Danny, you're so sweet."

"I love you, Laurel."

"Well, not really. You mean, you *like* me a lot."

"No."

"You don't like me at all?" she asked playfully.

"I mean I love you."

No guy had ever told her that, not that she didn't feel loved. She had wonderful parents, as parents go, and brothers, and a sister, grandparents, and a whole retinue of aunts, uncles, and cousins. Love was a bountiful crop in the Grady family. Rain or drought, it grew. The more it was harvested, the more it flourished. Laurel's mom had that printed on a Christmas card one year, then needlepointed it and hung it on their kitchen wall. But family love just wasn't the same as being loved by a boyfriend. That moment was maybe the happiest Laurel had ever felt.

And after they'd dispensed with the cooing words, there was a lot of "white-on-white" in the front seat of Dan's mother's Jeep, with the gear shift jutting up in awkward places.

By the time Dan walked her to the door — and her father had swung the door open to greet them — Laurel felt pulverized, her lips swollen, her cheeks raw from his bristly face, her clothes baggy and wrinkled, her fingers frozen celery sticks, her teeth sore after combat.

At the door, Laurel's father made a big exaggerated scene out of looking at his watch. "Have we forgotten about curfew, miss?"

"No, Dad."

"I'm sorry, Mr. Grady."

"I thought I saw the car drive up at least, oh, say, two hours ago?"

"Couldn't be," Laurel muttered.

"It's our monthiversary, sir."

"I see. Well, come in out of the cold. Your mother has some hot chocolate on the back of the stove for you. You, too, young man. Everyone else is long since asleep. So, tell me about this year's Mall Crawl, while your mother's out of earshot."

"We couldn't describe it, Dad," Laurel said, kissing his cheek. In the light, Dan was clearly battle-worn, with lipstick all over his face. Oh, God.

Her dad seemed amused. "Well, let's just sit

here and have a mug of chocolate, eh?"

"I really have to get home," Dan said. He shook her father's hand and quickly bolted for the front door.

When he was gone, her dad said, "That's a fine boy." He rubbed his glistening bald spot, which every morning he tried to weave his hair across. "Has a fine, thick head of hair. Awful short, though." Why was *hair* always such an issue with parents? "What do we know about his family? Catholic, by any chance?"

"I think they're members of a satanic cult. Either that, or they're Gypsy fortune-tellers."

"That's a relief," her father said. "I was afraid they were Protestants."

CHAPTER FIVE

Dan's mother was going out on her first date in six years. "His name is Mr. Carlotti," she explained, and Sudi asked, "What's he, eighty-seven?"

"No, about my age."

"What do you think, Danny, should we let her go? What if he has his way with her?"

"Mr. Carlotti is a gentleman," their mother huffed as she dabbed Evening in Cairo behind her ears.

Mr. Carlotti arrived on a motorcycle, and Dan stood at the curb, stunned as his mother flung her leg over the seat to straddle the Harley-Davidson, with her arms wrapped around the skinny middle of Mr. Carlotti.

Now Sudi and Dan sat on the cement slab of their back porch, eating baloney sandwiches for lunch. Obviously Sudi had made the sandwiches; there were slices of pickle and chopped olives and American cheese plastered on to the mayonnaise.

Sudi said, "Wasn't the Mall Crawl amazing last night?"

Dan pried a piece of bread glue off the roof of his mouth. "Sure beats the James Dean Daze in Limon."

"Did you see those skinheads?"

"Pretty impressive." Not like the Coke, which was lukewarm because no one had remembered to refill the ice trays.

"Impressive? I'm drooling down to my knees. The one with the flag on his gut? I'm definitely going out with him as soon as I meet him."

"They were kind of rough on that Rastafarian guy."

"Oh, it was just a lot of *macho* posturing. Besides, the guy in the dreads was pretty repulsive. When's the last time he washed that hair?"

"Probably the last time I washed my sheets."

"See what I mean? They'll be after you, next."

"Yeah, but I guess the Rasta had a right to play his drums — "

Sudi interrupted him. "The man's a druggie, for sure. He probably brings it in from Jamaica and sells it to junior high kids. Hey, get me a pair of those Docs for Christmas, okay?"

"Sure," Dan promised, though he didn't know how he was going to scrape together the money to get *himself* a pair. Now he rolled up his jeans just above the hairline, the way the skinhead guys wore theirs, and he tried to imagine how much better the black boots would look instead of these scuffed-up old junior-year Reeboks.

Laurel waited for Dan at his locker. It was seven-thirty, and they were going to hang the Bella Donna Prozac posters before the first bell rang and the halls clogged with kids. He wasn't a step into the building before she noticed the new rolled-up look, and she burst out laughing.

"What's the matter?"

"It's you!"

"This is the new retrograde look," Dan snarled.

"Um-hmn," she said. "I think my mom might have a poodle skirt I could pull out for Saturday night. Let's go to the hop."

"Let's get the stupid posters hung." He ignored her snide remark and opened the ladder. They had twenty posters to hang.

The rickety ladder bounced from leg to leg as Laurel reached up to tape the last Bella Donna Prozac poster above the cafeteria door. Dan helped her down and folded the ladder against the custodian's closet.

Laurel stepped back to admire her work. Of course, there were Homecoming queen posters all over the walls. The Lampoon Club had put up pictures of Tomboy Garrett, the Drag Queen Candidate, but Mr. Herrington made them take those posters down. Marlene Burke stared back at Laurel from just about every square foot of wall space, but her posters were in high-resolution black-and-white, which made her eyes look beady, and, well, ferret-like.

The Bella Donna posters were on bright lemon-yellow paper, and beneath each smiling picture of Limon's own Tracy Maris were the words:

BELLA DONNA PROZAC
The Uncommon Homecoming Queen
She's so gorgeous, it's not
"ferret all"
to the ordinary candidate.
VOTE FOR HER!!!

Once the posters were up, the whole school seemed to be talking about Bella Donna, but no one could actually remember meeting her. So, Joy and Laurel and Dan created a social life for the mysterious Ms. Prozac.

Laurel told people gathered at The Slab, "Bella Donna was at my party Saturday night. You must have seen her. She actually had on fur. Oh, that's right, you weren't there."

"Of course not," Marlene said, with a pout. "Melissa Pandowsky had a party at Briarwood. Most of *us* were there."

"Oh," Joy said, groaning lazily, "I couldn't have endured another deadly evening at Briarwood. It's so stuffy, with all those crystal chandeliers and those fraternity men waiters in tuxes. Bella Donna prefers more down and dirty parties, anyway. It's more like what she's used to in Barcelona."

"At the bullfights," Dan added.

Laurel admired that touch and built on it. "Isn't it cute the way she says 'Bar-*the*-lona,' just like a real Spaniard?"

Then Mark Moore said, "You know, she called me the other night."

"Bella Donna did?" Laurel squeezed Dan's hand. This was too good to be true!

"Asked me to the Homecoming dance, I mean, if she doesn't win. If she wins, I guess she belongs to the king, right?"

"Oh, what a nineties idea," Joy said dryly. "Like that poor Japanese princess nobody's heard from since 'ninety-three."

Dan said, "You're a lucky guy, Mark. Bella Donna doesn't call just anybody. I'd sell my blood plasma to get a date with her."

"Whereas I demand whole blood," Laurel retorted.

But now there was a problem. All the Homecoming king and queen candidates were to parade across the stage at an assembly the next day, so the voters could eyeball them lustily. It would not do to have Bella Donna led across the stage on a leash, her short little brown legs churning away, vulgarly sniffing after the odd rat that might come out of the woodwork.

"Think, THINK!" Joy had hissed in Dr. Millwood's class, when the afternoon announcements brought news of the fateful assembly.

And then Mark gave them the perfect alibi. "The only thing is, she said she was coming down with the flu or something. Wouldn't it be rotten luck if she lost Homecoming *and* missed the whole dance? I guess I'd have to dig up another date."

Gary was at soccer practice, and Booser was upstairs sleeping off his measles, so there were only seven of them at the dinner table when Laurel asked, "Do you know anything about skinheads?" She saw her parents exchange Meaningful Glances, the kind she and Dan were learning to perfect.

Patrick said, "They're losers."

Her dad laid his fork carefully across his plate. "They're anti."

"Anti-what?"

"Anti-Catholics," her mom said. "And anti-Jews, anti-blacks, anti-Asians, anti-Hispanics. They're hate-filled people."

"They shave their heads," Jonathan announced. "They're as bald as a bowling ball. They're Coneheads."

"They're white supremacists." Mrs. Grady began brushing crumbs off the table into her hand, and Laurel noticed her lips pressed tight.

Laurel asked, "You mean plain old racists?"

"As usual," Patrick said, "you oversimplify. They're a socioeconomic violent counterculture gang menace."

"Talk English," said Jonathan.

Patrick summed up his case: "Scum."

"What's your interest in them?" Mr. Grady asked.

"Oh, there were some skins down at the Mall

Crawl." She shouldn't have mentioned it; now they'd get hysterical.

"Laurel! I knew we shouldn't have let you go."

Patrick jumped in, to take the heat off Laurel. "These skins are really spooky. They get tattoos inside their lips."

"Gross!" yelled Jonathan. "I'm gonna lose my dinner."

"And those steel-toed boots? Guess why they wear them?"

"To look like Nazis," Mr. Grady said irritably. No one was eating anymore, except Kim, who clutched a wedge of potato like a knife. Loc tapped out a tune on his milk glass, using his chopsticks as drumsticks.

Patrick said, "They say a few good kicks to some black or Asian guy can do as much damage as brass knuckles or steel pipes, but hey, they don't have to worry about getting splashed with blood, see? These guys worry about AIDS, too."

"He said *blood* at the table," Jonathan whined. "It's against the rules," and he began a fake wretching.

Loc asked, "Why would these guys want to kick Asians?" A silence as heavy as fog hung over the table.

Finally, Mr. Grady explained, "Because they think only white people have a right to live in this country. They're dead wrong, of course."

Mrs. Grady said brightly, "So, who's ready for some banana pudding?"

"Am I Asian?" asked Kim.

"Only half," Loc replied. "Which half of you are they gonna kick? Oh, yeah, they hate your black half, too."

Kim began to wail. "You may be excused, Loc," Mr. Grady said sternly. "Rinse your plate and put it in the dishwasher and go to your room. I'll be up to talk after dessert."

Two of them found Dan at school, as if he had a sign on his back that said, "I'm ripe." Their names were Butcher and Baker.

"Yeah, and I'm the candlestick maker," Dan said.

The one named Butcher stuffed a crumpled paper into Dan's back pocket. "That's for reading when you're on the can," he said. "Call me if you got any questions." He grabbed Dan's forearm and wrote his phone number across the vein.

"Now you're like them Jews with numbers on their arms," said Baker, and the two of them hurried out the school's side door, before they got caught. Dan slid into his chair in stats just as the bell was ringing.

"Well, Penner, you just made it under the wire," Mr. Moreland said. "My chickadees, I want your problem sets right now. Pass them up before you have a chance to change any answers."

Dan glanced over at Laurel, then pulled the paper out of his pocket. The copy was fuzzy; he slipped his glasses on to read it better. It was a crude drawing of a hard hat type lifting his boot to stomp on a cringing boy with a huge Afro and grossly exaggerated lips. Under the picture were the words, LET'S KICK SOME BLACK ASS!!! WANT TO KNOW MORE? CALL ME, I'M FREE AND WHITE. (JEWS NEED NOT APPLY.)

Dan crumpled up the paper and stuffed it back in his pocket.

"Pop quiz, chickadees," said Mr. Moreland.

He *knew* he shouldn't have taken stats. He couldn't concentrate at all. The words *I'm free and white* kept going through his head, and nothing on the quiz made sense. He turned it in to Moreland, facedown. As soon as the bell rang, Dan darted out of class and down the hall. He sensed Laurel trying to catch up to him, but he kept going and cut seventh hour.

Once he was off campus, he took the picture out again and studied it more closely. Sick. Sickening. He ripped it to shreds and commended it to the blustery winds.

CHAPTER SIX

Bella Donna Prozac was not only Laurel and Joy's candidate, but she was also the Favorite Daughter of the FemPower Coalition. For days they'd marched all over the school protesting the Homecoming queen contest. "A woman is not an object! Beauty isn't where it's at!" their placards read. So, of course, they were one hundred percent in favor of putting up a ferret as Homecoming queen. And FemPower had inside women all over the school. It only took a hint of a suggestion from Joy, and the FP's were able to enroll Bella Donna Prozac in six classes and a study hall. Besides that, they gave her a 3.8 GPA and a full scholarship to Bryn Mawr.

Most important, the FP's saw that Bella Donna was in Dr. Millwood's seventh-hour political science class, because the ballots were to be counted in Mr. Herrington's office during sixth hour, and by seventh hour, he'd be sending for the winners to give them the big news privately. It was supposed to be a state secret, of course, until the right time.

Poor old Dr. Millwood had taught just a year or two too long. When the office proctor came in with a note, Dr. Millwood got a bit rattled. Pushing his glasses up from the tip of his nose, he studied the fresh new class list that had miraculously appeared on his desk.

"Bella? Are you here today?"

This is it! Laurel thought, and Joy clutched her arm.

"Bella Donna Pritzic?"

"Prozac, sir," Joy said.

"Ah, yes, Bella. Mr. Herrington wants to see you in his office."

Joy got up, pulling Laurel along with her. "Dr. Millwood, Bella's absent today. She has a strep infection."

"Oh, dear." He seemed confused, until Laurel explained, "We're her best friends. Would it be all right if we went to talk to Mr. Herrington?"

"Yes, yes, by all means." It was obvious that they were no more familiar to him than Bella Donna. They wrote their own passes, which he signed, and he waved them on.

And that's how they found out that Bella Donna Prozac was to be crowned queen at the Homecoming game on Friday night. And Greg Gunther was to be her king.

There was one convenience store that had given Dan a nibble of hope, and he checked back with the manager before meeting Laurel at the Homecoming game.

A sullen clerk, probably a C.U. student, tapped her nails on the counter while Dan waited for the manager to come out. "My shift's supposed to be over," she said, glaring at Dan.

Finally the manager appeared and recognized Dan. "I'm sorry, really. One of my students needed more hours. He's got to work a certain number of hours to keep his scholarship. Here he comes now. Don't say anything. We wouldn't want to embarrass him, right?"

Right, because he was about seven feet tall and as black as a cast iron skillet and had an arm like a ham. Dan felt the fury rise in his chest as the manager said, "Lerone, you've just got to try to get here on time from now on. Will ya try, son?"

Dan slammed the door so hard that the store windows rattled. It wasn't fair, wasn't even a level playing field. The whites slogged through the mud at the low end, and the blacks and foreigners claimed the high ground, right under the goal. When had things turned around for white guys?

"Where's Lover Boy?" Joy asked, ten minutes into the first quarter of the Homecoming game.

"I don't know." Laurel kept a spot on the bleacher for Dan. He should have been there way before the game started. But eying the FemPowers around her, it was probably better if Dan never found them.

Of course, FemPower considered football a degrading exhibition of masculine brawn, and they were trying to get a female kicker onto the team.

So far no luck, so the plan was to boycott the whole season until they could infiltrate the team. But that night, the whole FemPower Coalition showed up to see the Homecoming queen crowned.

People all around them yelled and cheered, while the FP's discussed their business: shaving vs. going naturally furry, and whether men were more afraid of women who'd had babies, or women who were virgins.

Laurel only half-listened as she scanned the crowd, head by head, looking for Dan. Maybe he'd been called over by a group of guys. Well, that was okay; he needed to spend some time with guys now and then. Or maybe he'd just decided not to come. He *had* been kind of unpredictable and moody lately.

Good question. When *had* things turned around for white guys? Didn't they used to be king of the hill? Now, it seemed like someone else had captured the flag. A white guy couldn't even get a stupid, minimum-wage job flipping hamburgers or selling Slurpees.

Dan walked away from his last hope for a job. His collar was pulled to his ears, and he wasn't even aware of the streets he was crossing. Then, somehow, he was home, but just as he started to open his front door, he stopped. His chest felt heavy, the way you feel when the dental hygienist lays the thirty-pound lead apron across you before taking X rays. Things were piling up on him. And inside that house, everything was piled up, too.

Sudi had her back to the window and didn't see him study the familiar jumble of their home. Papers were tossed on top of wobbling towers of books. Unpacked boxes were stacked to the ceiling behind the couch. The TV uneasily perched on its Styrofoam crate. Even their feelings, Dan thought, seemed packed down and stacked up in that dump. One morsel of anger, one hurt, one hurled accusation piled on top of another, and the stack never went down much. How much did it take to topple a stack?

The Prancing Panthers came out on the field, tooting and drumming out "Pinball Wizard" from the Who's *Tommy*. Tall overheads brightened the field, turning the mud yellow. Mr. Herrington took the mike, and his voice echoed off the canyon of the bleachers.

"Panthers, we're ahead twenty-one to six!"

"Yayyyyyy!" The crowd went wild.

"Panthers, shh, Panthers, this is a very special night, because tonight is the seventy-fifth annual Homecoming!" He was interrupted again by cheering, but quickly subdued the crowd. "In a minute, we'll have the traditional parade of king and queen candidates — oop — here they come now."

The band began playing a schmaltzy Strauss waltz, as the Homecoming marshal, Todd Evergreen, announced the candidates one by one. Laurel stood in the wings, Joy behind her, and behind Joy was a rustling box with three big airholes.

Laurel watched Marlene Burke's heels sink into

the mud. Each step was like lifting her foot out of molasses, but finally, all the beauties and studs lined up in the middle of the field. On a signal from the band teacher, they all did an about-face to bow to the visiting-team fans, then turned back to their adoring schoolmates.

"Hey, Panthers," Todd Evergreen said, "I guess you can see there's a king and two queens missing, if you count Tomboy Garrett." Just then the Drag Queen candidate trotted out onto the field, in sequins and furs, and was heartily cheered, until Mr. Herrington firmly escorted him/her back to the gate.

"So, uh," Todd continued, "it's my pleasure to announce this year's Homecoming royals" — big drum roll — "Greg Gunther and Bella Donna Prozac!"

Laurel saw Greg straighten his tie and look around for the babe he was to escort onto the field. Joy opened the box and wrapped a black-studded leash around Greg's wrist. Bella Donna made her appearance.

"What the — " Greg cried.

"This is Bella Donna Prozac," Laurel explained triumphantly. "Joy's pet ferret."

You could feel the expectation in the crowd as everyone waited for the king and queen to appear. Laurel shoved a stunned Greg onto the field. Beside him, Bella Donna stretched out her extremely long neck, nobly raised her head with her little black nose pointed in the air, and began her victory march on the other end of Greg's leash.

Some of the loser queens rushed forward to pet Bella Donna, obviously relieved that they hadn't lost to a bigger beauty. But ferrets are not user-friendly, and the wannabe queens had to pull back their fingers, or lose them.

Mr. Herrington apparently decided to let this caper go. He grabbed the mike and announced, "Ladies and gentlemen, it appears that Boulder High's Homecoming queen is some sort of animal. What is it?" he whispered to Joy.

"A ferret, sir."

"Yes, a ferret." He made great ceremony of crowning Greg and Bella Donna. Greg just looked silly, but Bella Donna let her crown slide down her long neck and over her front paws. She simply stretched out her body like a dachshund and stepped through the hoop of the crown. She came out of it with great dignity.

By now, fans on both sides, and all the football players, rushed on to the field, and Bella Donna was getting a bit nervous. Greg was trying to be a good sport, but he made a wide berth of his queen, as if he were afraid she'd use his leg as a fire hydrant.

The newspaper and TV cameras caught Bella Donna in her hour of glory.

Laurel yelled to Joy, "Right now, I think she could get elected governor of Colorado."

Laurel was probably spitting mad that he hadn't shown up at the game, Dan thought. He should go home and call her, leave a message at her house.

But he just couldn't bring himself to go inside his own house. He had a feeling that if he went in, he wouldn't be able to loosen his clothes fast enough to avoid suffocating.

He turned away from the house and walked to the Corner Store, where he'd started his job search so many days ago. Maybe the guy who spoke Farsi had learned three or four words of English by now.

There was only one car in the lot. Everyone else had the good sense to be at the Homecoming game, or at some college party, or back in their cozy little houses on this miserable night. The lone car in the parking lot was a rusted-out gold Buick sedan that hadn't seen a showroom floor in maybe ten years.

The bell over the door jingled as Dan went into the store. He thought he'd warm up a little, read a magazine, maybe buy a jawbreaker for a nickel and make it last half an hour. Odd, but the store seemed totally empty. A video game flashed its tempting come-on across the screen.

Then Dan heard something that chilled him to his gut: the clear sound of a fist thudding into human flesh. A groan burst from the victim, from deep within the belly.

Time to get out, for sure. And yet, Dan crept quietly toward the curtain at the back of the store. Under its hem he saw sneakers kicking at the cement floor, then landing with a sickening clunk until they lay still. Other shoes moved quickly, like a boxer in a ring. Two pairs, black. Boots.

Dan was no hero, but it was a weird night, and he felt enough rage to be dangerous. He whipped back the curtain. In a flash, he recognized K.C., the skinhead leader, just as the guy pulled a switch-blade out of his jeans. He grabbed Dan's right arm. His eyes were fiery as he held the blade at Dan's throat.

Jesus, I'm dead. Dan glanced at the pulverized foreign student in the grinning buffalo sweatshirt. *We're both dead.*

Then the other guy said, "Come on, K.C., let's ditch this hole."

"Without the dude? You got to be stupider than I give you credit for if you think we're leaving a witness behind."

Dan inched back from the knife, saying, "I don't care what happened. Just get the hell out. I'll cover for you."

"You believe him, Scott?"

"He looks like a straight white man."

"I don't trust him," K.C. said, twisting Dan's arm behind his back. It pulled at his shoulder, could snap out of joint. No problem, compared to the knife at Dan's throat, as close as a hair. If he swallowed too hard — and his throat was so dry, he desperately needed to swallow — he'd lose his Adam's apple.

"We're taking him with us," K.C. said, jerking Dan around until he lost his balance.

From the front of the store, Dan heard, "Yoohoo, anybody here?" Suddenly Dan was yanked and dragged out the back door. The last thing he remembered was the toe of a boot landing in his belly, and sour bile rising in his throat.

CHAPTER SEVEN

Joy and the FP's were taking Bella Donna out to celebrate after the game, though she'd be going in a box.

"Gee, I sure hope the Half-Moon Café serves prairie dogs," Joy said. "I'm sure Bella Donna's starved."

Laurel said, "She'll have to celebrate without me. I'm frozen and just want to take a hot bath and go to bed."

"Also see if Lover Boy has turned up?" Joy teased.

At home, Laurel should have made a straight path from the front door to the stairs, but she couldn't resist checking out the garble coming from the family room.

Patrick's red swirls spiked all over his head. He sat on the floor, record albums spread around him, dubbing *The White Album*. At high speed, the Beatles sounded like Theodore and Alvin Chipmunk.

Laurel wasn't excited about getting into a conversation with Mr. World's Authority, but she asked, "Where's everyone?"

"At the Donnellys', the only family brave enough to invite all of us."

"You didn't go there or to the game?"

"Are you kidding? And miss a chance to have this house all to myself? I ran through every room totally nude, belting out four hundred medieval Japanese war chants. Or, the one chant I know, four hundred times."

Laurel flipped through the cable directory. Maybe she'd watch a late movie after the hot bubble bath. "Did I get any calls?"

"You mean did Dan call? Not exactly."

"Exactly what, then?"

"Well, his mother called, looking for Dan. Wait, I've got to turn over the tape." The Chipmunks started up again. "Mama Penner was playing it close to the vest, you understand, but I figured out that Dan didn't exactly check in with the local authorities at his house. She said she hadn't heard from him since he left for school this morning."

Laurel frowned. "Now I'm worried. He's been acting really strange since he got cut from the swim team. And I know he's had no luck finding a job. It's been a blow to his ego."

"That fragile male ego," Patrick said, twisting his doughlike face into something wounded and pained.

"I know Dan's upset, but he wouldn't do anything crazy, would he?"

"Sure he would," Patrick assured her. "You got

your basic adolescent hormonal imbalance, added to a crushing blow to the male ego, and anything's possible."

"You forget, brother, Dan's way past puberty, whereas *you're* the adolescent."

Patrick straightened up his rounded shoulders, and his gangly arms folded at his sides like an orangutan's. "Yeah, but on me it looks good."

"Oh, pa-lease. I'm going to call and see if Dan's home yet. It's not like him."

Dan woke up, felt icy cold and sick to his stomach. It was dark around him, but an eerie glow came from the far end of the room — maybe a kerosene lamp? He thought he smelled kerosene, and also manure.

Where?

Beneath him he felt something hard and rubbery, like a tumbler's mat, and his head rested on a rocky pillow. He groped behind him, found that the pillow was his wooly jacket, rolled up. He sat up and put the jacket on, his hands brittle with cold.

Where? Why?

Something stirred near him, and suddenly he remembered. The skinheads! He scrambled to his feet, but could see nothing except a mound moving like a dark wave.

"Relax," a voice called out. "You're okay." There was a scratchy sound, a match being lit, and then K.C.'s mean face burst into view. He lit a fat candle that had melted into the dirt floor. Dan became aware of another mound covered with a horse blanket.

They were in a barn. The candlelight revealed rafters, a hayloft, some dilapidated tack. Was the other form a dead horse?

"Wake up, Scott," K.C. yelled, poking the horse blanket.

"Hunh? It's still dark."

"Yeah, but our guest is up. Be a gentleman, we got company."

"Forget it, I'm getting out of here," Dan said, not sure how.

"Right." K.C. threw one leg across Dan's lap, and it landed like falling timber.

Scott maneuvered his way into a sitting position, the horse blanket pulled up to his chin. His shiny head gleamed in the candlelight. He quickly reached for the stocking cap that had fallen off in his sleep.

"You guys are crazy," Dan said. How convincing could he sound, with his teeth chattering? His mouth tasted like the inside of a hot shoe. "You killed that guy in the store."

"Killed, no. Let's get the facts straight," K.C. said.

"He wasn't moving or breathing. Good imitation of dead, if you ask me."

"Hunh-uh," K.C. told Dan. "It's not our style to put their lights out one hundred percent."

"What percent were you going for?" Dan asked sarcastically.

"Oh, man, you're so quick to judge. Jesus, I

hope you're never on my jury. Want to know what happened?"

"Yeah, I've got a certain curiosity about the whole thing. I was there."

"Right. Here's the blow-by-blow."

Scott chuckled.

"Me and Scott, we go into the store to get some gum and see if the guy will sell us beer. Some of them do, you gotta check 'em out. So Scott plunks down a six-pack of Keystone, and the guy shakes his head. Doesn't say anything, just stands there like a dummy, shaking his greasy little Arab head."

"He didn't say anything, butthead, because he doesn't know a word of English," Dan said.

"Right, so me and Scott, we decide it's hopeless. Maybe we'll just have a little fun with the Paki."

"You call beating the crap out of him a little fun?"

"You're getting ahead of the story," Scott protested. "The good part's still coming." But he seemed as eager as Dan for the details, as if he had no idea what the good part would be.

"Scott, shut up and boil us some coffee."

Scott ambled to his feet and began rummaging through some provisions behind Dan. Out of the corner of his eye, Dan saw the horse blanket hung over Scott's shoulders, and he yanked it off.

"Hey!"

K.C. smiled his approval as Dan wrapped himself in the blanket. "Survival of the fittest, hey, Scotty?"

Dan asked, "Then what?"

"Well, me and Scott, we're wondering what's it like in the freezer, like how long until you feel like an Eskimo Pie? So Scott shoves aside all the pizzas and spick dinners and the Sara Lee crap, and he climbs on to the freezer shelf, like he's going to hibernate."

"I wasn't any colder than I am now," Scott muttered.

"Then the Arab goes ballistic. Comes running over and shouting at us in this foreign language."

"Farsi," Dan said.

"Yeah, whatever. Next thing I know, the bastard pulls a gun."

"That little wimpy engineer?"

"You can't trust these foreigners. They live like barbarians over there. Shoot anything that moves. Talk about the jungle! No wonder they all want to come over to America, where we've got laws and people don't go around overthrowing the government, and the Red, White, and Blue really means something." Dan saw that K.C.'s eyes had begun to glow in the candlelight, as if he were ignited, or close to tears. Then his voice turned hard.

"So we had to take care of him, or we'd both be dog food. We did it in the back of the store, discreetly, right?"

"I guess." It sounded plausible, if you didn't look at it too closely. "Maybe it would be easier to believe if I knew for sure that the guy was okay."

"Let's see if we made the morning news," K.C. boasted. He turned on a battery-operated boom box. Voices scrambled up and down the dial like coded messages. Finally, K.C. tuned in to a station, and Dan heard the announcer say, "News at the top of the hour. Time now is 6:57 on a cold and frosty, beautiful Colorado A.M." Then the smarmy voice of an Oxy10 commercial filled the barn, along with the smell of coffee. Hot coffee would sure feel good going down.

"We have an update on Hafiz Bihzad, the clerk assaulted in an apparent robbery at the Corner Store on Twenty-eighth and Arapahoe. Bihzad suffered severe lacerations on his face and neck and is in peril of losing one eye. According to a spokesperson for Boulder Community Hospital, the extent of Bihzad's internal injuries is unknown at this time, but he appears to be out of immediate danger. Police will be questioning him as soon as they find a Farsi interpreter."

K.C.'s laugh bounded off the rafters of the barn.

"There are no suspects at this point, but police are investigating reports of a person seen entering the store around midnight."

Dan's stomach clenched.

"He's described as a white male, six feet tall, sixteen to twenty years of age, light brown or dark blond hair, wearing blue jeans and a brown plaid wool jacket. Among the objects found near the location of the attack was a small penknife with a mother-of-pearl handle. It may have fallen from the pocket of either the suspect or the victim. Police are still attempting to identify the knife."

"Jesus, that's me!" Dan cried, but K.C. gently put his arm on Dan's to calm him.

"You're okay here," he said. "No one knows about this place except our own people."

Scott handed Dan a mug of muddy coffee, as if to console him. Funny how it had turned; *they* were the ones that beat up the guy, but the police were looking for *him*. He warmed his hands, watching the coffee grounds float at the top of the greasy mug.

"We're your friends, we'll take care of you," K.C. said, almost like a father chanting a lullaby. "What are friends for?"

Laurel was surprised to see how small Dan's house was. The front doors of the duplex units on Arapahoe Street hung side by side, like bathroom stalls. She knocked on Number One, and a wornout woman opened the door. "Mrs. Penner?" The woman nodded and stepped back for Laurel to go in.

The room was a jumble. It wasn't dirty, just crowded with things, a lot like the Gradys' attic. Furniture lined the walls, arm to leg; boxes towered behind the couch, and books, albums, magazines, and mail were stacked a foot deep on every surface. A bag of knitting lay sprawled in pastels at the foot of the easy chair.

"I'm half crazy with worry," Mrs. Penner said. She shuffled in oversize furry slippers, and Laurel followed her a few steps into the tiny kitchen. Distracted, Mrs. Penner poured her a mug of cocoa. It wasn't even warm to the touch.

"I knew he was upset about the swimming thing.

He told you about the swimming thing?"

"Yes, I guess he was really hurt by it."

"And then he's been having some runaround over a job. He wants to help us out." Mrs. Penner vaguely waved around the room. "He ate some Cheerios yesterday morning and left for school as usual, but here it is more than twenty-four hours later. Where does a guy go for the whole night? He doesn't really have any friends. You, of course."

"Maybe he came home and left, while you were asleep," Laurel asked hopefully. She forced herself to take a sip of the cocoa, through the layer of milk scum.

Mrs. Penner nodded. "Walls this thin, we'd have heard him. Besides, I sleep in the living room." Tears filled the corners of Mrs. Penner's dark eyes, ringed in day-old mascara.

Laurel felt like the mother here, the caretaker. "Did you call the police, Mrs. Penner? Maybe he had an accident." Her throat tightened at the image of Dan freezing in a ditch. Someone could have been out walking, mugged him, tossed him into a ravine. It was below zero last night.

"I'm afraid to call the police," Mrs. Penner whispered. "You haven't heard the morning news, I guess."

Then Laurel was sure something horrible had happened to Dan.

Mrs. Penner leaned over to the radio–tape player on the counter and rewound a short tape. "It's been on every half hour since four A.M. I taped it for Sudi when she wakes up. Didn't see any point in waking her, yet."

Laurel heard, "We have an update on Hafiz Bihzad, the clerk assaulted in an apparent robbery at the Corner Store on Twenty-eighth and Arapahoe. Bihzad suffered severe lacerations on his face and neck and is in peril of losing one eye. According to a spokesperson for Boulder Community Hospital, the extent of Bihzad's internal injuries is unknown at this time, but he appears to be out of immediate danger. Police will be questioning him as soon as they find a Farsi interpreter. There are no suspects at this point, but police are investigating reports of a person seen entering the store around midnight. He's described as a white male, six feet tall, sixteen to twenty years of age, light brown or dark blond hair, wearing blue jeans and a brown plaid wool jacket. Among the objects found near the location of the attack was a small penknife with a mother-of-pearl handle. It may have fallen from the pocket of either the suspect or the victim. Police are still attempting to identify the knife."

"That's Danny," Mrs. Penner said, twisting a napkin. "The pocket knife was his father's. He always had it with him."

CHAPTER EIGHT

"Once more, in case you're too dense to get it the first time, here's the plan." K.C. squatted beside Dan and outlined it all in a calm, clear way, like a guy presenting his campaign to a vanload of paint salesmen.

Scott refilled their coffee mugs. The coffee tasted like it had been drained from a truck axle, but it was hot.

"Forget it," Dan said, emboldened by the fact that he was finally starting to defrost.

"You are one stupid idiot," K.C. yelled, leaping to his feet.

"It'll never work," Dan said, even while he measured each plank of it against the logic of the world before the Paki was beat to a pulp. Maybe it would work. Maybe he had no other choice.

K.C. must have seen the flicker of hope ripple over Dan's face, because he softened and knelt on one knee beside Dan again. "Go over to the police station on Thirtieth and Baseline, over by the high-rise dorms. There's a nigger who mans the morning desk over there. Spread a little sweet butter over him. He'll believe anything, as long as he thinks it's coming from a nigger lover."

"Long as you don't use big words," Scott said, chuckling. "He ain't exactly Alfred Einstein."

"Just tell him what I said, every detail," K.C. barely whispered; his words came from his blazing eyes more than his throat.

"I don't know." Dan lay back down on the ground, with his hands propping up his head.

"Okay," K.C. said, crackling with irritation, and Dan was reminded that this wasn't a guy you wanted to see mad. He cantered back and forth in front of Dan, like a Doberman pacing his pen. "Just storm right into the police station and turn yourself in. Hell, sell us out while you're at it. All for some Paki fag who can't even speak the King's English? Some friend you turned out to be."

Friend? Who said they were friends? And yet, Dan could have tried to get away, could probably have outrun the two of them. What kept him there? It sure wasn't the hot cocoa around the crackling campfire, or sitting around singing bus-trip songs with these two hoods. What, then?

Dan got the feeling he wasn't responding fast enough. K.C. was starting to sizzle, and he yanked off his coat and the sweatshirt under it, sniffed it and tossed it aside. Dan's own body temperature dropped about twenty degrees as K.C. stood there, bare chested. The American flag rippled over his tight belly. He had rings through both his nipples and scar tracks from his right armpit to his waist.

What was he trying to do, show off how tough he was, how strong? Dan let himself believe he could take both these guys on, as long as nobody pulled a knife, but in the next second he knew it wasn't true.

Scott huddled near Dan, warming his hands on his coffee mug and frankly ogling K.C.'s chest.

"Can't you stare a little harder, you fag?" K.C. said with disgust.

"Not me! It's just that it's, like, twelve degrees in here."

"Yeah, he's worried those rings are going to freeze onto your skin, and some doctor will have to rip off your nipples."

K.C. laughed, flexing the rings like pasties. Then, his voice suddenly turned as hard as packed snow. "You don't have to be cold if you don't want to. You don't have to get caught if you don't want to." He ran his hand over the flat of his belly, his fingers covering only the red stripes of the flag. "You don't even have to be alive tomorrow."

"I'm supposed to take that as a big threat, right?" Dan reached for a bravado he didn't feel. But he'd been in fights, he knew the lingo, the rules, the fakes.

K.C. stood with his boots planted wide. His arms hung down, away from his body, as if he had a two-by-four stuck under each armpit. He towered over Dan, who watched him closely in case K.C. decided to spring. Dan met his eyes defiantly, vowed not to look away.

"There's a place here for you," K.C. said.

"Thanks. Me, I prefer having a real bed in a nice warm place where you don't pee icicles."

"You can't go home," K.C. said quietly, almost sadly. "Not 'til you get this thing cleared up. Otherwise, you can figure on having your mail forwarded to the county jail temporarily, until they send you up to the state prison for about forty years. Face it, you're their prime suspect, Sweetie Pie."

"Now who's the fag?" Scott joked.

"How many of you are there?" Dan asked, sizing up the opposition.

"Hundreds, thousands," Scott replied, making a worldwide circle with his stubby arms.

"We're everywhere. We're in Boulder, we're in Denver, we're clear across the U.S. of A. Don't you see the ABC news? We're real big in Germany."

A picture flashed through Dan's mind: crowds running helter-skelter; skinheaded kids in Nazi uniforms splattered with blood. Whose blood?

"We're a family, Dan. You can count on us anywhere, anytime. Brothers."

"Chicks, too," Scott added. "They do whatever we want? No problem."

"And they're going to be the mothers," K.C. said dreamily.

"Your bald-headed girlfriends are pregnant?"

K.C. ignored him. "The mothers of the pure . . . white . . . Aryan . . . race."

"After the revolution," Scott said.

K.C. continued, "We're going to get what's due

us, what we deserve, what the niggers" — he corrected himself, like a southern gentleman stumping for David Duke — "what the Negroes and Orientals and Jews and fags have cheated us out of." Suddenly, the dreamy glaze slid away from K.C.'s eyes, and he sprang from his coil. "They'll suck out your lifeblood and your manhood, Dan." He clutched Dan's shoulder in a steel grip. Dan felt the imprint of each finger dangerously close to his jugular. How much pressure would it take to cut off blood flow to his heart?

Gradually K.C. loosened the vise and whispered, "Do you know what I'm talking about?"

"Sure, sure," Dan said, massaging his shoulder.

"I'm talking about our white birthright, Dan. But we'll get it back, trust me, if we have to wipe every trace of their scum off the face of the earth."

"They're just mud people, anyway," Scott murmured.

"Don't be fooled," said K.C., boring his eyes into Dan's. "They're dangerous, all of them, because they want our jobs, our women, and our asses."

If K.C. hadn't looked so rabid, Dan would have burst out laughing. Nuts, these guys were as crazy as starved rats. Dan had to lighten it up. "Yeah, well, maybe . . . when you're getting your birthright, somebody will toss you a shirt, too." He crawled over and picked up K.C.'s sweatshirt, which was cold enough to take the swelling out of a football injury. He whipped it at K.C.'s chest.

K.C. slid the shirt over his head. The rings jangled. He knelt beside Dan again and pinned him with his eyes, those eyes that could make a snake shed its skin out of season. Scott instinctively backed out of the way.

"Talk to the nigger cop. I'll tell you exactly what to say."

Dan weighed it. He could probably live with it. Maybe *not* live without it. For a second he flashed on what Laurel would think. "Goody Two-shoes" Sudi called her. True, she was just a little too good and decent to be real, as though she'd never longed for anything in her life enough to hurt someone else to get it. Well, she'd just have to adjust, if she wanted to stay with Dan. Jesus, he had a mother, two sisters, two grandmothers, and a girlfriend. He glanced at K.C., who was grinning in his face, knowing that Dan was about to give in. K.C. sure wasn't a guy who'd let himself be whipped by a bunch of women, no way.

Dan nodded.

K.C. picked it up right away. He put his arm around Dan's shoulders. "Tomorrow morning's soon enough. We'll just hang out today. I've got a few things to show you, and I want you to meet some of the guys."

"Thanks," Dan said. Thanks for what, for setting him up to lie to the cops?

"Hey, what are friends for?" K.C. squeezed Dan's shoulder, an iron grip maybe just a little too hard to be entirely friendly. And then he outlined the plan for the third time, until Dan had every detail memorized.

CHAPTER NINE

Laurel didn't expect to fall asleep, since she was so worried about Dan, but suddenly she was deep into a dream about an oil refinery — the acrid smell stinging her nose, the flames tearing into the sky — when she heard something outside her window. She bolted up, her heart pounding. Silence. It must have been part of the dream.

Across the room, Kim was curled into an S under her covers. Her sleep sounds were like an untuned motor. Laurel slid back under her down comforter, still alert as a pointer. Then she heard a sharp ping and saw her window web out into a dozen hairline cracks. Someone was out there! Why hadn't she pulled the shade down? But she never did; her window looked out onto the trees of the backyard, and no one could see in, unless someone sat in the crotch of the giant elm.

Oh, God, someone *was* out there. Laurel opened her mouth to yell "Dad!" but was afraid she'd scare Kim too much. She decided to slide out of the bed onto the floor. Whoever was out there wouldn't see her crawling toward the door, even with Kim's stupid nightlight bombarding the room with brightness.

But another stone hit the window, and then Laurel was mad. Whoever it was had made his point. Enough; this was verging on harassment. She picked up a vanity chair and lunged across the room, ready to hurl it out the window at the intruder.

It was Dan's face she saw in the moonlight, laced by the few leaves still on the elm.

Laurel pulled her robe off the hook in the closet and raced downstairs and out the kitchen door. Dan had scrambled out of the elm and seemed like another bare and hulking winter tree.

"Are you crazy?" Laurel whispered. It was freezing. Why hadn't she taken a minute to get a coat? But none of this was rational.

"I have to talk to you." Dan put his arms around her, which helped a little, but she still shivered feverishly. He pulled his wool jacket off and draped it over her shoulders.

"You *are* crazy," Laurel said, giving the jacket back. "I don't dare take you in the house. My parents would slaughter me."

Dan nodded, trying to snap his jacket with fingers that must have been frozen and brittle. How long had he been out there? How long could someone survive outside at this temperature? A few hours, maybe, and if you hadn't frozen to death by then, you'd be delirious with hypothermia.

Laurel needed to get him to some shelter. There

was a shed in the backyard, padlocked for show, but the whole family knew the padlock didn't work. She gave it a good yank. Inside, the lawn mower, several bikes, and a snowblower just about filled the dark space. Shovels and hoes and a rake hung on the wall, like rotting carcasses. But at least they were protected from the lacy flakes that had begun floating in the black wind.

Huddled together for warmth, they leaned against the mountain bikes. Laurel said, "Tell me." She had a million questions. Had he been to the police? Where *had* he been for the last twenty-four hours? And — she didn't want to think it, yet it crept into her consciousness cruelly — had he actually beaten up that store clerk? She kept her questions to herself.

"I'm in trouble," Dan began.

"I was at your mother's. I heard the radio."

"I didn't do it."

Relief warmed her. Of course he didn't!

"But I know who did. And I've been out here all night trying to figure out what to do."

"There's no question. Just go to the police."

"Don't you think I'd have done that if it was so simple?" He took a step back, knocked a shovel off the wall. She heard it thud into the soft earth floor. It stood straight up like a soldier.

"Who did it?"

"I shouldn't tell you. What if they come after you?"

"Well, Dan, it looks like I'm already involved. I mean, you scared me to death by pelting my window, you *broke* my window. Now I'm standing out here with you, freezing in this shed, which, incidentally, if my father catches me, I'm grounded until I get married. I'm involved. Tell me." It was hard to make an impassioned speech when her voice was wobbling with cold, but apparently she'd convinced Dan, because she sensed him gathering his thoughts. He sighed and began his story.

"I went to the Corner Store, I don't remember why, maybe to get a bag of Fritos. I was upset last night, didn't want to go home. No one was in the store. I mean, no customers, and not even the kid behind the counter. Then I heard some sounds coming from the back. Somebody was getting hurt. There were these — thuds and growls."

"Oh, Danny." Laurel squeezed his hand.

"I should have run the other way, but no, I had to be some kind of hero. I crept up to the curtain that separated the front of the shop from the storeroom. The curtain didn't close all the way, and I saw two guys beating the crap out of the foreign kid who ran the store."

"What did they look like?"

"Huge, black guys, wild-eyed crackheads. Must have been looking for money, only the store clerk didn't know any English and probably didn't understand what the crackheads wanted."

"So you ran?"

"Yeah, but too late. One of them spotted me. I ran the half-block to the Jeep in my driveway, but now they know where I live."

"Daniel Penner, you've got to go to the police immediately."

"I can't. If they find me, I'm dead meat."

"The police will protect you."

"Where have you been living, in Mr. Rogers' Neighborhood? Crackheads don't exactly fight fair. They just drive by your house and fire automatic weapons through your windows."

"Come on, Dan, we're going inside and we're going to wake my father. He'll know what to do."

They stumbled through the shadowy equipment and back across the lawn. Ice crunched under Laurel's slippers.

Inside, she put the tea kettle on and went to wake her parents, while Dan called his mother and told her to come over.

Sitting around the safe fire in the Grady family room, warmed by spiced cider and Mr. Grady's reassuring words, Dan finally agreed to go to the police. Laurel's father offered to take him.

"We'll all go," Dan's mother said.

"No, I've got to do this alone."

"You know where the main station is downtown, son, don't you?"

"Yes, sir, I think so."

Mr. Grady gazed into his cider mug and finally said, "You'll need a lawyer." Laurel felt her heart lurch.

"Why? He didn't do anything," Dan's mother protested.

"There's no money for a lawyer," said Dan.

"You'll get a state-appointed lawyer," Mrs. Grady assured him. "Some fresh-faced young person still idealistic enough to give it his best shot."

"My daughter's a law student," said Dan's mother, with a mixture of pride and disapproval.

"*Her* best, perhaps," Mrs. Grady's voice was full of fake cheer as she clutched her husband's arm.

He said, "Let's wait until morning."

The clouds were breaking up, and the snow had stopped. Strips of purple and orange streaked across the sky. And then it seemed there was nothing to say until the sun came over the mountain and caused morning.

Laurel looked around at the unlikely gathering. Mrs. Penner sat primly on the love seat in raspberry sweat pants and a Colorado Rockies sweatshirt that came down over her hips; Danny's shirt? Laurel's mother gathered up the mugs and swept cookie crumbs off the coffee table onto a Lucite tray, her plaid quilted robe ballooning around her. Mr. Grady's thin blond hair stuck up around his head. He wore the navy sweats he usually slept in in the winter, and a white T-shirt. He looked solid and dependable, like an airline navigator is supposed to look. Captain, his friends called him, though he wasn't a real pilot. But with his sure bearing and his head held at alert, he seemed like someone who could organize the survivors of a plane crash, or go down with the ship if called upon.

Across the room, leaning against the TV, Dan seemed withdrawn, though he was the guest of honor at this weird party. Ten days, only ten days had passed since he'd given Laurel the red rose for their second monthiversary. They'd been through the whole Bella Donna Prozac campaign and Dan's bizarre fashion statement after they'd seen the skinheads. Now she wondered if he still loved her, or had too much happened, too fast? Was having your life threatened by vicious crackheads enough to stomp out any feelings except fear and the need to survive?

The three parents made small talk — mostly questions Laurel's mom asked and Dan's mom answered. What did a university gardener do in the winter time? What were her daughters studying? And wasn't Boulder a lovely place to settle?

Except for the crack houses, Laurel thought.

At a respectably decent hour, her father put in a call to the public defender's office, and an attorney agreed to meet Dan at ten o'clock at the police station.

"Not the one downtown," Laurel heard Dan say into the phone. "I'm going to the station at Thirtieth and Baseline."

There was a long silence, while the person on the other end of the line apparently tried to change Dan's mind, but Dan stood firm. "Thirtieth and Baseline," he said, as though it were an official proclamation, and finally the lawyer agreed.

Dan took his mother home so he could shower before the appointment. When they were gone, Laurel crawled back into bed, even though her room was flooded with morning sun. She listened to Kim's purring sounds, saw one small foot curled around the outside of the covers. She heard the furnace kick back on and felt the first blast of cold air before it heated up.

Those perfect two months were over. Something had changed.

She didn't know yet that the *something* was Dan, and that nothing would ever be the same again.

CHAPTER TEN

Dan thought he knew the way to their camp. If he kept going west on Canyon Boulevard, he'd come to Sunshine Canyon Creek, and it was in that area somewhere. The temperature sign on the bank said forty-two degrees — not bad for walking, though he knew the thin, selfish winter sun would be setting in about an hour, and he'd be a chunk of ice on the dark hike home.

At the corner of Sixth and Canyon, he considered turning back. K.C. and his buddies were major trouble. Dan had no business messing around with them. Bullies, they were. Bigots. Hell, fact is, they were freaks, with their shaved heads and nipple rings. And he'd even heard that some guys put rings through their balls. Sick!

The sun was slipping behind the *Daily Camera* building, and already the temperature was dropping. Dan pulled his knit cap down over his ears and thrust his head into the wind. He could make it to Sunshine Canyon Creek in fifteen minutes and wouldn't feel the cold at all if he picked up his pace.

Laurel waited with the motor running, her eye on the E of the fuel gauge. They'd probably make it home if she didn't have to waste too much gas waiting for Loc. Finally, after all the other students had cleared out of Catholic Social Services, Loc skulked toward the car, dangling his Vietnamese language book by its blue cover. He slipped into the car and seemed closed into his silence, as usual.

"Good class?" Laurel asked.

"Same as always." He hunched his feet up on the seat of the car. He could make a concise package of his body, its borders clear and impenetrable.

"Do you hate going to Vietnamese class, Loc?"

He flipped the workbook open and said something singsongy to her. He was probably cussing her out in Saigon street talk which he'd picked up from the other kids in the class who'd actually *lived* in Saigon. But he pretended to be reading from the day's lesson. Then he ripped a page out of the workbook and watched it float out the window until it was hurled against another car by a gust of wind.

Laurel sighed. How long would it be until Loc felt at home with them? Kim was already one of them. Everyone adored her, except for Loc, who made a point of loving no one. Maybe he ought to spend some time with Dan, thought Laurel. Two guys who'd lost their fathers — they had something in common. Like Loc, Dan kept a reservoir of anger banked inside of him. It spilled out occasionally, and instead of evoking sympathy in Laurel, it made her angry. Didn't Loc play her the same way? She was usually mad at him; everyone was.

"Loc, stop rolling the window up and down!"

"Air," he gasped, hanging his head out the window.

She resigned herself to blasts of cold air and decided to take a different approach. "You know that boy Dan I've been going out with?"

"Yeah, the creep."

She jerked to a stop when the light changed. Why did Loc always have to turn everything into a battle? "Why don't you come with us to a movie some time? I think you'd like Danny. He's a lot like you."

To her surprise, Loc shrugged and said, "I don't care," which, for him, was an enthusiastic response. He raked his fingers through his hair and turned his bare forehead to the cold night.

Something glowed red in the dim light of the barn, and it took Dan a few seconds to figure out that they'd gotten a space heater and jerry-rigged a couple of connecting extension cords into the light fixture that swayed in the rafters. K.C. and three other people Dan didn't recognize sat around the heater as if it were a roaring campfire. Dan stood tentatively at the door until K.C. spotted him.

"Hey, the big hero," K.C. said, jumping to his feet. Again Dan was struck by how animal-like K.C. was, doing things in a herky-jerky fashion, always about to spring. He led Dan back to the circle and pulled him down to the ground. The girl next to K.C. scooted over to make room. Nobody introduced anybody, but they all seemed to know who Dan was. He checked the girl out. A big clump of stringy hair bushed out and hung just over her eyes and ears.

"I'm Saffron," she said, looking off in the other direction, so that he could see that the back of her head had been shaved and was now starting to show a little dark fuzz.

Across from him were two guys in the standard uniform. Their heads seemed bony and small, and they wore their braces on the outside of their jackets so there'd be no mistaking that they were genuine skins. One guy's boots had white laces, tied in neat bows, and the other guy's were laced in red. Dan glanced at Saffron's baby-size Docs with the bright yellow laces. Did the colors mean something, like color wars at camp, or school colors? Dan tucked his Reeboks under his legs, out of sight.

Saffron said, "You're staring at my feet. Why? You're wondering if I really did it?"

"Did what?"

"Offed a cop."

"Oh, yeah, that's one of my first interview questions when I meet a girl."

"I'm no girl. I'm a woman."

"It's the yellow bootlaces," K.C. explained. "Means she's a cop basher. Look at Dolby over there — he wears red laces because he's a full-fledged card-carrying neo-Nazi." Dolby waved across the heater and sucked something up into his sinuses.

"And white?" Dan asked.

K.C. retied his boots in a slow religious ritual, reminding Dan of how he'd struggled to learn how to tie his sneakers in order to graduate from preschool. K.C. said, "I wear white. It just means white power."

"White power!" everyone yelled.

K.C. yanked Dan's foot out from under him. "Like I thought, Dan's got white laces."

What *else* would he wear? But he was about to find out.

"Pink's for gay bashers," Dolby offered. "And some skins'll tell you yellow's not because you kill cops, Saffron, but because you're a chink basher."

"I don't have anything against the yellow race," she said.

"What you want to look out for," K.C. explained, as if he were offering fatherly advice about women, "is guys with black laces, or dark blue laces. They might dress like us and look like us, but they're not us."

"Who are they?"

Saffron pushed her face right up to Dan's nose. "Antiracists. They'll stab you with a jagged knife if you give 'em a chance." Her breath was foul, as if she'd been sucking garlic. Dan lightly pushed her away, and she sank back into her spot around the campfire, her knees spread wide and her holey-mittened hands hanging between them.

The mother of the pure white Aryan race, Dan thought.

"We've got a lot to teach you, Danny boy. The best teacher's Odin. He's in charge of the Denver ForeSkins. We're WhiteSkins, they're ForeSkins. You gotta keep it all straight, right?"

"Hey, I can't wait to meet them."

Saffron dug around in her boots, yanking up stale nubby gray socks. "Yeah, Odin's an amazing guy. He stutters." She apparently thought that was hilarious, and they all waited while she wiped tears of laughter out of the corners of her eyes. She sneered at Dan. "Odin's the size of two of you."

"That would make him about twelve foot two," Dan said.

"*He's* got a body."

The skin who hadn't said a word yet suddenly got inspired. He shoved his legs out in front of him so they slammed into Dan's knees. "You've got a Jew name."

"Dan? Daniel? No, it's from the Bible."

"Uh-huh. It's what the kikes name their boys just before they circumcise 'em. That, or David, sometimes."

"And Izzy," K.C. said.

"Manny."

"Seymour, Isadore, Sol, Bernie."

"Jesus, where do they come up with these names?" said the guy whose boots were leaving tracks on Dan's Levi's.

Dan glared at him and said, "Your name's something real manly, like maybe Bruce? Dick? Peter?"

"Steve," he said, spitting the word in Dan's direction. Then the Steve guy changed course and smiled. The smile made Dan's palms sweat. "I say we christen you all over again. I'm taking away your Jew name and from now on you're Demon. I hereby baptize you Demon," he said, flinging what was left of his beer in Dan's face. "Baptized in the holy font of Coors," he said with a laugh. "Demon!"

"Demon, Demon, Demon, Demon," they chanted, with their arms flung out in the Sieg Heil position.

"Okay, now you and Steve shake hands," K.C. commanded, "because we're all brothers. Even Saffron."

Scott came in with two big bags of food. "From the Chinaman," he said proudly, and he began passing out white cartons. Then, as if every statement were a question, he said, "This is the lo mein? And here's your lemon chicken? And this is shrimp fried rice? Anybody like egg foo yung, because I didn't get any. The slant-eye tried to give me some of those chopsticks they use, but I shoved them into a plant." He handed Dan a carton of something steamy.

Dan opened it. Fried prawns, oh, God. He pushed it away. "I don't have any money," he said, his mouth watering.

K.C. said, "Hey, we don't any of us have any money. *They* get it all."

"Yeah, the Jews," Dolby said.

"And the welfare mamas," Scott added.

Saffron said, "You don't see me taking no handouts."

"And the ones who get the jobs, the ones who'd only recognize English if it came out of a can of refried beans — they're the ones who're getting rich, not us good old white Americans," said Steve.

K.C. shoved the carton of prawns closer to Dan. "It's okay. It doesn't cost us anything anyway. The old Chinaman at Ming Dynasty gives us whatever we want."

"He's real fond of his wife and daughters," Steve added, slurping up broccoli-beef.

They all ate out of the various containers. Saffron didn't bother with a fork. She just scooped it out with her fingers and licked them after each bite.

"Soy sauce?" Scott offered. He tore a hole in a little plastic pouch and squirted soy sauce at Dolby. That started the Soy Wars, and before long a salty-sweet skin covered Dan's face.

Steve said, "Be careful, you go out like that and someone's gonna think you're a member of the NAACP!"

After dinner, the guys took off in different directions. Some of them actually lived in homes and had jobs or curfews and had to account for their time like regular citizens. Scott went out to take a leak, and that left Dan/Demon and K.C. alone in the barn. K.C. dragged a stick through the dirt floor but seemed disinclined to talk. Maybe he was a deep thinker.

Finally, Dan felt loaded down by the silence. "Did Saffron really kill a cop, K.C.?"

"Says she did. Last year, when she was with the Romantic Violence Skins over in Chicago. But I don't believe it. She's got a kid. Mothers don't kill."

CHAPTER ELEVEN

White handprints started showing up on the outside school walls. Rosie Merren, who took violin over at the university, said the handprints were on the walls outside the University Memorial Center, and then suddenly they began appearing on trees and on cars and all over school.

At Taco Bell, Laurel and her friends speculated. Karen Gilardo said, "It seems like some mysterious advertising campaign for a new restaurant or a show that's opening up."

"Yeah," Erika Bennet agreed, "like the TV and magazine ads before the Infiniti car came out. No one knew *what* the point of that campaign was."

But the white hands had begun turning up on the doors and windows of places like Nagel's Bagels and the Eritrean Restaurant and the Uhura Book Shop which specialized in African folktales and African-American politics.

Mike Gutierrez said, "Hey, look at the evidence. We're talking a white power trip here, racism, pure and simple."

Laurel thought about the skinheads from the Mall Crawl. "You think they're trying to recruit at school?"

"Even closer to home than that," Mike muttered, and Laurel asked, "What's that supposed to mean?"

"Just keep an eye out, that's all I'm saying."

In the chaos of the cafeteria, Joy sat across from Dan and Laurel and was prattling on about the handprints and how she'd spotted one on the black toilet seat in the girls' john. "Personally, I think it's revolting. I mean, who needs narrow-minded, ignorant, prejudiced, pea-brained bigots?"

"Well, aren't you just the model of tolerance," Dan said, smashing his burrito into mush. It was obvious that Dan didn't much like Joy, and being around the two of them together made Laurel uncomfortable. She always seemed to be defending one against the other.

"I don't care," Joy said, climbing on her personal soap box. "Racists don't deserve common courtesies. They are pond scum. Well, it's been great, but I've got to go. The FemPower Coalition is meeting before fifth hour to work out our attack on the porno bookstore that just opened up on Walnut. I wish you'd come, Laurel."

"Pass."

Joy jiggled into a standing position, with her tray balanced on an out-thrust hip. "Well, personally I just won't tolerate the sexploitation of women," she said, fluttering her eyelashes at Dan. They watched her slink out of the cafeteria, her hips swaying in the tight jeans, and Laurel couldn't help but laugh.

After a while she said, "You know my brother Loc? He's eleven. Would it be all right if he came along with us sometime? He needs a strong male influence."

"Your brother? I guess. What's Loc short for?"

"Just — Loc. Loc Grady. His name used to be Loc Nguyen until we adopted him."

"Wynn?"

"N-g-u-y-e-n. It's like Smith or Jones, in Vietnamese."

"Your brother's Vietnamese?" Dan nearly choked on the word, or else he had a piece of taco shell stuck in his throat.

"Um-hm. And my sister Kim's half Laotian and half African-American."

"Wow! I see why you've kept this a secret."

"It's not a secret, Dan. It just never came up. I don't talk about my other brothers, either, and they're all pure white Irish-American. Why is it a big deal?" Laurel protested, even though she knew it *was* a big deal to some people.

"It's not."

"He's a lot like you, Danny."

"Must be a great kid," Dan said absently.

Time to change the subject. What a crab Dan was turning into. It had to be the business over that poor store clerk that was weighing on his mind. "What's happening with the case, Danny?"

"I can't talk about it." He gathered up his milk

carton, his straw wrapper, a bunch of crumpled napkins.

"Not even to me?"

"The lawyer, Aurelia Phoenix, says I'm supposed to keep my mouth shut."

"Do you think she's handling this right?" Days were flying by, and nothing seemed to be happening. It was all so unfair. Laurel worried that the crazies who'd just about killed the store clerk might still be looking for Dan because he'd been courageous enough to turn them in. Anybody else would have just kept his mouth shut, refusing to get involved in something so dangerous. Why didn't everyone understand that Dan was the hero here? But he'd been falsely accused, and he was the one who had to get a lawyer when he hadn't done anything wrong.

She asked, "Any progress? Have the police found the guys yet?"

"What guys?" Dan snapped.

"The crackheads, Danny. Where *are* you today?"

He stood up abruptly. "I've got to get to my locker before the bell rings. I forgot my stats homework." He brushed her face with a dry kiss. "Catch you later."

Aurelia Phoenix, who had to be close to thirty, looked at you and away at the same time, since her tinted glasses were as thick as ice cubes. Besides, she seemed distracted by the bustle in the surrounding cubicles of the public defender's office, as though the story just on the other side of the divider were a whole lot juicier than Dan's.

Great, I've got a lawyer who's bored to death with my case. "I'm telling you the truth."

She stood up and sent her chair rolling off the vinyl floor protector. She yanked her navy skirt smooth over her hips. With hips like those, she could pop thirty-pound babies.

"It's the absolute truth, I swear."

"Oooooooh. Ordinarily I'd be thrilled. I'd be dancing a jig on the window ledge, Penner, but I don't want to hear anything that would make me swallow bile in the courtroom."

"Hey, this isn't going to get to court, is it? I mean, I'm not on trial."

"Penner, Penner, get a grip, Babe." She had one shoe off and limped toward him. "Somebody's going on trial, and somebody's testifying under oath. The who-what-where-when-why are still up for grabs."

"I don't understand, Miss Phoenix."

"It's *Mrs.*, Babe. Don't get any ideas." She went back to her desk and swung her chair around to the side. She wriggled her dark nylon toes at him. Strains of the case next door wafted over the divider. ". . . after they found two quarts of the stuff buried under the tool shed . . ."

Of what, motor oil? Bootleg? Fingers and toes? Classic Coke? Aurelia Phoenix seemed intrigued by the possibilities also.

Dan said, "Maybe you can still get that case next door."

"And maybe you can quit bullshitting me." She settled back behind her gun-metal desk. "Why is it that your story stretches credulity, Penner?"

"I can't relate to your vocabulary, Mrs. Phoenix."

She stared at him a good long while, drumming her fingers on her ink blotter. "I'm looking across the desk at a guy who's making a flashy fashion statement. Giorgio Armani he's not. In a land where the popular prejudice runs to hair, he's got skin. There are things in the back of my fridge growing more hair than he's got on his head. Don't tell me, you had chemo?"

"A friend shaved it all off for me after school today."

"Jeez, he oughta win a prize. Barber of the year."

"So?" Dan had his arms crossed over his chest, aware that he appeared sullen and faintly belligerent. No, not faintly; aggressively.

"Well, then, let my eyes drink you in." She took off the glasses and stared at him. She had eyeballs after all — black buttons in a sea of bloodshot white. "And what I see is a punk who looks like a leftover from the Hitler Youth Brigade."

"You're confusing punks and skins."

"Common mistake. Try to overlook my ignorance."

"Anyway, what's your point?"

"Well, how do I put this?" She aimlessly flipped through her Rolodex. She obviously didn't know very many people. Finally, she said, "You and your type hate all kinds of minorities."

"Hey, I'm not one of a type."

"You've got nothing going for you, Penner, so just shut up and listen. Doesn't it strike you as just a tad coincidental that you're a white supremacist racist pig — all right, maybe you're not, but you sure *look* like one — and you just happen to walk in on a scene where two black crackheads are beating up on an Iranian store clerk? It's like the Church Lady used to say, how con-*veen*-yent."

"Iranian? I heard he was a Pakistani."

"Oh, right, it's okay to beat up a Pakistani."

"I'm not a racist!" he shouted, then realized the people one cubicle over had stopped to listen. More calmly, he added, "The style fits me, that's all. And sometimes I hang around with guys who happen to think whites aren't getting their fair share."

"Hey, I may not be Martin Luther King, Junior, but I can smell a pack of racists when I get close to one. You-all have a distinct aroma, Penner."

Dan jumped up. The cubicle was so small that he practically knocked over the divider. "Can I get another lawyer?"

"Oh, Penner, Penner, don't we both wish for that." She pulled a pencil out of her tangled web of black hair and jotted something on her blotter. "But you see, we drew straws, and I lost. Sit down."

He didn't.

"I'm damned good, Penner, so sit down and tell

me the story again, and I'll wait until you trip yourself up on a key detail, then I'll pounce." She beamed at him and put the glasses back on. Once again he started to tell her what didn't happen.

It was Loc who opened the door when Dan came over, while Laurel lingered upstairs so the two guys could meet each other without her muddling it up. She'd heard the doorbell and murmuring voices, then seconds later Loc bounded up the stairs and burst into her room.

"That boyfriend of yours? He's got no hair."

"What?" Laurel grabbed her purse and followed Loc down the stairs. Sure enough, Dan stood there, facing her astonished parents, with his head shining as pink as a baby's behind. There were blue veins at his temples, and his ears stuck out too far.

"Told you." Loc pointed to the obscene head, which made Dan look as naked as if he'd stripped all his clothes off.

"It was such a fine head of hair," Mr. Grady said, shaking his own head sadly.

"Ringworm?" asked Mrs. Grady, in a hushed voice.

"Oh, Danny." Laurel clutched the banister, reluctant to go any nearer.

Dan pulled a red ski cap over his head, and it crackled with electricity. He jumped slightly at the little shocks that must have smarted on that newly bare flesh. The cap clung to his head like plastic wrap.

"Why did you do it?" Laurel was still trying to

get used to the buzz haircut, and now there was nothing, not even prickles, to run her cheek across.

"People shave for swimming," Dan said. "Guys even shave their legs and chests."

"But you're not swimming anymore."

"Not for the Boulder Panthers, but I'll still be working to keep my times. I may try out for the Neptunes."

Laurel's parents discreetly drifted into the family room and turned on the TV. Laurel saw her mother bite the knuckle of her index finger. To keep from laughing? Crying?

"You look like those guys we saw at the Mall Crawl," Laurel whispered.

"Skinheads, yeah!" Loc cried. "The guys who kick Asian butt."

"Hey, it's only hair," Dan said irritably. "We'll be late for the show." He snapped his jacket shut.

Loc grabbed a jacket from the hall. "She hates it, but I like it that way. Tomorrow I'm shaving my head."

As long as he kept the cap on, Laurel was okay, but she couldn't bear to look at him without it. She kept flashing on pictures of Nazi death camp survivors — bald heads, sunken eyes, skin like paste, flesh so wasted you could count their ribs. And then she thought of the guys at the Mall Crawl, with eyes like ice holes.

Good thing Loc was with them tonight. The Silent One kept up a steady stream of chatter, and Dan seemed enchanted by him, flattered, full of confidence and experience, like the big brother initiating the little brother into the ways of the real world.

Dan asked Loc, "Do you like sports?"

"Not white sports," Loc replied. "That martial arts stuff, that's my sport."

"What do you think, white guys aren't into karate? I know a few moves myself."

"Whites ain't got the coordination, man." Loc trotted along, full of energy and bounce. Laurel had never heard so many words come out of his mouth.

"Oh, yeah?" Dan challenged him. "I saw this white guy on TV, and he kicked his way through a piece of board six inches thick. Clean slice."

"Brutal," Loc conceded. "I'll bet you can't do it."

"Bet you can't, either."

"How much you wanna bet?" Loc asked.

Laurel sighed loudly, but they both ignored her. She walked around to the other side of Loc so they wouldn't have to keep darting in front of her for their fascinating conversation.

Dan said, "Okay, here's the deal. If you can kick a six-inch-thick plank in two, I'll give you — "

"A Honda bike?" Loc suggested.

"I was thinking of something more like a strawberry sundae."

"Aw, it wouldn't be worth a busted foot just to get a blob of ice cream. No deal."

By now they were at the movie theater, and neither of them seemed to realize that Laurel hadn't spoken in the last fifteen minutes. They carried on their conversation while she paid for three movie tickets.

Through the movie, which was some high-tech violent fairy tale, Dan held her hand, but leaned across her to make snide comments to Loc about the movie.

Loc downed a huge barrel of popcorn, and after the movie he had a million technical questions. Dan invented answers to them all, while Laurel seethed and counted how many stores were already decked out for Christmas before the Thanksgiving turkeys even went on sale. Sure, she'd wanted them to be friends, but somehow she thought she'd be necessary to keep it all going. Instead, she might as well have been in Katmandu, for all the guys noticed.

Back at home, she was eager to tell Dan just how she felt about the whole evening, but first she had to get rid of Loc. "Okay, time for bed."

"Hey, we're on a date," Loc protested.

"Not *we*, me. Good night."

Loc pulled himself into his square package again and made it clear he wasn't budging.

"Get out, twerp!"

He stayed silent just long enough to make Laurel uncomfortable, then said, "Why, so you and your boyfriend can make out?"

"Loc!"

"That's okay," Dan said, laughing. "I've got to get going anyway. We're heading for Denver around sunrise tomorrow."

"You and your family?" Laurel asked.

Before he could answer, Loc said, "Can I go? They never take me to Denver."

"No."

It was the terse way Dan said it that made Laurel feel he was hiding something. "Who are you going with?"

"Friends."

"Which friends?"

"You don't know them."

"Danny, I know all your friends." But then she guessed who these new friends were.

"What are you, my prison guard? My second mother? The one I've got is more than enough, thanks."

"A fight, yeah!" Loc unfolded himself and leaned forward with a big grin on his face.

Laurel snatched up her purse. "I'm going to bed. You two have a terrific evening, and next time you go out on a date together, *you* pay, Danny. I'm tired of being your banker." She ran dramatically up the first few steps, then spun around. It was like that big scene in the movie, *Tootsie*, when Dustin Hoffman pulled off the wig and showed he was really a guy. Laurel almost laughed to herself. From the top of the steps, she shouted, "And your bald head is ridiculous. Get a wig. You look as pathetic as the rest of the skinheads!"

CHAPTER TWELVE

The sky was just starting to lighten as they rolled down U.S. 36 to Denver. If the speedometer in the ancient pickup had worked, it would have shown them hitting at least eighty. But it was Saturday, and there wasn't much traffic.

"It's lucky there's no cops out." K.C. peered out the window, watching the majestic sunrise over the open field.

Dolby had one arm hunched over the steering wheel, and the other clutching a Styrofoam cup of coffee. "I see cops are still sucking up their bribes in the truck stop restaurants." He swallowed gulps of his coffee, which had enough sugar in it to make a crater in Dan's stomach. Talk about a jolt.

Dan had been uneasy to find Dolby waiting for him outside the house, looking like something right out of the German army. Caught in the headlights, he looked natty and tight in his tan shirt and pants, his black tie knotted perfectly, and a pair of German jackboots. One sleeve had a swastika armband. Sitting next to him in the truck, Dan was able to study the insignia on his other sleeve. It was some complex design of a crown and a sword and a cross on a deep blue shield. Dolby took his hand off the wheel to tap it with his beefy finger. "Aryan Nation," he said. "Hot stuff."

Compared to Dolby, K.C. looked like a slob in his usual getup. It was hot in the pickup — the heater worked *too* well — and K.C. was down to a well-worn T-shirt that said HITLER'S EUROPEAN TOUR, 1939–1945. Pretty clever take-off on concert shirts, Dan thought.

Dolby drove like a maniac, speeding up to pass the occasional car, then slowing down just ahead of it. Good thing the road wasn't icy. It was thrilling to be with these guys who weren't afraid to take a few chances. They had an edginess about them that really pumped Dan up.

Shimmying down 36 in the steamy truck, they didn't say much. Sure, K.C. said what was on his mind, but with these guys, a lot was left unsaid, too. Packed in the truck, practically hip-to-hip, their jeans swishing against one another every time one of them moved, Dan felt really relaxed — for the first time in months, maybe. It could have been a hunting trip, a male thing in the woods, where you just experience it, get dirty and wet, shoot it, smell it, cook it, eat it, without analyzing it all to hell the way women did.

Minutes passed in companionable silence. With Laurel, one or the other of them had to be talking all the time, unless they were going at it hot and heavy. Silence made her nervous, maybe because she came from that crazy, overstuffed family.

K.C. had a way of reading Dan's mind. "How 'bout that woman of yours?"

"How do you know her?"

"I make it my business. I saw her the other day with some chink."

Dan sensed trouble here, but he tried to blow it off. "Yeah, he's her personal laundry boy."

"Sure seems like the kid lives at her house," Dolby said. "Some other half-breed bitch, too."

What were they doing, spying on Laurel's house? "She's got a really complicated family. I guess her parents are these do-gooder types."

"Well, if you ask me," K.C. said, "it's obscene putting a kid that's a half-breed, and some Chinaman dude, too, into a clean white family, even if they *are* Catholics. Should be illegal."

"Something oughta be done about it," Dolby agreed, swerving around a dead furry thing in the road.

"Like what?" Dan asked, wondering how far these guys would go.

"Hey," K.C. said, "trust us. We'll think of something. I got a creative mind."

Dolby passed a mobile home that had sped up when the driver saw the pickup gaining on him. He flipped them the universal sign of his contempt, and Dolby leaned out the window and shouted every cuss word he knew, until Dan and K.C. were laughing and holding in their guts.

It was too many months since he'd had good times like this.

And yet, there was also something menacing about being with these guys. They were intense, full of themselves, full of crazy ideas, dangerous. On balance, Dan decided he liked the danger, the unpredictability. Sitting between them, the flesh on his neck crawled with nervous anticipation.

After a few more miles of silence, he asked, "So, where are we going?"

"Denver."

"Yeah, I know that, K.C., but *where*?"

"Me and Dolby have a surprise planned for you. We're gonna get you jumped in."

"What's that mean?" He felt just a twinge of nervousness, a curl in his stomach.

"You'll find out," Dolby warned. "By then, it'll be too late, right K.C.?"

Dolby careened through the Denver streets while K.C., map propped against the window, tried to direct him. K.C., as it turned out, had no sense of direction, and he was mad at his own stupidity. Naturally, he blamed Dolby.

The tension was mounting, and Dan asked, "What are you looking for?"

"Projects," Dolby muttered.

Projects. The word brought memories of Dan's Cub Scout days back in Limon, when they'd spent Saturdays doing projects for badges. Once he and his dad had made a soapbox derby racer, every corner notched and joined perfectly, without nails. The wood was as smooth as polished stone, and stained, not painted. They called it The Zephyr.

"About a mile down this road," K.C. muttered.

Another Saturday the troop spent the whole day cleaning up wreckage after a violent windstorm had torn through Limon. The weather service wouldn't dignify the storm by calling it a tornado, but several buildings were in shambles anyway. Dan had lifted and carried planks, shards, chunks of stone, and twisted metal until his back was killing him and the blisters on his hands had burst. The Cub Scouts really knew how to have a good time.

"There, across the overpass," K.C. pointed. Dolby shifted lanes, ignoring the blasting horns all around him. They turned right, into a whole other world of windowless brick buildings and filthy graffiti; of peeling billboards advertising pomade and help for high blood pressure; of cars with blown tires, tilting like three-legged dogs.

People filled the sidewalks and swarmed at every corner, and there wasn't a white face in sight. An old woman struggled up the street dragging an upright shopping cart. Dan watched a kid go up to her and gently relieve her of the load, then run off in the other direction with her groceries. The old woman just shrugged and kept walking. But then two other guys in red berets jumped the thief and knocked him to the ground and rolled the shopping cart back to the woman. An older man dragged the bloodied kid toward the curb, out of the way of a bus that inched along the jammed boulevard. The man left him there, and others stepped around him as if he were a dead cat.

"Law of the jungle," Dolby said with a sinister

chuckle. "Jungle bunnies, every one of them."

They came to a stoplight, and fierce black faces surrounded the pickup, glaring into every window.

"Just stare straight ahead," K.C. muttered under his breath. "No eye contact, hear?"

Dan heard. The light changed, and Dolby hit the pedal. Bodies flew in all directions, but nobody was smashed. Dan let go of his breath as they tore through the streets.

Dolby rounded a corner, brakes squealing, and all of them slid toward Dolby's door. "There," K.C. pointed, "the Cheyenne Project."

Dan's heart sank. Ahead lay a sprawling collection of huge concrete boxes, painted pink and reaching ten or twelve stories into the sky. Lawns, brown and bare and stony, lay between each pair of buildings. Laundry hung everywhere — people's personal items flapping and tangling in the wind.

K.C. said, "Don't they just live like pigs? Sure am glad I was born white, how about you, Demon?"

"Yeah." Dan swallowed, his eyes everywhere. A couple of Oriental girls, younger than he, sat on a stoop while their babies played in the dirt. None of them wore shoes. There was a broken-down clump of playground equipment, and Dan watched a young black man gently swinging a little girl in a red ski jacket. The man (her father?) shifted from foot to foot, maybe to keep warm, because he wore only a T-shirt and shorts. A woman in a bulky robe came out to collect her mail and brought a steaming mug of something to a boy who paced nervously back and forth in front of the entrance.

Black and Oriental teenagers clustered separately in every doorway, smoking, passing packets back and forth. "They're dealing," Dolby said. "Burning out what little brains they got with dope and ripping off their own brothers. What a way to live."

Suddenly, K.C. said, "I see them." Dolby swerved into a dirt lot and pulled up right behind a van, bumped it, in fact. Painted across the back doors, in crude rainbow letters, was the name DENVER FORESKINS. The van doors opened, and about ten guys and a couple of girls spilled out. There wasn't enough hair among the dozen to cover a tennis ball.

It felt good to be in the cold air after the stifling pickup, but Dan wasn't too sure about this crowd. One of the guys wore a military uniform like Dolby's, and the rest were in the standard government-issue skin regalia.

K.C. went over to the group, dancing on the balls of his feet. Dan followed. "This is Demon, our new man." Some of the ForeSkins shook Dan's hand; others eyed him suspiciously. "He's ready to get jumped in."

Dan pulled his hands into tight fists, wondering what they were going to do to him.

A guy about twenty was obviously the leader. He looked tough and forbidding. If he'd had to weigh in for a fight, he'd have been in the heavyweight division. So Dan was amused to hear that he had a stammer. This had to be Odin, the one

Saffron had warned him about while cracking up.

"You're l-l-lucky," he said, affecting a growl that obviously didn't come naturally. "Back in the old days when we j-j-jumped a new recruit in, he couldn't s-s-see out his eyes for about a week because they were s-s-swoll shut."

"Not much to see, anyway," another ForeSkin said, "lying there in the hospital with everything except your dick wrapped in bandages."

Dan took a deep breath to calm himself, but did it quietly. He couldn't let them see he was scared. "Well, I'm glad to know you guys have turned respectable."

"Oh yeah, we're damn near middle-class. Now we've got a b-b-better initiation rite. Nobody gets hurt."

"Not by us," K.C. said, slinging his arm around Dan.

"C-c-c-can't help what *they* do to you, though."

The ForeSkins made a circle around Dan and K.C., while Dolby stood guard on the fringe. He had some sort of army rifle slung over his shoulder, and a bandolier of ammunition across his chest. Dan was chilled to realize that these things must have been stowed right behind him in the cab of the pickup.

And then they explained what Dan would have to do in the projects, to get himself jumped in.

CHAPTER THIRTEEN

They put him on the seat between K.C. and Odin, and the rest of them stuffed themselves anywhere they could in the van. "We'll be waiting for you in the p-parking lot of the Fillmore Theater. It's not b-b-but two blocks away."

K.C. reassured him, "I've done it, Demon, you can, too, buddy."

The van slowed down between the middle two tenements of the Cheyenne Project. Odin opened the door and shoved Dan out onto the blacktop. He scrambled to his feet, dodging cars, as the ForeSkins raced away. This was it.

People watched him from doorways, windows, balconies, cars, like they were waiting to see what the white kid would do. The man who'd been swinging the little girl snatched her up and ran inside with her. Bad sign.

Dan summoned any courage he could find and quickly assessed his chances. He could take off running, but these dudes would come after him with a gun, thinking he had some dollars in his pocket. Or maybe they'd think he was a cop, some undercover narc. Either way, he'd be just as dead.

And even if he got away from them, the skins would know he'd chickened out. What had Dolby said? "If you don't do it, we've got no use for you. Those mountains up there? Pretty high up." He'd motioned toward the snowcapped Rockies, and Dan knew he wasn't talking about a ski trip. "Some poor buck tossed over the side would end up as chopped steak on somebody's barbecue grill." Dan got the message.

K.C. had tried to encourage him. "Hey, we've got confidence in you. Anybody as loyal as you isn't gonna screw up this far into the game."

Get your head together, he told himself, standing in front of Building F. He only had to do two things, then run like hell. After twenty minutes, the ForeSkins would come looking for him anyway. He could survive anything for twenty minutes.

Only two things. He sauntered over to the building. If he looked cool, if he looked confident, maybe they wouldn't mess with him. He slowly unzipped his jacket; nothing jerky, wouldn't want them to think he was pulling a knife or a gun or anything. He slipped the can out and sprayed his message in big loopy white letters: NIGGERS GO BACK TO AFRICA.

One more thing he had to do. He ran down the brittle grass strip between the two buildings, shouting, "White pride! White power!" His knees wobbled, but the sound of his voice echoing off the buildings gave him courage. "White supremacy!"

Suddenly he was mobbed by a bunch of black guys whose eyes were murderous. One shoved him to the ground. They were all punching him. He pulled up his knees to protect himself, tried his best to cover his face, which felt wet and spongy and beyond hurting anymore.

A kick to his kidneys reminded him that he could still hurt plenty. He concentrated on staying alive, on not yelling out, on not showing his pain, on not showing his fear.

"GET OFF HIM," came this booming voice from beyond the mob. The crowd parted, and Dan tried to focus on the black face that now hung over him. The man wore a white collar. Some sort of minister? His fingers probed Dan here and there, and then he turned and said to the hoods, "I expect your mamas are waiting dinner on you." The guys made a few brave sounds, but began drifting away, obviously scared of this man.

"You — Sledgehammer and Otis — carry this boy to my car."

Dan felt himself being gruffly lifted. Everything hurt like hell. He hoped there were no major bones broken, because they weren't doing much to support him, hauling him as though he were already in a body bag.

They dumped him on the backseat of the car, which smelled like other people had bled there before him. Dan might have blacked out. He opened his eyes to see the preacher, younger than he remembered, kneeling over the front seat.

"Don't you croak on me," he threatened. "Where are your folks?"

"Boulder," Dan said with a groan.

"Lord, don't ask me to go that far with this boy."

"People waiting. Fillmore Theater." That's all he could manage, before he swallowed a tooth.

In the Fillmore parking lot, the preacher stopped the car and murmured a prayer just before he got out. Dan heard him say, "I've got your friend. I hauled his white ass out of the fire."

The ForeSkins opened the car door and slid him onto the ground.

The preacher said quietly, "I'm saying this just once. This is *my* neighborhood. Don't you be coming back here, ever."

One of the ForeSkins lurched forward as if to attack the minister, but Odin grabbed his arm to restrain him.

The preacher turned his back on the mob and climbed into his car. Rolling up his window, he said, "I pray God forgives you," and he drove off.

The next time Dan woke up, he was in a four-poster bed with a patchwork comforter drawn up to his chin. A gray-haired lady sat by his bed, and as soon as she saw him open his eyes, she reached for a bowl nearby.

"Just some lime Jell-O, Hon. You need a little fuel." She spooned a sliver of it into his mouth. "I know, I know, Darlin'." She wiped his forehead with a cool cloth. "There." Dan heard voices in another part of the house. "My boys," the lady said proudly. "All of 'em just like my very own Harve." Another spoon of Jell-O slid between his lips, and she smiled approvingly. "I'll bet you're pretty sore, Hon, but it'll go away."

He tried to sit up; her firm hand held him down. He became aware of a radio playing something country/western, maybe Garth Brooks or Hank Williams.

"Believe you-me, I've seen a lot worse," the woman said. She'd taken his hand and pulled it up to her cheek. At least his arm wasn't broken. "A whole lot worse. You're lucky they didn't take you out there at night."

Dan groaned and turned his face away.

"Now don't you worry, Darlin'. I'll look after you 'til you're on your feet. I used to be a nurse's aide, you know."

Dan drifted in and out of sleep while she held his hand and talked to him in a low, soothing lullaby. Once he woke and heard her say, "I'd never let my grandchildren miss out on Christmas, Lordy no, even if I had to steal to give 'em a Christmas." Another time he heard, "The sad thing about being a white supremacist woman, Hon, is that all our men are in jail or dead."

Hours must have passed before Dan woke up and was fully conscious. The woman still sat by his bed. When she saw he was alert, she called softly, "Harve, Hon, he's awake, and I'm guessing he's good and ready for a trip to the little boys' room."

Odin poked his head in the door, K.C. and Dolby and the others right behind him.

"Harve, be gentle, hear?" Odin's Christian name was Harve? He helped Dan sit up. Felt like everything was broken inside. Relieved that he had the use of both legs and both arms, Dan tried swinging his legs over the side of the bed, but something stabbed at his chest.

"We're gonna tape up your ribs, Hon, soon as we can turn you over without it hurts you too much." She pulled off the covers, and Dan was surprised to see that he had nothing on but his underwear and some bloody socks.

Odin supported him as far as the door and left him alone in the little cupboard of a bathroom with the heart-shaped toilet seat and wallpaper of pink hearts and blue kittens.

Afterwards, Odin led him back toward the bed.

"I want to try sitting up," Dan said weakly.

"Ma, clear the easy chair," Odin commanded, and the woman dashed over to toss a few coats on the floor. They eased Dan into the chair.

"You're getting back some color, Hon. I do believe you're over the worst of it."

"I better call home."

K.C. said, "Don't worry, Demon, I already talked to your old lady."

"Kevin Cabot, is that any way to refer to a white woman?" the lady scolded.

"Sorry, Miz Beaumont," K.C. said, hanging his head. "Anyway, I told her you were spending the night with me. Only I said I was Rick Sweeney, that football star? Your old — your mom was real impressed."

Dan tried not to laugh.

Mrs. Beaumont and her three daughters, who were all nearly the size of Odin, brought out big bowls of chicken fricassee, and green beans with ham, and apple walnut salad. The only thing Dan felt like eating was the mashed potatoes, because his ribs hurt with each chew and swallow.

The next morning he felt a lot better. He struggled into his jeans and pulled the T-shirt over his taped ribs. He finally looked in the mirror. Wait until his mother and sisters saw him, swollen and red as a tomato, and with that front tooth knocked out. He looked around for his Reeboks.

K.C. said, "Hunh-uh, you won't find them." K.C. opened a closet door and pulled out a scruffy pair of black boots. Dan reached for them. They weighed a ton and tore at his ribs. "Same size as those old Reeboks, Demon. Not a bad trade, hunh?"

CHAPTER FOURTEEN

"Hey, no, you've got it wrong," Dolby was saying as they bounced along in the pickup. On the way back from Denver, the cab didn't overheat; it didn't heat at all, and Dan's hands and feet were numb. That was an improvement, since the rest of him hurt like crazy. Each rut, each pebble the truck rolled over, was a stab to his ribs, to his kidneys, to the sealed cuts on his face and arms that felt like they'd be ripped open at the next pothole. He was aware of his heart, a thick, throbbing lump, hanging heavy between his bruised ribs. And he itched under the tight bandages.

Dolby had turned the wheel over to K.C., freeing himself to yammer on, while Dan craved only silence and a warm bed that wasn't moving down a highway.

"Like I said, you've got it all wrong, Demon. We're not racists, we're racialists."

"What's the difference?" Dan asked drowsily.

"Big difference. Racists hate people because they've got a different color skin, but racialists just believe in separation of the races. You gotta have pride in what you are, whatever you are. But, you look around, and everybody's saying nigger pride is okay, chink pride is okay, goddam anything hyphenated pride is okay. Just try to talk about white pride, and the cops are looking for excuses to bust you. Hey, equality's all we're into."

"That, and the fact that whites are just naturally superior," K.C. added. "We can't help it, it's in the genes." He reached out the window, adjusted his side mirror, and grinned at his grubby image. "We're just better-looking."

"And a hell of a lot smarter," Dolby said. "And we were here before all the rest of them."

"Except the Indians," Dan reminded them.

"Well, they *say* they were here first, just so they can rip off the white man's land and smoke that peyote stuff without getting busted." Dolby leaned against the door and turned slightly toward Dan. Not fair; Dan should have had the door to lean against, since he was the one in pain. Dolby said, "Bet you didn't know this. The first man and woman were Aryans. Adam and Eve, no kidding, blue-eyed blonds with skin as white as the sand."

"You've seen pictures of them?" Dan asked sourly, but the sarcasm escaped Dolby.

"God is white, too, of course. All you have to do is look at His picture that that guy painted on the ceiling of some church in Rome or wherever the hell it is. It's got a white God pointing right to a white Adam. Case closed."

Dan remembered seeing pictures of the famous

Sistine Chapel painting, and had wondered how Michelangelo *knew* what God looked like.

Dolby was on a roll. "And a lot of people say Jesus was a Jew, but how can that be, when his name was Christ, for Christ's sake. I mean, Christians came from Christians, not from kikes. You see what I mean?"

There was a pretty logic to it, even though Dan's seventh-grade Sunday school class had done a whole project called "Getting in Touch with Our Jewish Roots." They'd made unleavened bread and they'd ground up horseradish until their eyes and fingertips burned, and they'd re-enacted the Last Supper as a Passover seder. Was it possible that the church was wrong? That the church had been deluding Christians all these hundreds of years?

K.C. slammed on the brakes to keep from hitting a slow-moving horse trailer. Two stupid-faced cows stared out at them without a flicker of curiosity as K.C. waited for a clear road to pass them. He looked at his watch, which had old-man huge numbers and no crystal. "If we hurry, we can still make it to church, and you'll have a bigger audience to preach to, Dolby. Lay off Demon a while and let him just sit there and heal."

Dan was grateful for K.C.'s common sense. He thought, *This must be what it's like to have a big brother looking after you.*

The cornflakes were soggy as Laurel shifted her spoon through them. Booser ate his dry, crunching annoyingly. Laurel concentrated on the Sunday crossword puzzle. She absolutely had to get it done before her dad came downstairs and filled in all her blanks. A five-letter word for pygmy antelope. Würtemberg measure, three letters. A word that means obfuscate, too many squares to bother counting. Did anybody really know stuff like this?

Something sputtered to a stop outside the kitchen window. Booser glanced up, but was more interested in the comics. Everyone else was still upstairs dressing for church. Laurel craned her neck to see who'd pulled up outside. The first thing she noticed was a huge, gallomping guy rolling out of a rusty old pickup truck.

"This her house?" His voice tore through the brittle, still air, and Laurel rubbed a circle in the foggy window to see better. A pair of black boots now hung down from the seat of the cab. Whoever was in those boots was slowly easing himself into a standing position. Was he drunk?

Dan! Laurel grabbed an afghan from the rocking chair and ran outside, before she remembered how mad she was at Dan. She slowed as she saw his face: pulpy and swollen; brown jagged gashes in his cheeks; one eye barely a slit.

The big guy — one of *them* — supported Dan by placing his hands on each of Dan's shoulders, as though he were helping a baby take its first steps. What had they done to him?

Dan attempted to twist his face into a smile. A blood-red hole gaped between his front teeth.

"My God, Dan." Laurel reached toward him,

not sure where it was safe to touch him. He stood slightly crouched. Hairless head, face gashed and burly, shoulders hunched, he could easily have passed for a Neanderthal, or something out of a *Godfather* back alley.

"I don't dare go home yet," he whispered, and Laurel could tell that the words cost him precious energy. "My mother would have a stroke if she saw me now."

A wave of sympathy rose in Laurel's belly. Then someone jumped down from the driver's seat, and she recognized K.C. from the Mall Crawl. He was the leader, the one with the flag tattooed across his belly.

Laurel stepped back to look these guys over. What, exactly, was going on here? Had the skins beat up Dan for some reason? But why? He wasn't black, or Jewish, or Hispanic, or any kind of foreign, not even Catholic. Even violent racists had a sort of code of ethics, didn't they? Moral limits? And if he'd become one of them, they wouldn't brutalize him this way, would they?

"You gonna be okay?" K.C. asked. Laurel watched his eyes, read the kind of detached concern you'd show for a pup run over by a bike. The other guy, the huge one, picked up a bulky paper sack and handed it to Dan, who took it with effort. "Want the chick to carry it?" he asked. This was their first acknowledgment that Laurel was even on the same planet.

"Take it slow," K.C. cautioned.

They weren't behaving like hoodlums who'd just

beat up Dan. They were acting more like fraternity brothers bringing a drunk pledge home. *So what's wrong with this picture?*

Dan raised his arm, shallowly waving them off. "You guys go on. I'll be okay." He nodded to Laurel, as if to say, "She'll take care of me, because that's what women *do*." As evidence for his case, Laurel took the sack, which was filled with clothes that smelled damp and musty.

The two skinheads climbed back into the truck. Laurel noticed a large gold and blue emblem on the driver's window, a swastika interwoven with a sword.

She heard the front door open and her father's voice: "Everyone into the van, we're late for Mass. Laurel? Where's Laurel?"

The skins had to be gone before her father came out. "Get going," she cried, pushing K.C. back into the pickup. "You've got to get out of here fast." She led Dan around to the back door. "I don't know what's going on, Dan, but if my father sees you, we're both dead."

"Wait, wait," Dan said, trying to straighten up.

"You hide in the kitchen, and as soon as you hear us leave for church, get out, do you hear? Don't *ever* come near my house again. Don't call me, don't write to me — "

He reached forward, hands in supplication, as if he were receiving communion.

" — and don't love me, because I hate you, Dan Penner. I hate you for being one of the haters."

CHAPTER FIFTEEN

Erika and Joy and Laurel sat in the back of the Big Brothers/Big Sisters truck, waiting for customers to buy Thanksgiving pumpkins, the ones that were recently known as Halloween pumpkins.

Joy said to Erika, "I guess you heard about Laurel and Dan?"

"You don't have to whisper like you're in a funeral parlor," Laurel said.

Erika squeezed her hand. "I'm really sorry about it."

Laurel smiled thinly. She felt numb; was it because of Dan, or was it the fact that they'd been freezing outside on this haystack since before the sun came up? She wrapped her woolen scarf around her face.

Joy explained, "It's like my father says, Dan Penner's just gotten mixed up with the wrong crowd."

"I heard," Erika said quietly.

"Heard what?" Suddenly Laurel was angry that her friends were talking about this so self-righteously. And yet, Laurel knew that at this very minute, Dan was wherever the skins were. What were they doing? Why was he even with them?

"I mean, admit it, Dan hasn't been himself," Joy said. "Everyone's noticed."

Laurel asked, "Who's 'himself,' anyway? Are you 'yourself,' Joy? It sure seems to me you try on different selves every day."

"Oh, you're just upset about losing Dan."

"I haven't *lost* him, Joy. I ditched him. I spun him off."

A father and son scrambled on to the truck to pick out a pumpkin, and Laurel forced up a glimmering smile. She hefted a good twenty-pounder and said, "This guy is a great pumpkin," to which Joy added, "He's *the* Great Pumpkin."

"No kidding?" The boy was wide-eyed with respect for such a world-famous vegetable.

After the father paid, Laurel turned to Joy and asked sarcastically, "No objection to the sexploitation of pumpkins?"

Aurelia Phoenix, the lawyer Dan had pulled out of a Cracker Jack box, sat in his cramped living room. She wore baggy jeans rolled above her thick ankles, and an enormous hot-pink sweater with the sleeves bunched up at her elbows. "Emily — can I call you Emily?" Dan's mother nodded, still holding the coffee pot in midair. "Your little sweetcake's in deep sh-shoot, Emily, we've gotta have a plan here in a minute."

Dan's mother only looked confused, and when she started to ask a question, he jumped in. "What's the deal? I'm not the guilty party." He fixed his gaze on his mother, avoiding the lawyer's eyes. He had to choose his words carefully, because there was truth, and there was *truth*. Technically, he wasn't guilty of assault. He'd never laid a hand or a foot or a weapon on the Pakistani — or was he Iranian? — store clerk. But, as the lawyer had explained earlier in her boxy cubicle of an office, he wasn't exactly innocent, either. Aiding and abetting. Accomplice. Harboring known criminals. She'd tossed nasty words like that at him. "Home free you're not, Penner," she'd said.

But she'd also promised professional discretion. "The can of smelly worms you've spilled on my desk is what we call privileged information. It's between us. Hey, if I have to, I'll carry it to my grave." She faked zipping and locking her lips and tossing the key in her Far Side mug. Until Dan gave her permission to dig the key out of the coffee dregs, she couldn't tell his mother the truth. And his mother still believed the black crackhead version of the story; was probably the only one who did.

Now the lawyer looked from Dan to his mother and back, obviously hoping Dan would signal her to spill the story. His back was still killing him. The projects dudes might have smashed something inside, like a kidney, maybe. Could you get along with only one and a half kidneys? As he shifted in his chair, he tried not to breathe too hard, or even to wince, since his face was still yellow and purple and tight as the skin of a drum.

He simply glared back at Aurelia Phoenix; he'd learned a few things about being tough. But there was a band tightening around his head, and it seemed like every day someone pulled it a notch tighter, and it had nothing to do with healing up after Denver.

"Say, I couldn't help noticing there's a tooth missing in your colorful head," Aurelia Phoenix said. "Most of us try to have front teeth all the way across our smiles." What a sarcastic bitch.

"Danny hit it on the side of the swimming pool doing an underwater turn," his mother said. "Really banged himself up."

"Right." Aurelia Phoenix took a deep sigh. She gathered her papers, which were in a circle around her feet. "Give him lots of chicken soup, Emily. Or carbs. The baby's gonna need lots of fortification before this is all in the can." She winked, actually *winked* at Dan, as if to say, "I can do it if you can do it, only I can do it better."

The frigid barn echoed with emptiness. Dan rifled around, looking for some sort of message, some clue. There wasn't a spoon, a gum wrapper, a soy sauce pouch, a scrap of paper, anything to tell him where the other skins were and why they were gone.

Dan kicked the dirt and a wooden post, noting that he could kick the post hard enough for the ceiling lightbulb to rattle, but feel nothing in his toes. This had to be one small measure of power. Of course, it hurt his back like hell. He still worried about his kidney and checked everyday to see if he was peeing blood.

Now he sat on a sagging bale of hay that still held the shape of a lot of other bodies, trying to reason this all out and to fight back tears of frustration, which only enraged him.

Just like when his father had left, nine years earlier. One Sunday they were bowling, betting a penny a pin on the point spread, and on Monday after school, there was nothing of his dad's left in the house, not even a wrench in the garage. Danny wondered, on that black Monday, what he'd done to make his father take off so suddenly. He'd sat on his bed, trying to figure it out before his mother and sisters came home to discover the emptiness.

Sorting through nine years of memories, and sifting out every detail of their bowling day, he'd finally isolated the cause. Once Dad had said, "If I hear any more smart-ass talk out of you, I swear, I'm outta here. I had enough of that stuff in the Army, guys mouthing off and cussing and being disrespectful of my rank as sergeant." That was it; Danny had mouthed off once too many times on Sunday, when his father's ball landed in the gutter on a spare. Or maybe he'd cussed too much, thinking it was okay since Dad was "damning" and "helling" all over the bowling alley. It didn't even have to be anything Danny had actually said. His father had probably read his mind — fathers could do that, couldn't they? — when Dad had padded his score on nearly every frame.

Now Dan shifted his weight on the hay bale and saw a figure nearing the half-open door. He compressed himself, willing himself invisible in case the farmer was coming to reclaim his barn. The door creaked open, and someone loomed dark and large against the dimming four o'clock light. Dan held his breath until the figure was nearly in front of him, then he jumped off the haystack.

"Jesus H. Christ, Demon!" yelled Scott, and Dan just grinned at him. "My heart's beating like a clock."

"Where's everybody?"

"Over at Dolby's. Some cop came sniffing around here? K.C. told him we were having a fraternity meeting?"

It was annoying the way Scott made every statement sound like a question, but everything about Scott annoyed Dan.

"But the cop didn't believe him? Especially when he got a close look at Saffron. The cop says, 'Is the lady in your frat?' He's real sarcastic, you know?"

"I guess K.C. had a snappy comeback."

"He said, 'Oh yeah, she's one of our guys, 'cause we're not into sexism or sexual harassment. Chicks can be in our fraternity, as long as they stay in the kitchen.' "

"Did Saffron kick him in the gut? She's got that soft, feminine touch."

"No, she was saving it up. So the cop said,

'Lemme see your charter?' And K.C. didn't have any idea what a charter was? So the cop asked, 'What's the name of your fraternity?' And that's when Saffron landed one. 'KKK,' she said, 'Kappa Kappa Kappa.' I swear, K.C. and me were cracking up, then Steve, you know, he hardly ever says anything? So he pipes up with, 'Yeah, we're the Grabba Thigh chapter of the KKK.' By now, Saffron and K.C. are rolling on the ground, and the cop knows he's outta his league, so he just shakes his head and slinks out of there?"

Dan was getting impatient with the story. "So, everybody's at Dolby's. Where's that?" It was safe to ask Scott; Dan would never have given K.C. or Steve or Dolby, or even Saffron, the satisfaction of fishing for information.

"Dolby's folks have a rooming house over on Mapleton? They're, like, everybody's mom and dad? They're big shots in the White Aryan Nation? Come on, I'll take you over there, as soon as I find that crowbar K.C. left under one of these haystacks. It works almost as good as an aluminum bat."

"For what, hitting grounders?"

Scott gave Dan one of his looks that said, "If I weren't so dumb, I'd be laughing."

"Hitting grounders, sure! Or cracking the heads of spicks or niggers or queers, your garden variety vermin."

His offhand attitude toward violence disturbed Dan. This skin thing was okay as a club, as the Grabba Thigh chapter of the KKK, as a bunch of guys who hung together because they were all poor, and everyone else, who wasn't white, seemed to be doing so much better. But beating up people with a crowbar? That seemed like something out of the movie *A Clockwork Orange*, which had been a cult classic among his friends in Limon. Back when he had normal friends. These new friends were the sterling characters who'd put a store clerk in the hospital with a shattered spleen and too many broken bones to count in the first go-round. He'd just have to shove that thought to the back of his mind, just as he'd shoved all thoughts of Laurel clear out of the picture.

"Really, a baseball bat works better," Scott said, slipping the crowbar out from under a stack of hay. He lifted it as if he were going to slam it down on Dan's head, but Dan outsmarted him — he called Scott's bluff by refusing to flinch.

PERFIT, the pink-and-black box said, Classique Style 8½ B. All Laurel's memories of Dan fit into one of her mother's old shoeboxes. Before she taped it shut, she inventoried the remains, the ashes of their relationship. A small stack of pictures lay at the bottom, wrapped in a Kleenex tissue. One photo was taken at the lake, the day Joy compared Danny to a well-roasted turkey. Great build, Laurel thought, then imagined him eighty-six years old, shoulders rounded as he hunched over his cane, sparse gray hair on his chest, face wrinkled and pocked. That helped.

The second picture was from Dan's eighteenth

birthday, when Laurel had treated him to dinner at Winston's, in the Boulderado Hotel. The doorman took the shot of them under the stained-glass canopy, which washed them in blues and pinks and yellows, like dressed-up angels or saints. "He looks jaundiced," Laurel said aloud.

The last picture had just come back from the drugstore. It showed a 3 Musketeers bar standing as close as its rectangular edges would allow to a crummy rendition of a Coors can, six feet tall. Out of sync. If she'd known he was going as beer, she'd have made herself a pretzel. That proved it: They never did really fit together.

She wrapped the pictures in the tissue again and laid them down in the box, among dozens of notes scribbled in class. She absolutely would not read the infantile banter, wouldn't unfold a single one of the notes.

She picked one up. He'd written, "Moreland looks like a locomotive," and below it Laurel's scrawl said, "Choo choo!" In Dan's precise black script: "Chug-a-chug-a-chug-a-chug," and her purple ink response, "I-think-I-can, I-think-I-can, I-think-I-can!" Finally, he'd written, "I lost my TRAIN of thought."

Laurel remembered sticking the note in her stats book because Mr. Moreland was chugging down the aisle, blowing off steam, and saying "Chickadees, chickadees, I'm disappointed in you," as he passed out their disastrous problem sets.

Well, no wonder Laurel was making a C in stats. Now she could concentrate again and catch the gist of Mr. Moreland's lectures, because she was liberated from Dan. Wouldn't the FemPower Coalition rejoice! She jammed the lid down on the box, then opened it again.

Inside were a few cards; he specialized in handmade cards with puns. There were also some ticket stubs, and a folded poster from the big football game with Fairview, showing a panther with its ferocious mouth gaping open. The caption read, FEED ME FAIRVIEW!!!! And finally, on top of everything else, were two roses, one for each monthiversary, their stems bent to fit in the box. The first rose was already gray and crunchy, but the second was still red, as though the relationship weren't quite totally dead yet.

But it was. This was the flotsam of a shipwrecked romance, Laurel told herself. She must have read that in a poem somewhere. She sealed the box with duct tape and stowed it on the highest shelf of her closet, on top of a carton filled with her elementary school clothes, which Kim would someday grow into. The past and future, piled there on the top shelf. "How symbolic," she muttered. But if she'd learned anything from having five brothers and a sister, it was not to wallow in self-indulgent sentimentality.

She slammed the closet door shut.

CHAPTER SIXTEEN

Dolby's face glowed green and ghoulish in front of his computer, while across the room, K.C. flipped through TV channels. Scott was in the kitchen, raiding the fridge. Juice or Coke or something splashed over ice cubes. Dan's stomach growled, and he was on his way into the kitchen when Dolby said, "Hey, Demon, check this out." He pointed to a few words in the middle of a busy field of dotted sentences.

Dan put on his glasses and read, " 'White woman wants to have white babies with a real red, white, and blue guy. Dial Terri, TR8–9406.' Maybe that's your woman, Dolby. You think she looks like a pit bull?"

Dolby ignored him, scanning through messages on the electronic bulletin board. Tiny lights on his modem flashed like radioactive redhots. Dan caught stray words flitting by: GFTT — Go for the Throat. ZOG — Zionist Occupied Government. White Revolution, the Only Solution.

"This is beautiful," Dolby said. "Listen to this,

Demon. It's the Aryan Nation Oath of Allegiance." He read from an ornately bordered document that slowly scrolled upward: " 'We hereby invoke the blood covenant and declare that we are in a full state of war and will not lay down our weapons until we have driven the enemy into the sea and reclaimed the land which was promised of our fathers of old, and through our blood and His will, becomes the land of our children to be.' Jesus," he said, clearly moved by the majestic poetry, "it almost makes you wanna go out and smash some skulls."

Scott was crunching something in the kitchen, maybe tortilla chips; maybe he had a jar of salsa he was dipping them into. Dan's stomach growled.

"You got a tapeworm?" Dolby scanned a few more screens and stopped on an article called HOMETOWN HEROES. "Look here, Demon. A couple of skins in Pittsburgh grabbed this Afro chick on her way home from school. One held her down, the other guy sprayed her with white shoe polish." Dolby chuckled as he read the message on the screen. "Know what they said to her? 'Now you're white like us!' Is that a riot, or what? Some people will do anything just to be white, hey, Demon?"

From across the room, there was a low symphony of fragmented notes as K.C. flipped through the TV dial. You deserve a break today . . . thank you, Thing . . . possible airstrikes over Sarajevo . . . he's makin' a list, checkin' it twice . . . he's dead, Jim . . . just keeps going and going . . . plight of the Palestinians . . . you're not fully clean unless you're Zestfully clean.

"Oh, this one's rich, Demon." Dolby pointed to the message stretching itself line by line across the screen. "Look here. Two guys in BASH, that's Bay Area Skinheads in San Francisco, they broke every damn window in a Jewish church. Just ran around the building with baseball bats smashing stained-glass Moses Noses all over the place. What a scene!" He elbowed Dan for some reaction, and Dan said, mustering what enthusiasm he could, "Yeah!"

He pictured the pile of colored glass ringing the whole synagogue, maybe enough to fill a couple of wheelbarrows. Or maybe the windows shattered into the building, and inside they were crunching glass under their shoes. What was the inside of a synagogue like, anyway? Were there pews, like in a real church? Or was it like you saw on TV, where the old man Jews all stood around rocking back and forth with their white scarves pulled over their heads. What were they hiding from? From us, Dan thought, and felt a thrum of blood course through his heart. *This is what white power means*.

"There he is!" yelled K.C., and Dan jerked his eyes away from the computer screen. "Zack Decatur himself." This must have been big news, because Dolby slid his rolling chair over to the TV. Dan followed.

Zack Decatur proved to be a clean-cut guy, eight or ten years older than Dan, with a face made for TV. His smile lit up the screen.

"Who is he?" Dan asked.

"Used to be a skinhead. Shut up and listen."

He was apparently some kind of local hero, head of the KKK in a Denver suburb. He was dressed in a business suit and black loafers, though his blond hair was close-cropped. "We don't hate blacks," he said earnestly into the camera. "We just love whites." A neat sign was propped on his lap: RIGHTS FOR ALL; SPECIAL PRIVILEGES FOR NOBODY.

The interviewer said, "Mr. Decatur, you appear to be an ordinary middle-class man, maybe an entry-level executive. You're dressed conventionally. Tell us about your tattoos."

The Decatur guy smiled almost sheepishly, flirting with the camera like a shy girl. "I got those when I was a kid. Kids do things like that."

"And could you describe those tattoos for our viewing audience?"

"Well, they're here," he said, moving his hand suggestively up and down his chest. "Faces of people I've admired."

"Such as?"

"Hitler, Himmler, Mussolini, heroes of long ago. What's important is not what happened during World War II — "

"You mean the Holocaust?"

"Oh, I wouldn't call it that. People try to tell you twelve million folks died. I don't think it was even a million."

"But Mr. Decatur, there's documentation on the evacuated ghettos and death camps. Hundreds of books have been written by survivors, and even now, fifty years later, they're uncovering memoirs and poems and pictures done by people who died in those camps. Perhaps you saw *Schindler's List*?"

"Didn't it win some Academy Award or something? Just like *Dances with Wolves*? Good stories. Hats off to the directors of both those movies."

"Mr. Decatur, how can you deny the overwhelming evidence? Surely you've seen the photographs of those emaciated, haunted people, and the bones, the piles of gold fillings and teeth and hair?"

Zack Decatur sat up straight and assumed an expression of deep concern. "My heart goes out to those individuals who've suffered in any war. But you know, most of those pictures you're referring to were trumped up. Oh, sure, some were killed, mostly Gypsies and homosexuals and a few of the Jewish persuasion, but most of *them* died of natural diseases. They never were a healthy people."

The interviewer cleared his throat, obviously to regain his composure. "Do you hate Jews that much, Mr. Decatur?"

Zack Decatur looked thunderstruck by this suggestion. Then the interviewer must have gotten a signal in his earphone, because he jumped into a bring-it-to-a-close mode. "Do you have any final words for our audience?"

"Sure." Decatur gazed right into the camera and went into a prepared speech. "People think of the Klan as those good ol' boys who ride around on horseback with torches and all. That era is long gone. I'm an average middle-class suburban guy, your neighbor. The Klan is full of people like me."

"Thank you, Mr. Decatur."

"Oh, and one other thing."

The interviewer looked annoyed, but nodded.

"Within ten years I hope to be a Colorado U.S. senator. Who knows, maybe it'll only take half that time." He grinned at the camera, like a pitcher whose Little League team had just won the World Series.

"And he'll be here for our rally, Demon," K.C. said worshipfully, as though he were talking about Adolf himself. "He's going to be our center ring, showcase, hotshot, white man, main man, keynote speaker. We are really gonna kick butt on December eighth."

CHAPTER SEVENTEEN

Dr. Millwood had a reputation to protect. For thirty years he'd held the record as the most boring teacher at Boulder High. Now he droned on in his flat, choppy exploration of the principles of American government, while Laurel practiced sleeping with her eyes open. Next to her, Joy dashed off a letter on her lavender stationery. On the other side, Mike Gutierrez contemplated moves on a palm-sized chessboard. The faint hum of somebody's earphones came from behind Laurel. Everybody kept busy with something that involved ignoring Dr. M.

The minute hand could go around the full circle while Dr. M said "amendments to the United States Constitution." The word "constitution" alone had at least seven syllables and three pauses as it dribbled, drop by drop, from his lips.

But what was this? A guest speaker? Laurel pulled out of her slump and investigated the tall young woman who shook Dr. M's hand and was now arranging papers on his lectern. She had a lot of untamed hair wrestled to the back of her neck and held in place by a black bow. Crimps of dark blond hair framed her face. Her gold granny glasses hung low on her nose, even though she couldn't have been more than twenty-two or twenty-four. Her gray flannel suit was all business, like Boulder High debaters at tournaments, but the blouse of deep pinks and reds and oranges reminded Laurel of stubborn weeds in a perfect garden.

"Ladies and gentlemen," the guest began, and then, as if surprised by the pitch of her voice, her next words were an octave lower. "I present to you the First Amendment to the United States Constitution." What took Dr. M a minute came out of her mouth like short toots from a clarinet. "I'm not an expert. I'm only a first-year law student. But we're required to make a presentation to a high school class on the Bill of Rights, so — here I am." She smiled warmly and seemed to relax. Laurel liked her immediately.

"Now, who knows what the First Amendment says?" She looked over the rims of her glasses, but no one raised a hand. Dr. M attempted to come to her rescue. He studied the seating chart. Laurel was sure he'd call on Bella Donna, but his eye fell on another name.

"Edward Boyd?"

"I dunno."

"Perlita Sanchez?"

"What was the question?"

"Let me rephrase it," said the speaker. "Who can tell me one thing the First Amendment guarantees?" She took off her glasses and was waving them around, as if to fan the flames of interest in her subject.

After an embarrassing silence, Monica Doane volunteered, "It says you can meet anybody you want, or something like that."

"Can you meet Tom Cruise?" asked the speaker. "Can you meet Jeffrey Dahmer?"

"I mean, like clubs. You can belong to any club or sorority and meet whenever you want to."

"Can you belong to the Ku Klux Klan?"

Monica sank in her chair. "I guess not."

"Of course you can! What else does the First Amendment guarantee?"

Someone from the back of the room was obviously reading from his textbook. "The free exercise thereof, I mean, of religion."

The speaker nodded. "Um-hmm. But what if your religion is Satanism? What if you practice the Cuban religion of Santería and part of your ritual is sacrificing live chickens?"

"Oh, gross!" yelled several kids.

The law student must have sensed she had them fired up, so she pounced. "And what else?"

Joy said, "I'm personally into freedom of speech."

"Ah, my favorite." The speaker had now moved away from the lectern and was pacing the front of the room as if she were arguing a case in court. Her heels clicked across the tile floor in counter-rhythm with her words. "Now, if we're guaranteed freedom of speech, when does the government have the right to abridge that freedom? Come on, guys, you know this!" She stopped and stared them down.

Erika offered tentatively, "When someone says something that hurts other people?"

"Actually *hurts* them? Can you wound somebody with words?"

"Sure!" several people yelled.

"Give me an example."

Mike said, "Well, like, if you say, 'you're really ugly' enough times, the person starts to feel ugly. Maybe even look ugly."

"But can you prove that *really* hurts? What about racial slurs?"

Laurel leaned forward, her heart tapping out a beat she thought the whole class might pick up.

The speaker continued, "Does the First Amendment stop me from telling an anti-Semitic joke when there are Jews in the room?"

"Well, no."

"What about if there are Holocaust survivors in the room?"

They weren't so sure about that one.

"Does it stop me from telling African-Americans they're lazy and shiftless?"

"Watch what you saying!" Edward Boyd cried out, and Laurel could feel the class growing uneasy.

"Let me put it to you another way. Does the First Amendment protect me if I burn a cross on the lawn of a black family?"

"That's illegal!" someone yelled.

"Only in seventeen states. And it's not illegal in Colorado."

There was a general rumbling in the class. Even Dr. M perked up.

"And if I belong to a neo-Nazi organization, can I call a rally on the steps of this school to spew my hatred for minorities?"

"I guess so," someone murmured.

"But what about the principle of 'time, place, and manner'? Suppose my rally, my right to free speech, interferes with the higher good of the learning going on in the school?"

"No problem. You just hold your rally after school, or during lunch," Monica said.

"We'll talk about this in a minute. Okay, can I have my rally if my hate speech threatens to kill or maim a racial or ethnic minority?"

"No!"

"What if my hate speech is against gays and lesbians?"

"That's different," said Wayne Bisoni, who'd just done an oral report on homosexuality in the military.

The speaker cleared her throat and launched into another relentless attack. "There's a disbarred lawyer in Topeka, Kansas. This guy, Fred Phelps, hates gays. He calls them 'sodomite scum.' He and his henchmen, who are mostly his family members, parade outside the funerals of gay men who've died of AIDS. They carry signs that say 'GOD HATES FAGS.' "

Wayne said, "It doesn't matter what you think of gays, you can't let people picket at a graveyard. I mean, doesn't the guy have any decency or respect?"

"That's what the Kansas State Legislature thought when they passed a law saying it's illegal to picket near a cemetery, house of worship, or mortuary during and after a funeral."

"All right!" someone yelled, but Rosie silenced him quickly:

"What about the guy's First Amendment rights — freedom of assembly and free speech and all that?"

"Ah, good point," the speaker affirmed. "Remember a minute ago I mentioned the precedent of 'time, place, and manner,' back when we were talking about demonstrating at a school? Well, I think this cemetery law is perfectly constitutional and the courts will uphold it when the challenge comes, because the time and place of Mr. Phelps's demonstrations are inherently harmful to the mourners. Did you know that he even picketed the funeral of President Clinton's mother?"

"Wait, I'm confused," Mike said. "Is this law a good thing, or a bad thing?"

The guest speaker smiled. "Shades of both. It's called justice." She paused for dramatic effect, then calmly said, "Personally, I think all gays should be shot."

"What?!"

"I think you should all pick up a gun — it's your

Second Amendment right — and shoot every fag you come across."

Kids were shouting and jumping to their feet, and Dr. Millwood turned bright red. Finally, the speaker whistled through her teeth to bring the class back to order, and while the rage was so thick in the room you could reach out and grab it by the handful, they did begin to settle back into their seats.

"I've just given you an example of fighting words, words intended to provoke immediate violence, to create a clear and present danger. Such speech, ladies and gentlemen, is not, I repeat, is *not* protected by the First Amendment."

Dr. M sat down, visibly relieved, and the speaker went back behind the lectern to refer to her notes.

"As you know, a local group of skinheads wants to hold a rally on the steps of this school on December eighth."

Joy's head snapped in Laurel's direction, but Laurel just stared straight ahead.

"Their leader, a young man by the name of Kevin Cabot — his buddies call him K.C. — has applied for a permit to assemble. It's all legal and clean. He's planning to bring in some minor bigshot, Zack Decatur, to lend his little display some credibility among adult white supremacists. Cabot's stated purpose is to drum up support for his separatist ideas."

"What is he, a neo-Nazi?" Monica asked.

"He doesn't claim to be. He says he's a white

supremacist, that's all. So far, the city of Boulder has denied him the permit because of a law on the books — unconstitutional, of course — banning the public display of symbols that are offensive to the community, and parades of political organizations in military-style uniforms."

"What's wrong with outlawing that stuff?" asked Jamie McPherson, who ordinarily never said a word in class.

"Well, here's the problem. Suppose a civil rights group wanted to march through a lily-white suburb under a banner that showed a black hand holding a white hand. Now, to you this might be a beautiful symbol, but in White Haven, USA, it would be rather offensive, right? Under a law like this, Dr. Martin Luther King wouldn't even be able to march. Never mind Dr. King; the Cub Scouts couldn't hold a parade. And this, in a town that has the Mall Crawl every Halloween? Think about it. Anyway, it doesn't look like Kevin Cabot and his buddies are going to get their rally."

"Why would they want to? Who would listen to them, anyway?" Jamie asked.

"Well, their stated purpose is to make speeches that advocate their white separatist ideas, ideas a lot of folks believe, but which I personally find repugnant, repulsive, ignorant, and obscene."

"Like what ideas?" Joy asked, shooting a glance at Laurel. Her look said, *I warned you about this guy*.

"They believe that all African-Americans are inherently inferior and should go back to Africa."

"We'll show them who's going back where!" Evelyn Lewis yelled. "I be glad to cuss 'em out in Swahili." Everyone laughed, needing this comic relief. But the law student pressed on.

"They believe that Jews have too much economic power, and that there shouldn't be so much control in the hands of Christ-killers."

Laurel saw Rosie Merren shift in her seat, fingering the gold *chai* she wore around her neck.

"They believe that all Jews should go to Israel, or better yet, die, and that all Asians and Cubans and Haitians and other immigrants should go back, even if their lives were threatened in their native lands."

Laurel thought of Kim and Loc and a couple of Cambodian guys who sprawled in their chairs at the back of the room.

The speaker continued, "Kevin Cabot and his cohorts want to establish a pure white nation, a nation of blue-eyed blonds." She looked around the room, studying each face. "I don't think all of you would fit into Mr. Cabot's America."

At that very point, with Laurel clutching her elbows and barely able to breathe, a crackling came over the P.A. system, signaling the afternoon's announcements. The law student was clearly angered by the interruption, and when the nasal voice of the announcer got to the message about selling Christmas poinsettias for the National Honor Society, she muttered, "There's the First Amendment in action."

The speaker tapped the podium with her pencil,

while the announcements finished up. "And the Activities Group Thought for the Day comes to you from the Future Farmers of America: Every Colorado farmer feeds 107 people plus YOU."

After the announcements, Dr. M corraled his waning energy. "Let's give our speaker a hand."

They were all feeling confused and agitated, and Laurel joined the tentative round of applause for the speaker. Then Dr. M said, "It's been a most provocative presentation. Food for thought. Thank you, Miss Saralyn Penner."

Laurel clapped her hand to her mouth.

Joy leaned across the aisle. "Isn't Dan's sister a first year law student? In fact, isn't her name Saralyn Penner? My, what a coincidence."

CHAPTER EIGHTEEN

"Well, well, well, look who's here."

Dan looked up from his statistics book, bristling at his mother's prickly tone, while Saralyn wrestled her key out of the front door.

"Excuse me, but would that happen to be my oldest child, the one who used to live in this house?"

The keys jangled when Saralyn dropped them into her giant canvas bag. "I have to pick up a computer disk." She disappeared into the room she and Sudi shared, and Dan was — as usual — torn between going to talk to her and staying in the living room to pacify his mother, who solved the problem by stomping into the bathroom. When the lock slid into place, Dan knew she'd be in there as long as Saralyn was in the house. They all used the bathroom that way, as the only quiet cave in their crowded zoo.

He heard the desk drawers slamming shut, one after another, and then Saralyn came out with a red muffler slung around her neck and a floppy disk in her hand. "Any mail?" She was already thumbing through a stack of envelopes on top of the TV.

Dan thought she seemed more distracted than usual. "How's law school?"

"It's a grind, same as always." She worked her finger into a corner of an envelope and ripped it open. "Damn, it's the bill from the bookstore. Do you know how much the average law book costs? Forty-seven dollars. What's Mom's problem? I see she's locked herself in the throne room again."

"She misses having you around. Weird way to show it, I guess."

"Still making excuses for her? Save it for Sudi." She tore up the bookstore bill and tossed the scraps in an ashtray.

"Where do you sleep every night, Saralyn?"

"Who says I sleep? Sleep's a luxury law students aren't allowed."

"You're pissed at me."

She sank into a chair and unwound one ring of the muffler. "Slightly. No, hugely. I was talking about you today."

"Where?"

"At your school. I did a thing in some government class on the First Amendment. Wouldn't you know it, the WhiteSkins rally worked its way into the discussion. I, who find your scum buddies totally reprehensible, had to defend your free speech rights. How ironic."

"The December eighth rally? It's all legal."

"Legal, but slimy."

"Off my back, Saralyn." He feigned avid interest

in the book, but he stole glances at her over the top of it.

"Right." She leaned forward, studied the label on her disk, then sank back into the chair, whose springs boinged indecently. "Remember, Danny? I'm the one who used to toast your English muffins until they were just right for the butter to melt down to the bottom. You used to take a bite and say 'Fanks' with such a sweet, greasy grin. How did you turn into such a shit?" Her eyes traced him, from his head to his boots. "Look at you."

"It's just clothes," Dan said irritably. His ankle itched. He longed to stick a pencil into the boot, but he wouldn't give her the satisfaction.

"Not just clothes," she said. "They're clothes with an attitude. Clothes with a political statement oozing out of the fibers. How do you live with yourself?"

He slammed down the textbook. "How do you live with *yourself*? I mean, you've had it all, like you've got it coming to you. You're the brain, you're the promise, the star. Sudi and I, we're just props. We're just the backup group. You're the main attraction."

"I don't know what you're talking about."

"Simple," Dan said, pacing the small cage of a room. "Everybody else around here does whatever's best for you. I had to leave all my friends in Limon, in my senior year, so you could go to law school and live at home, not that you bother showing up here unless you need something from Sudi or Mom or me."

"I came for my own disk. And sit down, you're making me nervous."

"Sudi can't live in the dorm because of you, Mom has to work two jobs, and we've got this pen to live in, snarling at each other like vicious dogs all the time. We're all tired of making sacrifices for you."

"Don't give me the sacrifice routine, Danny. It makes you sound like a whiny old maid."

He grabbed her muffler and a handful of her coat, jerking her harder than he'd meant to. "Then don't trash my friends."

She pulled away from him, and the muffler slid to the floor. "They're not your friends, Danny, face it."

He thought about the terrific care he'd gotten in Denver from the ForeSkins. Sure, they'd tested him, but that was part of the game. When it came right down to it, they'd gotten him out of danger and taken care of him. And K.C. was more like a big brother watching out for him, someone to open up to about most things. You talk to women, and they pounce on your vulnerabilities. But K.C. just listened and agreed, because he'd been through it all before. The Boulder WhiteSkins were his real family now, a circle of people who felt the same about things. When he was with K.C. and the other WhiteSkins, he was *himself*, powerful and important. What a change from this house, where the oppressive woman-smell rose and expanded to fill every molecule of the air, stifling his freedom and turning him into a whipped puppy. Like now.

And still Saralyn was relentless. "Would they be your friends if you turned out to be Jewish?"

"We're not Jews, that's stupid."

"What if they found out you were gay?"

"Me? You've got to be kidding." He puffed up his chest, nearly strutting. The floorboards creaked; a vase rattled on the mantle.

Saralyn stood up and rewrapped her scarf around her face. Only her angry eyes were exposed, like a harem woman's, and her words were muffled by the soft wool. "They're despicable, Dan. They're filled with hate and vile ideas."

Dan shrugged. "It's a free country."

Saralyn tugged at the scarf until her lips were free. "It sure is, baby brother. And you know what else your so-called friends are full of, besides hate and disgusting ideas? Fear."

Dan turned on the TV, to show her how unimportant her words were to him. *Gilligan's Island* was just ending. Jeez, Gilligan must be a grandfather by now.

"They're scared little sparrows, Danny, pretending to be hawks and falcons."

Maryanne probably weighed two hundred pounds and had sagging boobs.

"Pay attention!"

"I hear you," he said, his back still to Saralyn.

"Then respond. Stick up for yourself, before they brainwash you and you haven't got a millimeter of free thought left in that spongy brain of yours."

He spun around, felt the hum of the TV on his

back. "Guys like Dolby and K.C. aren't afraid of anybody."

"*Au contraire, mon frère*. They wouldn't be spouting all that poison about races and religions and nationalities if they weren't scared little rug rats, worried that their Tonka trucks and Tootsie Pops are going to be taken away from them. They're pitiful, Danny."

Anger rumbled in Dan's stomach. He wanted to smash her face, tighten that scarf around her throat, hurl her facedown in the slush of the front walk.

She yanked open the door, and a blast of frigid air hit him, along with her icy words. "Get some hair, brother. In fact, get a life."

CHAPTER NINETEEN

Dan was getting a life, all right. In fact, he was getting a tattoo, a gift from K.C. and the rest of the WhiteSkins who'd each tossed five bucks into a Broncos hat.

"It means you're one of us," K.C. told him. With the American flag rippling across K.C.'s entire belly, he could have been two or three of them.

K.C. jerked the pickup around the block a couple of times, looking for a parking place. "I know what you're thinking, Demon."

No, he couldn't know. What Dan was thinking was how the tattoo was going to hurt like hell and last forever.

"You're wondering, can you get AIDS from a tattoo needle."

Jesus, he'd never even thought of that!

"Miss Donarene runs a clean operation, trust me. She cooks all that stuff in her autoclave and uses a quart-and-a-half of antibiotic cream on you."

"Sounds cool," Dan said casually, though his

heart was thumping. It passed through his mind that he wasn't well-suited to this WhiteSkins stuff, or maybe it took time to grow into it. Look how far he'd come already.

K.C. parked the truck in a handicapped zone. RIGHTS FOR ALL; SPECIAL PRIVILEGES FOR NOBODY — that was Zack Decatur's motto which K.C. took to heart. He led the way down the street to the tattoo parlor. Not parlor, *studio*. The sign said DONARENE'S STUDIO OF SKIN ART. A little bell tinkled over the door, and a voice from nowhere said, "Hold on."

The waiting area looked like an old-fashioned barbershop, the kind Dan's father used to take him to. His father always said, "I don't trust his 'n' her joints where a woman cuts your hair. The hormones are all mixed up in places like that." At eight and nine, Dan had wondered what hormones actually were; guessed they were a certain kind of clipping shears, or maybe hair goo.

The place smelled like a printing shop — the rusty-blood smell of ink. There was a faint moan from behind a screen that had a map of the old world on it. Spain and Portugal were in the center of the world. Africa and Asia were minor inkblots. Then a husky voice called out, "I'm just finishing up this courageous pigeon. Be right there."

"I know what else you're thinking," K.C. whispered. " 'Does it hurt,' right?"

Dan shrugged. "I'm not going to let a couple of needle jabs spook me."

"Look over Miss Donarene's flash and pick

one." Flash, it turned out, was what they called the samples of the tattoo artist's work. "See anything you like?"

There was the usual array of flags and Lady Columbuses, roses and tulips, skulls and crossbones and serpents, naked women, butterflies, anchors, Yosemite Sams, crucifixes, and cannons shooting off red and blue and jaundice-yellow fireworks. "Can't decide," Dan said.

K.C. must have picked up on the wobble in Dan's voice. "You're not chickening out, are you?" He put his arm around Dan and nodded decisively, like a father urging his son to hand the store clerk the pack of Juicy Fruit he's just palmed.

"I just don't see anything I like yet."

"You will." K.C. thumbed through a magazine so worn that the pages barely whooshed when he turned them.

Then he heard Donarene murmur a bunch of words behind the screen to someone who seemed to be slipping back into his clothes. In a minute the back door slammed shut, and Donarene peeked out around the screen. "Just need to wash up." Water splashed, some metal tools clinked into a container, and there was a whirring sound, like a centrifuge. Donarene must have ripped off a huge slice of butcher paper, which she was crumpling into a wad. It sounded a lot like a nurse getting an examining room ready for the next patient. Encouraging, familiar, *clean*, Dan assured himself.

Finally, Donarene came out. "Kevin Cabot, I thought that was you. Back for more work?"

"I'm covered, Miss Donarene. But I brought you a new victim."

The woman's age and weight were about the same, seventy, and she raised her glasses to her forehead to get a better look at Dan. Her polyester bellbottoms flapped around the skinniest ankles that ever held a woman upright. Stilts, her legs must have been. A white T-shirt covered a flat chest. Maybe she used to have breasts, or maybe she used to be a boy. She lifted Dan's chin tenderly. "Kevin, I do believe you've brought me a virgin."

"She means in the tattoo department," K.C. said gruffly.

Donarene patted Dan's right arm, stretching the skin across his bicep. "Good elastic skin. Light, supple, not like chicken hide. No prickles. You're a fine tatty specimen."

"Yeah."

K.C. clunked Dan's knee, and Dan added, "Thanks, Miss Donarene."

"Where do you want it?"

Behind the screen, where K.C. couldn't witness his cowardice. But then he realized she was getting anatomically specific.

"You'd have to hold Donarene's feet to the flame to make me mark up that pretty face."

On his face? Never, although Dolby had a dime-size swastika tattooed just in front of his left ear, and one of the Denver ForeSkins had "Sieg Heil!" on his nose.

"I do a lot of gut work," Donarene said, pulling his T-shirt out of his jeans. "Nice flat white belly.

Be a breeze. I can do your girlfriend's name in a pretty heart, lots of lace, for, say, forty bucks?"

Wouldn't Laurel get a kick out of that! If he ever saw her again.

But K.C. wasn't amused. "Get real, Miss Donarene."

She screwed her eyes up at K.C. "Uh-huh. Something nasty. One of those Hitler things? Well, it's no skin off my nose," she said, laughing in toots and snorts. "What'll it be?"

She sounded like a waitress. "What'll it be, eggs over easy or a short stack?" But Dan suddenly realized that the *what* wasn't as important as the *where*. If it showed, his mother would have a fit, but mothers recovered. Coaches didn't. He might still have a chance to swim for the Neptunes. Hey, were skinheads competitive swimmers? In his new life, anything was possible, right? So he thought about his swim coach in Limon lining up all the guys, dripping wet, with towels wrapped around their suits and goose bumps as big as zits all over their chests. "If you put pictures on your God-given body where I or any alumni of this school, or any parent, or any other taxpayer, for that matter, can see them, you're dead meat. Off the team, and don't even *pray* for a swimming scholarship."

"I'm a swimmer."

Donarene understood. "Doesn't leave too many choices. You want it where the sun don't shine." She pulled him to his feet and spun him around. Patting his butt, she pronounced him suitable fodder. "But I won't know for absolute 'til I see it in the living flesh under my gooseneck lamp." Dan slipped behind Asia and Africa and unzipped his jeans, while K.C. said, "Keep it something simple, Miss Donarene. Maybe just a little 'Sieg Heil' with some scrollwork around it. We've only got twenty-five dollars."

Dan lay on Donarene's examining table, belly down and squashed on to a steamy white towel.

"My father's name was Donahue, and my mother's was Irene," she said, swabbing Dan's butt with alcohol. He held his breath, but sucked the fumes in through his nose. His left cheek stung cold, even though she'd pulled the lamp right down to it. "Oh, yes, I was their love child," she said dreamily. "They nearly got married because of me."

What was he supposed to say? Lucky they came to their senses?

"But it wouldn't have been right, and so they just married their names together. Donarene."

"You almost done?"

"Just cranking up, pigeon, like warm-up exercises those Jane Fonda types do. So, you want me to surprise you, hunh?" She snapped at her rubber gloves, waiting for inspiration, while he filed through every excuse he could think of to bolt from the table. He still hadn't finished *The Fixer* . . . only sailors and longshoremen got tattooed . . . he had to call the Neptune coach before the season got away . . . he promised Loc they'd go out for ice cream after their next karate lesson . . . there were cobwebs thick as safety nets in the corners of his closet. . . .

"I've got it!" Spurred on by her creative genius, Donarene was all business now. Dan felt a sponge on his skin and warm water trickling down and pooling under his hip, then something cold and sharp. He jumped slightly. "Lay still, pidge, I'm just shaving off a patch of hair no bigger than a pancake." The blade scraped across his skin in a place a guy never expected to shave — not even a swimmer.

After a few quick swipes with the razor, she washed the spot again and dabbed it dry with alcohol, then smeared it with some greasy stuff. "This cold part's just Neosporin. Kills the bugs." She massaged and massaged, as though she were looking for a vein to tap for blood. Already the spot felt tender from overworking. When would it actually *hurt*?

"Okay, I'm just gonna lay this acetate stencil down on your little bun. It's kinda powdery with ground up charcoal. And I'm gonna press it onto this greasy gunk. Good! That gives me a picture to work with."

"What is it, Miss Donarene?"

"Told you, a surprise. You won't be disappointed." Dan hunched up on his elbows to see behind himself, but couldn't unless he'd had a neck the length of Bella Donna Prozac, the ferret's, or a head that swiveled. He watched Donarene stir little smudge pots of dye — red, black, yellow, navy blue. He lowered his arms again when he heard her fiddling with the needles, pulling them out of the antiseptic and drying them and snapping them onto the vibrating tattoo machine. It was going to feel like a dentist's drill, only it sure wasn't happening in his mouth.

"Still breathing, pidge? Now, I won't be sticking needles into your muscles like a doctor shot. I'll just poke through the first three to five layers of your skin."

He tensed, pulled his cheeks together.

"Oh, relax." She slapped his rear affectionately, like the guys on the swim team did when you beat your best time by a tenth of a second.

His chin slid around in a puddle of sweat and probably some drool, too, as he heard the brushy needles clinking like melting ice cubes. "Is it going to hurt much?" he asked, even though he'd promised himself he wouldn't. He was practically whispering, so K.C. wouldn't hear him on the other side of the screen.

"Won't hurt me a bit," Donarene said, then cackled. "These suckers vibrate about five thousand times a minute. Just feels odd, that's all, kinda prickly and burny." With that, she began to outline the permanent design on Dan's rear end.

Mike Gutierrez stood on the porch, with a quart container of Ben & Jerry's Fantasy in Fudge frozen on to his fingers.

Laurel's face must have registered more surprise than hospitality.

Mike stammered out, "I thought the afternoon called for ice cream." He waved his bushy dark eyebrows. "It's — what? — eighteen degrees out here?"

Laurel laughed and pulled him into the house.

"Of course, if you want the ice cream, you're going to have to eat my thumb and forefinger."

Loc sauntered out of the TV room. "I heard ice cream," and he grabbed it out of Mike's hand.

Jonathan came running at the sound of the magic words. "What flavor?"

"It's mine," Loc said.

"You pig." Jonathan and Loc passed Ben & Jerry back and forth like a football, until it rolled under a chair.

Laurel retrieved it, with dustballs glopped on to it. "This was really nice of you, Mike." She led him into the kitchen, and the boys followed. Mike dropped his coat onto a chair and sat at the round oak table.

Loc and Jonathan each grabbed a spoon from the drawer and shoved each other to be first in line at the table.

"Out, you two." Laurel pried the ice cream open, and Jonathan was happy to take a swipe of Fantasy in Fudge with his spoon before he left the kitchen, but Loc wouldn't budge. He studied Mike closely, and finally said, "This guy your new boyfriend?"

"Loc Grady!"

He glared at Mike. "You dumped Dan?"

"Get out, or I'll rip your lips off and pitch them into the garbage."

"Okay, okay," Loc conceded as he backed out of the kitchen. Safely on the other side of the swinging door, he yelled, "I like Dan better. Me and Dan are friends, ya know. He's teachin' me martial arts stuff."

"Out! I'm really sorry, Mike."

"No problem. I've got two little brothers myself. I guess I should have called."

Laurel scooped out a mound of ice cream for Mike and absently licked the spoon. Mike slurped his ice cream as noisily as possible, to cover the embarrassing silence.

"It's just too soon, Mike."

"Yeah, I know. I'm not saying we have to get grafted at the hip. I just thought you might need a friend." His tongue darted out like a cat's, to lick ice cream off his upper lip. "Just friends," his words said, though his eyes pled a different case.

Laurel went around behind him and put her arms around his neck. "I couldn't ask for a better friend," she said. His neck felt warm and sinewy as a rope. Mike was a weight lifter; his strength was in his neck and arms. Dan's was in his legs. *His* neck was as soft as the underside of his arm.

When would it stop? Would there be a time when she could just go about her normal life without everything and everyone reminding her of Daniel Penner?

"You don't know the occupational hazards in a job like this," Donarene said while she shaded her design. True. Dan was just beginning to appreciate the hazards of being the tattoo*ee*, and it was way too early to realize how tough life was for the tattoo*ist*.

"There's no job security. No retirement, no sick leave, bad hours. Can't even get insurance." Dan winced. "Did I jab you, pidge?" She stopped for a while. "You know, it's all in the shading, never mind color. Shading's what makes it look three dimensional."

Great, he was going to have a three dimensional — what? — *thing* — on his tail, realistic as a bucket of live worms.

"We ought to have a union, but we can't get along well enough to agree on diddly squat." She got back down to work, shooting globs of dye under his skin with writhing needles. All he could think was that K.C. better be happy about this, and it better be a fantastic creation, because he was *never* doing this again.

"There's a lot of myths about tattoos," Donarene said. Her face was so close to her work that he could feel her breath on his raw skin. "People say it's addictive. They say once you've got the pigment under your skin, you get crazy until you get more ink. That's the stupidest thing I ever heard."

It made as much sense as any of the rest of this stuff, but she had other cheering news. "People say you can't get into heaven if you've had skin work. I've had guys in here with letters from their priests, can you feature that? Geraldo Rivera, that nut from TV? He's got a tattoo on his hand, and some rabbi told him he couldn't be buried in a Jewish cemetery on account of it."

"I didn't know he was Jewish," Dan said faintly.

"Half. Maybe they can slice him down the midsection and bury his clean half with the Jews, and the other part of him with us sinners. Okay, pidge, the rest is downhill."

Downhill from where she was working was *not* good news.

"I'm just going to finish up the coloring, that's the easy part."

And then, when he was just getting used to it, the way you get used to hearing jets take off outside your bedroom window, she tapped his back and ordered him up on his feet. Dan slid off the table, careful to wrap the soggy towel around his middle. Craning his neck like a cat doing her personal laundry, all he could see was a white bandage about four inches square.

"You'll see it tomorrow." She presented him with a paper, left over from mimeograph days, telling him how to take care of things when he got home. "Whatever you do, don't pick at it, hear? If you pick, you'll pull the color right off."

"Now you can tell me what it is, this big surprise."

"It's a daisy."

He had a *flower* tattooed on his butt? Somehow he didn't think K.C. and Dolby would be too thrilled.

"Relax," she said, sinking into a barber's chair.

"The work wears me out because of the arthritis. Another occupational hazard."

"A daisy?" he whispered. He'd rather be hung by his eyelids than have K.C. know that he'd be sitting on a daisy (she loves me, she loves me not) for the rest of his natural days.

"Yeah, it's because of that poem, that cummings guy who never uses capital letters. He says, 'i thank heaven somebody's crazy enough to give me a daisy.' That's me, Donarene. I gave you a daisy. God bless, pidge." She shoved him around the screen.

K.C. had been dozing and he jumped up. Dan heard his nipple rings jingle slightly. "What did she put on you?"

"I haven't seen it yet," Dan said, stalling for time.

"It's a red rocket," Donarene said. "Just gone off. And all that flashy fire's left in its wake."

"Nothing about white power, Miss Donarene?"

"It's a pretty powerful tattoo, Kevin. You wouldn't want to look at it without shades."

"Where *it* is, I wouldn't want to look at it, anyway," K.C. said, handing Donarene a clump of limp dollars.

CHAPTER TWENTY

Every kid was out of the building except Loc. Only one light still burned, on the top floor of Catholic Social Services. Laurel was furious, because she had to double-park in a bank of snow and trudge up two flights of clunky stairs to the classroom. The teacher, a birdlike lady named Mrs. Truong, smiled at her but looked blank when Laurel asked where Loc was. Then her face lit up as though someone had opened the refrigerator. "Maybe he went with that boy who brings him to class sometimes."

"Patrick? My brother?"

"No, the other one, the one who has no hair."

Laurel ran back down the stairs, powered by raging thunder. So Dan was picking Loc up at school and taking him to Vietnamese class! How long had *that* been going on? Patrick's head would roll. He'd be grounded until he was thirty.

And now Dan had picked Loc up *after* class, even though he knew that was Laurel's job. It was so rude and thoughtless of him. In fact, it was kidnapping!

She cut new tracks in the snow and drove like Mario Andretti. In Dan's driveway, she left the motor running. He opened the door quickly — maybe because she'd been leaning on the buzzer that sounded like a "strike" on *Family Feud*. "Where's Loc?" Laurel demanded, and then she saw his scrawny body behind Dan, with Dan's Toronto Blue Jays hat turned backwards on his head.

Dan said feebly, "I thought you were all at some Cub Scout dinner."

"You make everything a big deal," Loc said in his gravelly voice. He spun the Blue Jays hat around; it was way too big.

"I'm really sorry," Dan began, but Laurel cut him off.

"Get your coat."

Loc obviously debated with himself for a split second, then decided he'd better follow her. He grabbed his ski jacket off the cluttered couch.

All this time Laurel had stood in the doorway. Now she noticed a tape playing softly in a back room of the house — something Barry Manilowish — and she remembered sitting at the kitchen table with Dan's mother the morning after he'd vanished. She could taste the chalky cold-hot chocolate, hear the tape from the morning news talking about the store clerk who'd landed in the hospital. And she remembered Mrs. Penner saying, "That's Danny. The pocket knife was his father's. He always had it with him." And then Laurel knew absolutely what she'd been suspecting all along: There were no black crackheads in the store that night.

"Don't ever pick Loc up again!" she shouted, and Dan nodded.

Sliding past him out the door, Loc said, "He's got a tattoo, but I'm not gonna tell you where."

In the car, Laurel was too furious to make much sense, so Loc capitalized on her sputtering. "You don't want me to have any friends. You're just mad because he likes me better than he likes you."

She slammed the brakes on and all but smashed into a red Camaro inching toward the stoplight.

"You'll get us killed," Loc grumbled.

"Don't you know what Dan's into?"

"Swimming."

"He's a skinhead, Loc. They hate everybody who isn't white."

"He doesn't hate me."

"Shut your mouth and listen. They beat up blacks with baseball bats, they terrorize guys who own Chinese restaurants."

"He's my best friend."

"They shatter gravestones in Jewish cemeteries. A couple of years ago, right here in Boulder, three skinhead kids were arrested for killing *one of their own* who'd done something they didn't like."

"Like what?"

"I dunno — maybe hanging around with an Asian kid?"

"You're making up lies," Loc said. He refused

to look at her, staring instead into the cold night through the frosted car window.

"They hate anyone who isn't white and Protestant. They despise all foreigners."

Finally the Camaro turned left, and Laurel couldn't believe it, but tough-kid Loc was sniffling. She thrust a tissue his way, jabbing it into his ribs.

"You lie," he said, his voice thick as pea soup.

Laurel wanted to reach out, but he wasn't a touchable kid, and besides, she needed comforting as much as he did. So she stared at the taillights ahead, and he stared out his window, and they made their way through the slushy snow, with silent tears crusting on their cheeks.

At dinner, Loc and Laurel were both glum, but when it's feeding time at the zoo, no one notices if a couple of monkeys are off their feed.

Mr. Grady said, "The soup's hearty and delicious, Love."

Kim picked out the slithery chunks of tomato and laid them in a neat row across her place mat.

"That looks like roadkill," Booser said.

"Kim, Booser!"

"What is *this*?" Jonathan shrieked.

"Okra," Mrs. Grady calmly answered.

"OKRA?"

Patrick said, "Yeah, she has a talk show on TV. Last week she did 'Three-legged Hemophiliacs Who Love Gerbils Too Much.' "

"Come now, Pat," said his father, smiling, while Laurel glared at Patrick and reveled in how good it was going to feel to get him in major trouble after dinner.

"Okra," Gary repeated. "They're those things in the grocery store that look like lizards."

Booser whined, "I'm not eating lizards," and he lined the rim of his soup bowl with slimy green flecks.

To complicate things, Mr. Grady asked, "What's the main course, Love?"

Mrs. Grady's answer was abrupt: "Soup. I've been grading midterms all day."

"And cornbread," Gary added, his mouth full and squishy.

"A hearty winter soup. It's got your four basic food groups in it," Patrick said. "That would be sugars, fats, salts, and sodas."

Mrs. Grady speared a chunk of stringy beef and glared at Patrick. "Food groups are out. We talk about food pyramids, now."

Kim asked, "Is tomato a fruit or a vegetable?"

"Yes," they all answered. There were sloshing sounds around the table, then Patrick's crackly voice: "Where's the dairy part? It's on the food pyramid, isn't it?"

"In the Parmesan cheese you're dumping in your bowl," his mother said frostily. "See how it clumps up your soup? That's just the way it's going to turn your arteries into clogged sewers some day."

Loc stabbed at chunks of meat and beans with his chopsticks. Then Mr. Grady said, "Have you been following this brouhaha about the rally the white power skinheads want to hold on December eighth?"

Laurel's spoon clunked against her bowl, and Loc caught her eye, then turned away.

"They call December eighth Martyr's Day," said Dad.

"One of our Catholic martyrs?" Gary asked.

"No, this martyr's a crook and a murderer. It has to do with some shootout between an FBI SWAT team and a pack of gangster white supremacists over in Washington state. I read that the man was firing a machine gun at the FBI, so they burned his house, with him in it. Made an instant martyr out of him."

"Oh, Bradley, no."

"Every year since 1984 they've used this as an excuse to tout their warped ideas in public. Only this year there's a new spin on it."

Laurel didn't want to hear, but it seemed she wouldn't be allowed to escape. The little kids had all tuned out the conversation and were into their own stuff. Only Loc seemed to be paying attention.

"This year," Dad continued, "the ACLU's involved. I just don't get this. These punks who spew hatred and violence want to have a rally on the steps of the high school. No decent-living citizen of this city wants them there. And the city's stalling on issuing them a parade permit. But then along comes the American Civil Liberties Union, filing friend-of-the-court papers and saying these thugs have a right to dress up like sadistic Nazis and preach their brand of un-American prejudice and hatred."

Thoughtfully, Patrick said, "Well, we've got this Constitution, Dad."

He pounded the table. "I say Fascist propaganda is not free speech!"

"Yes, but if these guys can't say what they believe, how do we know that next week or next year we won't be stopped from saying what we think's right?"

Mrs. Grady stacked bowls and shooed the impatient little kids away from the table. Laurel was relieved to see Loc scurry away to the TV with the rest of them.

"What could we possibly have to say that would hurt anyone?" Mr. Grady, the gentlest of men, asked.

"Well, we're Catholics, right?" Patrick began. The parents had stern looks on their faces. "Feel free to help me out anytime, Laurel," he said, but Laurel looked down into her soup bowl circled with its reddish grease specks and let Patrick hang out to dry. "Okay," he was saying, "suppose we want to have a protest outside an abortion clinic?"

"Abortion's an abomination!" Mrs. Grady cried, and Patrick said, "But it's legal in this country."

"But it's wrong," his father said.

"Yes! And don't we have a right to speak out against a stupid law, even if all those legal types and pro-choice types say abortion's okay?"

"It's *not* okay."

"So *you* say, Mom," Patrick pounded on. "That's your right, but the majority of Americans disagree with you, and don't they have a right to say so, if they think you're wrong?"

Mr. Grady asked incredulously, "You mean, you believe these hoodlums should be allowed to hold their rally?"

"Sure." Patrick popped a crumb of cornbread into his mouth, certain he'd convinced them all.

"Oh Pat, where did we go wrong with you?" his mother said with the saddest of sighs.

"No, no, wait. I think they should have their rally, but all the rest of us should have the biggest, loudest, most bombastic, well-organized, incredibly amazing rally this city has ever seen. A counterdemonstration, get it?"

Mr. Grady shook his head, and Mrs. Grady studied the ceiling. It made some sense to Laurel, though.

"In fact, I'm already working on it," Patrick said quietly.

What? This was a whole chunk of his life Laurel didn't know a thing about. Funny how you can live with a person and not know him at all. But, then, it was also funny how Laurel could go out with Dan for two months and not know *him*, either.

Patrick continued, "I've been meeting with a bunch of people — synagogue kids, the Islamic students from the University, the NAACP, the Asian Center, even some community bigwigs. We work on it every day after school." He glanced up at Laurel, silently begging for mercy; obviously, Loc had already gotten to him. "You want to help, Laur? I promise you, it's going to be the biggest thing that ever hit Boulder, Colorado."

CHAPTER TWENTY-ONE

Dr. Millwood's entire seventh-hour class was in various stages of REM and non-REM sleep as he ratcheted his way through a lecture on po-li-ti-cal ac-tion com-mit-te-ees. Mercifully, announcements crackled from the speaker above Dr. Millwood's head, and Laurel opened one eye.

"Good morning, Panthers. Today is Tuesday, November twenty-third . . . tickets still available for the Turkey Trot tomorrow night in the north gym . . . Pom-pom squad's mums sale finishes up today at noon, if you want mums for your Thanksgiving . . . and don't forget the Christmas poinsettias . . . SOAR, Students Organized Against Racism, meets in the art room after school to work on posters and banners for the December eighth rally . . . Connie Bocker was MVP in a heartbreaker against Louisville yesterday . . . Today's Mr. Calhoun's birthday . . . won't say how old he is, but he says he's been teaching physics since before Einstein."

That brought a chuckle to Dr. Millwood, who was even older than Mr. Calhoun.

". . . and the Activities Group Thought for the Day comes to you from the White Student Union: The only good Jew is a dead J — "

Someone snapped the mike off, and the broadcast crackled out. Dr. Millwood pepped up considerably. "Well!" he said, the fastest thing ever to fire from his mouth, and people stirred uneasily in their seats. Joy went over and put her arm around Rosie Merren. "I'm sorry," she murmured, and Edward Boyd yelled, "What is this, Nazi Germany?" Dr. Millwood apparently sensed political action in progress, and he let them talk it out for the rest of the hour.

Laurel left the class with a throat that felt as sour as if she'd been throwing up all morning.

With the promise of Thanksgiving hanging in the air, and a four-day vacation, she agreed to go to a SOAR work session with Patrick at seven o'clock in the morning on Wednesday. He'd presented his case the night before while they were studying at the dining room table.

"Students Organized Against Racism is the only answer, Laur. We've got to fight fire with fire."

Laurel smiled at him, wondering how this total cutup had gotten so serious all of a sudden — but then things were pretty serious around school. She actually remembered Dr. Millwood once saying, "In every civilization, leaders have arisen when they were needed," in considerably more syllables than that, of course. Patrick, it seemed, was emerging as a political leader. So she told him, "The catch is, *they've* got fire. All you guys have got is a puny little flickering Bic."

"Just come once, just to feel the energy we've revved up to smash these scummy vermin."

She said she'd go, but in her heart she was afraid for Patrick and his friends, just as she was for Dan himself.

You can tell before you open a door that there's something inside you don't want to see. Patrick had parked in the school lot and was just catching up with Laurel when she stepped into the foyer of the school. A banner hung across the main hall:

RIGHTS FOR ALL
SPECIAL PRIVILEGES FOR NOBODY
HAVE A NICE DAY IN WHITE AMERICA!

Across walls and lockers and windows and doors were messages of such incredible hatred and rage. Laurel and Patrick moved slowly down the empty hall, fascinated and repelled by the evil all around them. The lockers of Jewish students had six-pointed stars on them and swastikas. A pink triangle hung on Gerry Dodd's locker with the message COME OUT OF THE CLOSET, FAG. The door to Mrs. Oliver's room gaped open obscenely; someone had shredded all the resource books on African-American studies. The scraps were blown all around the room. The map hanging on the wall had Africa circled in red lipstick, along with the words NIGGERS GO BACK. Mr. Goldstein's biology lab chalkboard said TOO BAD HITLER DIDN'T FINISH THE JOB.

A noose hung from the ceiling over Maurice Gannet's locker, with a card attached. Typed in some extra-bold computer font were the words **REWARD FOR RUNAWAY SLAVES!!!**

Coach O'Malley, pale as oatmeal, carried a stiff dead squirrel out of the gym. Grimly, he offered it up for Laurel's inspection. A note safety-pinned to its hide said ATTENTION ILLEGAL ALIENS — THIS ONE DIDN'T MAKE IT ACROSS THE BORDER.

"Oh, God." Laurel turned to her brother, whose face was resolute. He led her, no, *pulled* her, along to the art room where SOAR was already working on its responses.

By eight o'clock, metal detectors were set up at the main entrance to the school, and all the other doors were chained. "What if there's a fire?" people asked, and then panic rippled through the building as kids became convinced there *would* be a fire before the day was out. It was useless for teachers to try to teach, and so the classes became public forums and platforms and places to park the loose-tied knots of fear and anger they all clutched.

"Good thing we'll be off for Thanksgiving," the optimists said. "Let things cool down."

"By Monday," the pessimists replied, "this building will be toast."

A lot of parents, including Laurel's, were called in for an emergency meeting with the school board and the administration. Not just cops, but tough-looking fathers were deputized to patrol the halls, like MP's guarding the brig.

"It's a war zone," Laurel told Erika.

"Yeah, but where are the soldiers on the other side?"

Good question. In fact, where was Dan? Since no one much cared if they got to class on time, Laurel went to the office between periods to check the list of absent students. Dan Penner, sick. She scanned the list for other guys she thought were in the movement, others with shaved heads and braces and obscene tattoos. All the ones she could think of were out sick.

A bunch of them sprawled on the floor of Dolby's basement, while K.C. thrashed around, as jittery as if he'd been swallowing uppers. "Jesus, I really feel like I've done something for my country, don't you?"

"Yeah, it's like shooting Japs back in the war," Steve said. "My grandfather says that's when he felt most proud to be an American."

"Like shooting Japs, I like that," K.C. said.

"Or Koreans, or those gooks over in 'Nam," said a guy Dan only knew as Lionheart.

Butcher said, "Too bad we didn't smash any mud people's skulls today." He waved a foot of steel pipe around.

"We don't get no Brownie points," said Baker, faking baby talk.

"Awww."

"Except Butcher offed that squirrel pretty good. This late in the fall, it should have been hibernating in some knotty tree. Stupid squirrel, it was practically dead meat, anyway, right, Demon?"

"Right, K.C." It was all just a prank, Dan told himself. His dad used to say, "Boys will be boys," and that would excuse almost anything he did, from escaping a shower, to hurling a baseball through the front window.

The cops called it vandalism and a bias crime, and K.C. called it patriotic duty, but Dan knew it was just juiced-up kids going a little bit wild. He searched his conscience for signs of regret or remorse.

"Man, it was better than jumping off a cliff into a lake," K.C. said, blowing out shallowly to keep from hyperventilating. "It's gonna take them 'til Groundhog Day to clean that pup up. And people are gonna think about it, too. They can't get by with what they're doing to us."

Scott shoveled the end of a breakfast burrito into his mouth. "It's like, everyone has to stand up and take notice?"

Dolby was getting ready for work at the bottling plant, and he poked his head out of his room. "You guys have gotta be alert, though. It's all gonna hit the fan here in a minute. Scott and Demon, Butcher, too, they'll nail you first, since it's your school. Baker's already suspended."

"Way to go, Baker!"

"Okay, here's the plan," K.C. began, and Dan knew that K.C. was inventing a plan as he spoke. "First, when the TV people come looking for us, and they will . . ."

Again, Dan searched his conscience for signs of regret, remorse —

". . . And then we gotta have a statement, you know, and everybody says the same thing, so nobody goes off half-cocked . . ."

— and Dan found only that he was as pumped up as he'd felt in the old days when he'd won every swim meet and had his picture taken next to all those trophies.

Since she'd figured out that all the skins were absent, Laurel was stunned when she came out of the office and ran smack into two baldies in uniform. Fear sliced through her — *had Dan's friends sent them to hurt her?*

But then she realized that one of the skins was an Asian and the other was black. They carried a paper banner between them, like two soldiers preparing to fold a flag over a coffin. The banner said DEATH TO THE NAZI PIGS, and it was signed by SHAFT, Skin Heads Against Fascist Tendencies. One of the parent-guards confiscated the banner, backed up by a cop with his hand on his gun.

"Oh, man, we're just trying to help," the Asian kid said.

Crumpling the banner into a huge tumbleweed,

the father muttered, "You're just as bad as they are!" The cop stopped him with a firm arm and said, "You two punks get back to class."

By lunchtime the custodians and members of the Spirit Squad had scrubbed or ripped off most of the graffiti. Pale scratchings still showed in some spots, like traces of yesterday's eyeliner, or eraser smudges on a test paper.

During fifth hour, the speaker crackled, along with three bells signaling the unscheduled announcement. An unfamiliar fluttery voice — someone from the office, not a student — gave the word: "Tonight's Turkey Trot has been cancelled due to the . . . circumstances, and Mr. Herrington and the school board have decided to dismiss school at one-thirty today. Have a happy Thanksgiving, Panthers."

CHAPTER TWENTY-TWO

The furnace in the duplex cranked and wheezed, pumping out too much heat, which sucked the moisture from the air. The air sparked with dryness and tension, like the firings of rods and cones when you close your eyes. Now a blast of hot air hit Dan's face as his mother coaxed the turkey into doneness in their unpredictable oven.

Saralyn had brought a pumpkin pie — baked in who-knows-whose kitchen — and it sat on the counter with a fissure down the center growing wider as the kitchen got hotter. Sudi, of course, was mad, because she'd made a lemon cream pie.

The potatoes were already pulverized, but Dan kept on mashing and mashing. Clunks of the masher against the pot made conversation impossible.

Sudi impatiently tapped a copper ring mold against the sink. "My Jell-O molds never come out," she said with a moan. The pale yellow bumpy mess looked like a bombed out building, shimmering in the sun.

"Saralyn, hurry, turn the green beans down!" Mrs. Penner called across the room. Too late; the volcano hissed and erupted, and Saralyn ran to the stove with a towel.

"Sure the potatoes are mashed enough?" she muttered to Dan.

Finally, all their efforts more or less programmed to come together at once, Dan's family sat down to Thanksgiving dinner.

Mrs. Penner sputtered, "We don't usually, I mean, most meals we just — "

And Saralyn helped, "A prayer would be okay. It's Thanksgiving, for God's sake."

They closed their eyes. There was a long silence, until Dan was afraid they were all waiting for him to offer the prayer. He opened one eye, met Saralyn's, and she said, "Amen."

There was *that* to be thankful for, at least. And also for memories of when his father used to carve the golden-brown turkey at the table. Dan could still hear the crackle of the skin, see the juices that would run out when the knife first slid into the breast. Now he looked at the shreds and clumps of turkey he'd hacked off the carcass. His mouth watered at the memory of the thin slabs of white meat his dad had offered up right off the carving knife, meat so juicy, it curved around the knife.

Dan said, "It's too bad Mr. Carlotti couldn't come for dinner."

"Well, I for one am grateful just to have my whole family around me on this day," his mother replied.

Saralyn stirred slightly, but said, "It's good to be home."

Sudi reminded them, for about the sixth time, "All my friends went home for Thanksgiving vacation. What am I gonna do for four days?"

"There's lots of football on." Dan's words were garbled as cold, tart cranberries slid down his throat.

"Football is barbaric," Sudi said. "I have a better idea. Introduce me to your cool friends, Dan. Remember I told you I was dying to go out with the one with the flag on his tum?"

"Oh, my God," Saralyn cried.

"What? I'm free, white, and twenty-one. Almost twenty-one. In two years."

Dan said, "I don't think it's a good idea, Sudi." Not a good idea? It was a rotten idea! Sure, K.C. was his best friend, but Sudi was his *sister*. You don't let your sister go out with a guy who has nipple rings.

"He's so cool!"

"Haven't you met any boys at college?" her mother asked.

"How? You meet them living in the dorm, Mother."

But of course the nipple rings weren't the issue. Bottom line: You don't let your sister go out with a guy who makes dog meat out of a foreign kid's face.

"More turkey?" Mrs. Penner said, too brightly. She sighed and sank back in her chair, and Saralyn quickly said, "The mums on the table are gorgeous, Mom."

"Thank you! I nurtured them myself through all these freezes."

Freezes? The rest of them didn't have any idea how cold it was going to get before this winter melted away. Despite the stifling room, a chill ran up Dan's back as he thought about losing Laurel, and about the WhiteSkins and the rally coming up, and the lawyer Aurelia Phoenix, and the inconclusive fingerprint report on his penknife, and the store clerk who'd already told the newspaper that the guys who savaged him weren't black, but were white guys in black boots. His heart began to thump, and he kept reminding himself, *the guy was already unconscious; he couldn't have seen me there*.

Laurel's Connelly grandparents from Ohio had come for Thanksgiving, and there was an extra leaf in the table to accommodate Gramp's wheelchair. Gram was brown and leathery because she played on the Seniors Tennis Circuit, and Gramp was just starting a second career as a taxi dispatcher.

Kim and the boys tried to look reasonably normal in their dress-up clothes. Laurel noticed Patrick's slicked-down hair springing up here and there.

Where was Dan having Thanksgiving dinner? she wondered. Was he still connected to his family, or did the skins all hang out in some cave together?

What were the rules of skinhead life? *Were* there rules?

Gram squeezed Gramp's hand and said, "Well, Monty, I guess this is about the most unusual Thanksgiving dinner we've ever had, ay?"

Gramp agreed. He wrestled a hunk of spring roll to his mouth with the chopsticks since there were no forks on the table. Strings of cabbage and shredded pork hung out the back of the roll.

"Eeeyuu, it looks like guts," Booser said.

"He said *guts* at the table."

"Booser, Gary." Their mom was gentle as she struggled with the chopsticks herself.

Laurel watched Loc twist thick noodles around his chopsticks and pop them into his mouth expertly. He could nab a morsel of meat as small as a fly with those things. Amazing! "Loc, you're a magician."

Meanwhile, Booser and Gary picked up wads of noodles with their fingers and wrapped them around the chopsticks, while Kim simply leaned her face into the bowl and sucked the noodles up.

Gram had the knack. Maybe her skill came from handling a tennis racquet so agilely. But Gramp gave up in defeat and picked up the spring roll, with his pinky delicately curled.

"I wish we were having turkey like regular people do," Jonathan muttered. Gramp looked like he agreed, but Mr. Grady said, "We can have turkey any night. But this is Loc's first Thanksgiving with us, so we thought we'd do a traditional Vietnamese meal, to show how really thankful we are to have Loc in our family."

"That's the beauty of America," Gram said.

They had to force their way outside just to breathe because of the crushing mass of bodies inside. Dan took a few greedy gulps of cold air.

"They should have hired a bigger place," K.C. said, rubbing a handful of snow on his face and neck. The beat of the music pounded through the thin walls of the old Denver warehouse. It was just the first warm-up group, a ska band from Jamaica, but it was enough to pump Dan up. He was eager to get back inside. A bright light blinded him as a TV camera practically pressed against his nose. A reporter, trying to look very hip in jeans and an expensive Vail-type parka, thrust a microphone in Dan's face.

"I hear there's going to be a lot of skinhead action here tonight."

K.C. had maneuvered his way behind the cameraman, and he was making faces and obscene gestures. Dan had to keep a straight face, for the viewing audience. "Oh, yeah, a lot of action."

The TV man asked, "What band is that playing?"

"Some Jamaican no-name band. Sounds great, hunh?" He tried to slip away, but the camera followed him.

"You guys are racists, right?"

K.C. tapped the cameraman on the shoulder,

and he pivoted, nearly knocking K.C. out with the lens. K.C. stepped back and waved to the camera. "Hey, man, we came for the music, not politics. The Jamaican dudes are great, right? I'm telling ya, you can't like black music and be a racist."

Good answer. If only Dan could think on his feet as well. K.C. ducked under the camera and pulled Dan back into the hall. The ska band was folding, and there was a ten-minute intermission. People poured out into the snowy night, so it was comfortable inside for a while. They found Dolby and Saffron just inside the door. Saffron had her kid in a papoose on her back. Big buttons, dark as Eskimo eyes, peered out at them.

Dolby said, "You ever been to a Sharkbait concert?"

K.C. had heard of them. "They're that San Francisco band, yeah."

"They're not just a band; they're a f—— ing demolition squad!"

"Don't cuss in front of my baby," Saffron warned.

Dolby looked nervously at the kid, then carried on. "This guy in the band, he says, 'Step right up to Sharkbait's Crush Cage,' and you go up, you sign a release, they give you a helmet and an iron pipe, and they set you loose."

"In what?" Dan asked.

"In this, like, fenced-in yard, and you get, like, five minutes to bash in stoves and fridges and washing machines. It's so amazing. The crowd yells,

'CRUSH! CRUSH! CRUSH!' I mean, it's chaos, it's anarchy, man."

Another band was warming up. "This is more like it," K.C. said. "These guys are a cool Oi! band."

Dan had a couple of Oi! records, which Saralyn had given him. They were by English bands like Angelic Upstarts and Cockney Rejects. In fact, he'd listened to them that afternoon, to rev himself up for tonight's concert. "Yeah," K.C. had told him after dinner on Thanksgiving, "Oi!'s the grandpappy of white power music." He wondered if Saralyn knew that, and while he was wondering, he'd browsed through the words on the back of The Oppressed's *Dead and Buried* album. What caught his eye was the message: "This one's dedicated to all the Oi! bands and fans with the bottle to speak out against the racist right-wing scum." Maybe *that's* why Saralyn had given him the album.

Even turning the box up to ten hadn't prepared Dan for the volume and excitement of hearing these guys live. He was jumping around like there were hot coals under his feet.

Now the place was more crowded, and even in the throng of bodies, Dan felt an insistent tap on his smooth head. He looked up to find Odin, surrounded by a bunch of the Denver ForeSkins. "H-h-h-how ya h-h-angin'?"

Dan just flashed him a smile and shoved his way through the crowd to get a better view of the mosh pit. Must have been two hundred kids slam-dancing in the pit, crashing into each other hard enough to knock off glasses, knock out teeth. Dan ran his tongue up to the hole in his mouth. He'd have to get that fixed, but not until after tonight, in case he swallowed a few more teeth.

It had to be at least ninety-five degrees in the room, and guys were tearing off their shirts. The whole place stank of sweat and beer. The punks in the crowd rattled their chains. Some had hot-pink and purple dye running down their faces. Dan saw Odin pull out a barber's straight razor and shear off a handful of hair from one of the longhairs in the crowd. Another one wore a peace button, and Odin cut that right out of the guy's shirt.

A girl in spandex pants fainted, and someone dragged her out of the pit and over to the door for some air. Saffron, in an outburst of maternal protectiveness, stood with the papoose pressed to the wall.

Fights broke out. Punches flew, kicks flew. It was what Dolby said — anarchy. K.C. chopped through the crowd, with his elbows high. Dan looked up just in time to see K.C.'s hands reach out. There was nowhere to duck to, and Dan was shoved right into the pit. Bodies slammed against him with tornado force. One girl stage-dived into the pit and clipped his ear with her boot. His face on fire, his body aching, his head pounding with the rhythm, Dan couldn't remember when he'd ever had a better time.

He saw K.C. pressing some girl up against a post. Her lipstick was as black as her hair. No way he'd let his sister . . . In the split second he was off guard, a guy the size of a mountain rammed his chest into Dan, and Dan went out cold.

He woke up in the snow, his face pins and needles, and he stumbled back into the warehouse. The crowd had thinned out a lot, and then he knew why: the skins had taken over the night. Odin and K.C. and Dolby and Steve and Scott and the other guys — but not Saffron; this was no place for the mother of the White Aryan Nation — were pressed, arm to arm, into a tight circle in the center of the pit. Stripped to the waist, their braces dangling at their sides, they formed a kind of tribal dance, moving in lockstep in a circle, to the relentless beat of the drums. Sweat trickled down their backs, left their skin glistening. Their boots scraped the concrete floor, sending sparks into the air.

And a low thundering war chant rose from the body of the circle: "Skins . . . skins . . . skins . . . skins . . ." their collective voice rumbled, until Dan could swear they were deep in a trance, as raw and primitive as anything that might come out of the jungle.

CHAPTER TWENTY-THREE

Boulder High was still standing the Monday after Thanksgiving. Laurel thought Dan might have been suspended, but there he was in first hour. She couldn't help noticing his was the last problem set Mr. Moreland was handing back, which meant it was the worst one in the class. That gave her just a twinge of satisfaction.

By second hour it was clear that while most of Boulder was thinking of creative ways to recycle dried-out turkey, the school administration had been busy all during Thanksgiving vacation. As soon as the bell rang, Dr. Millwood turned his class over to two C.U. graduate students in sociology.

"We're from the Center for Human Relations," the older one said. His name was Mr. Patel, and he had a thick Indian accent that turned his W's into V's. The other student, who was introduced to the class as Geoff, was deaf and mute. He sat in the front row to read Mr. Patel's lips as Mr. Patel told Laurel's class that they'd be doing some exercises in prejudice reduction.

At first they laughed.

Joy leaned across to Laurel. "This is like stuff we did in Camp Fire Girls." But the man was a guest, and a foreigner, so people were pretty polite.

"Pull your desks into three groups," Mr. Patel instructed. "Seven or eight of you in each group." Joy and Laurel quickly slid their desks up next to each other and made a scraggly circle with Erika, Mike, Rosie, Tran, Edward, and Wayne. "You will need a recorder in each group. I am going to give you five minutes to do this task. Geoff will move through your groups and help."

How? Laurel wondered, since he couldn't hear or speak.

"Here is the task. For two minutes I want you to call out in your group every word or expression you can think of that uses *white* as a describer — for example, white sauce." Geoff showed them the sign for white, which was five fingers coming from the heart and closing into an O. "Recorders, you write everything down."

Rosie was the group's recorder, and Joy started it off. "White knight."

"Whitewash," Wayne added. And then they were all firing answers: white as snow, white as a sheet, detergents that whiten and brighten, White House, white flag of surrender, white lie, white man's burden, whiteout, white slavery, white chocolate, the White Cliffs of Dover and white water rafting. Geoff kept signing words to them and rewarding them with his toothy smile when they hit on a good one.

"Time!" shouted Mr. Patel. "Now, ladies and gentlemen, do the same thing using the word *black* as a describer." Geoff showed them the sign for black: the index finger moving across the forehead, as if you're wiping off sweat.

Black sheep, black magic. They came so fast. Blacklist, blackball, black-and-blue bruises, black bear, blackboard.

"Can't use it, because blackboards are all green now," said Tran Thui, and so they scratched it from their list.

The pilot's black box, black comedy, black plague, Black Death, black eye, Black Flag bug killer, blackmail, black market, black mass, black as the ace of spades, and black widow spider.

When they read their lists aloud, it got really clear, really fast, that most of the white images were positive and clean and comforting, and most of the black images were negative and dirty and dangerous.

"Now," Mr. Patel said quietly, "suppose you're not white-skinned." He let that settle in for a while, and then he asked, "What is prejudice?"

There was the usual silence, finally broken by Edward Boyd. "It's when you don't like someone who's different."

"And?"

"When someone's a member of another race or religion or nationality," said Tran.

"Or sexual orientation," Wayne Bisoni added.

Then answers were flying from all over the room.

"And you don't really know a whole lot about

them, but you decide you hate them?"

"It's discrimination against a whole group, not just a person."

"It's judging them before you know them."

After each answer, Geoff gave the sign for good, and finally Mr. Patel agreed, "All good answers. Now, I ask you to accept this definition of racism. Racism is prejudice with power behind it." Geoff's interpretation of *power*, which involved showing a tight bicep, along with his fierce facial expression, was pretty scary, so they accepted Mr. Patel's definition. "Now, my friends, I want you to turn back to your groups." He gave each group a piece of pink poster board and a bunch of markers. "Your task is to design a racist community."

Geoff went to the former *black*board and wrote in huge loopy letters, MONEY? SCHOOLS? LEADERS? DECISION-MAKING? JOBS? CLUBS? YOU-NAME-IT?

At first, Laurel's group couldn't think of a thing to write on their pink posters, until Rosie said, "Let's say we've got two social classes. They've got to have something that sets them apart. One's got — "

"One eye, and the other group has three eyes."

"All right!"

"Which group is superior?"

"The Three-Eyes, because there are more eyes per head."

"No, the One-Eyes, because each head gets one single powerful unit."

"So, the One-Eyes get the good jobs. They're

the doctors and stockbrokers and movie stars and architects — "

"And they build buildings that are designed just right for One-Eyes, but they're just impossible for Three-Eyes."

"Like, no windows, just single peepholes in all the doors."

"And — what are those things called you see in English movies? Oh, monocles. All the glasses would be monocles, and there wouldn't be any with three lenses."

"And if you've got three eyes, all the TV's and computer monitors will look blurry — "

"How could you even focus to read those inch-wide books that are printed for One-Eyes?"

"That means they couldn't get an education, which means they couldn't get decent jobs — "

"Which means they'd be stuck in the Tri-Ghetto and would never make it to the Uno-Palace on the hill."

"This is great stuff!"

Afterwards, when each group told about their model racist communities, most of the kids felt kind of sick inside, realizing how easy it was, and how much fun, to create a community where all the power went to one group and none to the other. Naturally, they all placed themselves in the power group.

Mr. Patel wasn't through with them yet. "Take a moment to look at how racism thrives in your school."

They talked about the graffiti and the destruction

from last Wednesday, but Mr. Patel wasn't interested in that. "Something more subtle," he urged. So they talked about bussing, and how people of different races hung out with their own kind at school, and how most of the cafeteria workers were Hispanic and Asian, while most of the teachers were white or black. Then Geoff stopped them abruptly; they'd learned to watch for his silent sounds. Laurel and the others turned back to Mr. Patel.

"Let's push the desks out of the way, and you three groups each form a circle." Joy and Rosie and Mike and Tran and Wayne and Edward and Erika and Laurel linked arms, facing one another. Around the room, the other two groups looked just like them, and Geoff and Mr. Patel were lonely islands.

"Now, I will ask one of you from each group to volunteer to break out of the circle. The rest of you must act as though your very lives depend upon keeping the outsider out. Outsider, your job is to get into the circle by any means you can, short of violence."

Mike volunteered to be their personal reject. As soon as he stepped out, the rest of the group closed ranks. He walked around the circle, obviously assessing its weak point. Laurel felt him tap her on the shoulder; everyone knew she was a soft touch. But she tensed her shoulders and refused to respond to him. He tried stepping over their hands; they raised them too high. He tried chopping through their linked arms, but they were like a steel fence. Their elbows butted against his chest when he tried to leap over their chained arms.

Mike was resourceful, though. He got down on the floor and tried crawling in. Of course, the whole group came down as a giant wave and closed the gaps, then stood up, tightening the circle until their legs and feet were pressed against one another.

"Hey, guys," Laurel heard him say. He didn't sound like he was having a good time.

Across the room kids were howling and grunting with their efforts to keep the intruder out. One guy made it in and immediately pushed another kid out of the circle, and that started the whole process over again. The third group was finally infiltrated and collapsed on the floor, laughing.

Meanwhile, Mike Gutierrez was getting nowhere against the Rosie-Wayne-Joy-Erika-Tran-Edward-Laurel fortress. And then a weird thing happened. Somehow a silent message passed among them. Laurel didn't know who started it; it may even have been Geoff. Anyway, all at once they dropped their arms and created a space for Mike. He came into the center of the circle, and they closed around him. He sank to the floor. They all got down on the floor and hugged him.

Mr. Patel drew the rest of the class into a quiet circle around Laurel's group, and he said, "This is the beginning."

CHAPTER TWENTY-FOUR

"I couldn't believe the stuff they made us do?" Scott was trotting around in his socks. He rammed a handful of popcorn into his mouth and mumbled, "All that holding hands and the white sheep–black sheep crap?"

Dolby's mother had left them bowls of popcorn and purple grapes, and Dolby spit the seeds into a tidy pile on the basement floor. "What do they think, a few pinko love-in games are gonna make it all right? We're talking global economic unjustice here."

K.C. said, "I'm sure glad I'm out of high school, aren't you, Dolby? I'd have split a gut if I'd had to do that touchy-feely, smoochy-moochy shit. How did you pull it off, Demon?"

"Didn't. I got sent to the office."

"Wow, I never thought of that," Scott said. "I coulda had the hour off."

"I'll probably get suspended." Dan said it with a casual shrug, as if the suspension were a treat he was looking forward to, like a check in the mail or a ski trip.

"Don't sweat it, buddy." K.C. punched Dan in the arm, nice and light, no bruising. "Hey, it's a free speech issue. We'll call up Zack Decatur and get it fixed. We need you there in the school. You're our inside man."

"What about me?" Scott asked.

"You're a moron. Here, Demon, I brought you a present." K.C. tossed a grocery sack at Dan. It was folded over like an envelope. Flat on the bottom was a T-shirt, and not exactly a new one. Dan held it up to the dim basement light. The front stretched longer than the back, and one sleeve seemed permanently bent.

Dan laid on the sarcasm: "How can I ever thank you?"

"Oh, it's nothing. Recognize it? It's from Skrewdriver's 1991 World Tour. I was gonna give you my No Remorse shirt, but it got munched in the dryer."

Dolby scattered the grape seeds with his foot. "Yeah, I got domestic problems, too."

Scott came over to have a look at the shirt. "Cool," he said enviously. On the front was a blue circle and the words "National Front's SKREWDRIVER," and under the circle were the lyrics from their best song: "Once we had an Empire, and now we've got a slum." The back of the shirt, shoulder to shoulder, was one giant swastika, in black and red and blue.

"It's pretty amazing," Dan said, pulling off his own shirt. The Skrewdriver shirt fit tight, but would probably look okay if he tucked it in.

K.C. grinned. "Happy Hannika, Demon. Hannika's coming up next week, ya know. I personally keep track of these things."

"Yeah, speaking of that Jew holiday, we had our own little celebration," Dolby boasted. "Did you see we made the papers?" He flung a newspaper at Dan, pointing to a small headline that said JEWISH FRATERNITY DEFACED. Dan scanned the article, something about spray-painting the front of the AEPi fraternity house with the words *Jews burn in hell*.

"Nice work," Dan muttered.

"Hey, it's the least we could do. Otherwise their house would look pretty dull, since those Christ-killers sure aren't going to be putting up Christmas lights."

"Just call it beautifying the neighborhood," K.C. said with a laugh. "Beats a burning cross, I guess you could say."

You could tell by the pinched looks on the teachers' faces that the assembly Tuesday morning wasn't going to be a pep rally to drum up spirit for Boulder's game against Lyons. Joy and Laurel filed into the auditorium with the rest of the seniors, while the lower classmen were streaming out.

"What's going on?" Joy asked.

"Just more Nazi stuff," one girl said, and Mrs.

Bower, the assistant principal, silenced her with a smoldering look that could have burned off the top layer of her skin.

Mr. Herrington called them to order even before the bell rang, meaning that he owed them two minutes which they'd be sure to collect at the end of the hour. "Seniors of Boulder High School, you are our hope for tomorrow."

Joy rolled her eyes.

"You are our hope for tomorrow in a world that doesn't seem too hopeful just now."

Laurel noticed that teachers stood in the aisles like prison wardens. Some of them had walkie-talkies, and they'd whisper something to another teacher across the auditorium. Spy, counterspy.

Laurel didn't try to find Dan, but he was a magnet. Light bounced off the shiny heads six rows in front of her. Her heart flip-flopped, as usual. Even when it was over, it wasn't *over*.

Mr. Herrington rolled up his shirtsleeves — his getting-down-to-business signal — and said, "We have a distinguished guest here today from the ADL, the Anti-Defamation League. He's here to share with you a remarkable story of courage and friendship."

"Oh, no," Joy moaned, "this sounds like a gutter-to-the-cross saga."

"Boulder High seniors, in true Panther hospitality, put your paws together and welcome Mr. Jerry Bamberger."

The speaker was barely tall enough to see over the podium; only his cotton-candy gray hair showed. Besides that, he had a gray goatee that pointed this way and that as he jerked his head around. He began, "Imagine, if you will, two enemies caged together . . ."

Dan had been waiting for the axe to fall. Why hadn't Herrington just gone ahead and suspended all of them? Instead, he had to sit through this propaganda, with Butcher and Scott next to him making stupid comments, like, "He's a Jew, isn't he?" The teachers in the aisles glared at them, daring them to make the wrong move.

"Jesus Christ, Demon, he doesn't even celebrate Christmas?" Scott whispered.

Dan saw Coach O'Malley say something into his communicator, and Coach Burns, on the aisle across from him, snatched a kid out of Dan's row. What was this, a warning?

"What do you think, Demon, do Jews have horns? I heard they have horns."

"Shut up, Scott."

"Well, the dude's got enough hair to hide horns."

Mr. Bamberger's voice, which was huge for such a runt, filled the whole auditorium. "Now let me tell you about two men who were, no question about it, sworn enemies before they even met. They come from opposite ends of the human spectrum. One of them is a guy by the name of Larry Trapp, the Grand Dragon of the Ku Klux Klan in Lincoln, Nebraska."

"Yeah!" Scott pumped the air in front of him.

"You can kinda understand where he's coming

from. Larry Trapp had a crummy childhood. He had diabetes, was sick a lot. Got sent to reform school for stealing. He tells about getting raped by some older boys there, some black boys."

"Figures," Butcher said.

"No one knows for sure if it's true, but anyway, Larry Trapp came away from that joint with a message etched by acid in his heart: In order to get what you want, you have to be able to inflict fear on others."

Butcher said, "*He* knows what it's like out there."

Bamberger continued, "Now, the other guy I want to tell you about is Michael Weisser. He's a Jew, a cantor in Lincoln, Nebraska, which means it's his job to chant all the prayers in the synagogue. And this is the story — it's a true story; you can read it in *Time* magazine — about the incredible friendship between Cantor Weisser and the Grand Dragon of the Ku Klux Klan."

Joy muttered under her breath, "Give me a break," and Laurel couldn't imagine any way the two men could be friends, either.

Mr. Bamberger raked his fingers through his hair and began again. "Larry Trapp isn't too happy when Cantor Weisser and his wife, Julie, and their three kids move to town. I take that back. Maybe he's deliriously happy to have a new target for his hatred, because up to now he's just been picking on Asian immigrants and calling them dog-eating scum. So, first thing Larry does is, he calls up the cantor and says, 'You're going to be sorry you moved in, Jewboy.'

"What does Cantor Weisser do? Well, what would you do?" Mr. Bamberger shaded his eyes to see out into the audience.

Someone in the front row called out, "I'd hit the road running!"

"No!" someone else yelled. "Let him stay and fight it out."

"Yeah, but Cantor Weisser doesn't do either one of those." The speaker yanked the mike off the stand and came out in front of the podium, trailing the mike cable like a stand-up comic. "Michael makes up his mind he's not going to be just another victim of religious hatred. In fact, he and Julie promise each other they will not hate back. So, they call Larry up. What do they get, but a ten-minute recorded message about the evils of blacks and Jews. They wait it out and leave him a friendly message. They keep doing this, over and over.

"Now, Larry's a pretty sick cookie, physically, not just mentally. He sits around in his wheelchair, in his rathole apartment, listening to these messages for four long months. Finally, he can't stand it anymore. The next time the cantor's voice comes over the machine, Larry picks up the phone. Well, the Weissers aren't expecting to hear his voice, after so many months, so they're caught off guard. What do they do? They do what comes naturally. They offer to bring him some food."

There was snickering in the audience.

"But it really throws Larry Trapp. Later he says, 'I could detect love in Michael's voice. I had never heard love from a stranger before.' Well, Larry sits around and chews on it like a dog with a leather bone, and then, a month later, he calls the cantor and tells him, 'I've got to talk to you.' So now what would you do?"

"Call the police?" someone ventured.

"Tell him what you think of him, then hang up on him!"

"Not what Michael and Julie do. They go right on over to Larry's house. Larry greets them like they're old friends. Later, he says, 'It was like a jolt, an electrical current. I looked down at my two swastika rings, and I took them off.' Michael and Julie stay four hours and leave with a promise that Larry will renounce his ties to the KKK. Unbelievable?"

"So what?" Scott muttered. "One old sick cripple gives up the Klan? The Jew musta cast a spell or something, maybe put something in the matzah ball soup."

Laurel thought it seemed pretty far-fetched, and wondered what Dan and his *friends* thought about all this. Joy had given up on the story all together and was doing her English homework.

"But the story ain't over yet, kiddies." Bamberger paused for drama, then launched into the rest of it. "Not only does Larry give up the Klan and let go of his hatred, but he starts to study Judaism with the cantor, like he's going to convert. Now, all this time, the guy is dying by degrees.

He's had both legs amputated, and he's totally blind. A societal throwaway, right? Wrong. The Weissers move him into their home, with their three teenage kids, kids just like you, and they take care of him."

"That's real Christian of them," Scott said. "Get it?"

"Got it," Dan mumbled.

"A magazine reporter asks Larry if his life's been in danger since he left the Klan. Larry tells him, 'I'm sure there's a contract out on me. Usually what happens is, the word gets passed around among the skinheads. They're the ones to worry about, because they're the ones who do all the dirty deeds.' "

"He's gonna try to pin this one on us?" Scott slid down in his seat, and Coach O'Malley moved in closer.

Mr. Bamberger was quiet for a long time. Some people thought he was done, and a few of them clapped politely, but he put his hand up to stop them. "Anyone want to know what finally happened to Larry Trapp?"

Bamberger let a heavy silence settle on the auditorium. Even Joy looked up. Even the bald heads six rows ahead looked up.

"He died in 1992. The man was forty-three years old. But here's the thing. He didn't die alone; Michael and Julie Weisser were with him. And you know what the poor guy said when he knew the end was near? He said, 'Love can do so much more than hate.'

"Do you believe that, kids?" Bamberger thumped the microphone three times. "*Believe* it." With that, he strode off the stage, and the crowd burst into applause.

"Very touching," Butcher said, snapping his black braces. "Makes me want to find that Jew and — "

Dan jabbed him, as Coach O'Malley signaled for Butcher to get up.

"What did you think?" Laurel asked.

Joy slammed her English book shut and said, "I just loved the sermonette. All I can say is, Herrington still owes us two minutes."

On Wednesday morning, Dan slipped the SKREWDRIVER shirt over his head, like a man getting into his battle armor. The shirt stuck to his damp back. Dan wiped a clear place in the steamy mirror. His eyes were gray and slightly gloomy; didn't they used to be blue?

This was a big morning. If he'd had any hair, he would have blow-dried it with special ceremony. To compensate, he shaved and shaved until his cheeks were red and stung when he splashed Aramis on them.

What else did men do when they were preparing for battle? Maybe they said a prayer. "Jesus, I hope I make it through this without throwing up." They wrote letters to the damsels left behind. In his head he composed a note to Laurel: "I'm doing what I have to, fair maiden. Keep a candle burning in the window for me." Talk about sappy. "I wish we still loved each other." Even worse. He mentally crumpled both notes and threw them in the toilet.

He grabbed a glass of juice and a piece of peanut-butter toast, scribbled a real note, and walked the nine blocks to school. Glancing at his watch, he estimated that in, say, twenty minutes, he'd be walking into the school, taking off his jacket, sauntering down the hall in his SKREWDRIVER shirt. What would it take — maybe another ten minutes? — before Herrington came tearing out of his office? Suspension, for sure.

Dan flipped the bathroom light back on and grinned at his face in the mirror. "What a stud," he told himself. "I've got a swastika on my back, and a daisy on my butt."

CHAPTER TWENTY-FIVE

Still shivering from the walk to school, Laurel watched Dan saunter down the hall in a short-sleeved T-shirt and jeans. He was close to her locker, and she busied herself with her combination; couldn't even remember the first number. He slipped a piece of paper into her coat pocket and walked past. When he was halfway down the hall, she felt brave enough to look up — and saw the swastika slashed across his back from shoulder to shoulder.

Joy came running down the hall. "Did you see him? My God, it's political suicide."

Laurel slipped the paper out of her pocket.

"What?" Joy asked testily. She read the note over Laurel's shoulder:

Today's the last day in November. There should have been a third red rose.

Joy said, "I swear, I'd sue the manipulative little bigot."

"For what, being a sentimental jerk? It's within his legal rights." Laurel felt her eyes harden into marbles.

The monitor was tilted at just the right angle so Dan could see his name but couldn't make out the rest of his dope sheet on the school computer.

Herrington rolled up his sleeves, then rolled them down again and buttoned them, while Dan sprawled in a chair by Herrington's desk, with his boots stuck out in front of him.

"Mr. Penner, why are you doing this?"

"Excuse me?"

"You're testing me, Mr. Penner. You're daring me to lower the boom. First there was the business with the graffiti, et cetera, and I know that you and your cohorts were behind it." Dan shrugged. "And, then, when we were trying to heal the raw feelings in this building, you refused to participate. What must I do, Mr. Penner?"

"Really, you can call me Dan."

Herrington sat back in his swivel chair with his arms behind his head in the hostage position. But Dan realized Herrington was faking relaxation, trying to unhinge him by refusing to get mad. Suddenly, Herrington lunged forward. "And now the shirt. You understand, son, that I can't allow you to roam about this building with that despicable symbol on your back."

"The swastika's an ancient design, sir. The Indians used it as a good luck sign."

"And Hitler used it as a symbol of tyranny and death!"

Dan stayed cool. He was definitely winning this round.

"That *is* what most civilized people think when they see a swastika, isn't that so, Mr. Penner?"

"Probably."

"Dan, how do you think our Jewish students and faculty members feel when they see you strutting around in that thing?"

"Your guess is as good as mine."

"All right, son." Herrington spoke through clenched teeth; a vein throbbed in his cheek. "I'm giving you one more chance. I want you to go to the pool and ask Coach for a Panthers T-shirt. Then I want you to turn right around and bring me the shirt you're wearing. Is that clear?"

"It's clear. But I won't do it."

"Then, will you go home and promise not to show up in this thing again?"

Dan shook his head. This was getting to be more fun than he'd expected. In a minute Herrington was going to explode like a nova.

"Penner, are you turning this incident into some big confrontational test case?"

"No sir, I just like the shirt."

"Then you leave me no choice. You're suspended for the rest of the week." He pulled a letter out of his desk and scribbled something across the top. "Take this home to" — he checked Dan's computer record — "your mother, and don't come back without her."

Dan reached for the letter. "Can I ask you a question?"

Herrington nodded in defeat.

"Why did it take you so long to suspend me?"

Herrington pressed his church-steeple fingers to his lips. "I don't know, son. Maybe because I like to think of myself as a just man. But I should have known that you and your kind wouldn't understand that sort of thing. Now, get out of my office and out of my building."

K.C. jumped around like a dizzy boxer. "Oh, man, this is the best thing that could have happened. The only thing wrong with it is I didn't think of it myself. This is dynamite, in case we don't get our rally next week. You don't know it, Demon, but you're a living, breathing goddam civil rights guinea pig!"

Dan was the headline story on the five o'clock local news, all three channels. One said, "Boulder High Senior Challenges the Bill of Rights. Details after World News Roundup." Another spliced a picture of Hitler on the screen with a close-up of Dan's face, and the announcer said, "Neo-Nazis in our schools — what YOU can do about it." The third channel featured a full-screen shot of the swastika, with the caption, "School Official Denies Student His Free Speech Rights."

At the first commercial, the phone started to ring.

"C-c-caught you on the news." There was no

need for Odin to identify himself. "Keep up the good work, brother. W-w-white is Right!"

There were calls from total strangers with strange messages. One said, "They ought to put you in front of a firing squad, only everybody's guns ought to be loaded until you're Swiss cheese." One guy, a Ku Klux Klansman in Elkhart, Kansas, happened to pick up the news on his satellite, and wondered if Dan would consider marrying his daughter. "Her poor husband, he was plowed under in the wheatfield last summer. You could have the back forty to farm, whaddya think?"

"Pidge, is that you?" Dan recognized Donarene's voice. "I just saw you on the *tee*-vee. Isn't that something? Whatever you do, you courageous pigeon, don't take off your pants!"

Another caller gushed and sobbed and said, "I'm calling the Pope to see about having you canonized." The American Civil Liberties Union called, offering free help. America for Americans offered sanctuary in one of their secret underground bunkers, if the heat got turned up too high for Dan.

"Penner? Aurelia Phoenix, here. Don't you think you're in enough trouble? Listen, I can deal with a criminal case, but I'm not in the civil rights business, you understand? You've got to fish in another pond if you want to keep your neck out of the noose on this one, Babe."

* * *

By the ten o'clock news, one of the local stations had cooked up a whole debate. On one side was Dr. Blaine, the superintendent of schools, and on the other side was some maverick civil rights lawyer who wore a button that said EXECUTE JUSTICE, NOT PEOPLE. The moderator set the stage by quoting from a dead Supreme Court judge. "Justice Abe Fortas had this to say in the decision in a 1969 school case not unlike the one young Daniel Penner is embroiled in. To quote Justice Fortas: 'It can hardly be argued that either students or teachers shed their constitutional rights to freedom of speech at the schoolhouse gate.' Gentlemen, were Daniel Penner's constitutional rights abridged? Let's hear from Dr. Blaine first."

Dan expected to sleep late on Thursday morning, but Dolby and K.C. came by to pick him up before seven o'clock. "Wear the shirt," Dolby said. "You're going to school."

"Maybe you missed the news last night. I'm suspended."

"Dolby didn't say you were going *in* the school. There's gonna be action outside. It's a sort of planned spontaneous demonstration."

He meant a mob. They heard shouts and general restless crowd croonings when they were two blocks away. From down the block, they could see hordes of people all over the campus lawn and the front steps of the school. TV trucks lined the street, including vans from Salt Lake City and Cheyenne. A National Public Radio stringer held her microphone above the heads of the crowd, pointing it this way and that to get some local color.

Dolby spotted a reporter with a KRON–San Francisco mike. "All the way from Frisco? Whoop!" He rubbed his hands together like someone who's about to come into a lot of money.

"Demon's a hero," K.C. said. "A hero. You all hear that, you out there in TV land? He's a political prisoner, a member of the oppressed white majority."

The TV cameras ignored K.C. as a shout went up: "There he is!" The crowd closed in on Dan and begged him to take his jacket off. It was Dolby's idea that he wear a black turtleneck underneath *the* shirt and, besides, the temperature was below freezing. The crowd cheered as Dan dropped his jacket and whirled around to show the swastika. People on his side cheered because he was so radical; people on the other side cheered because they could smell blood.

Lining the north side of the school steps were SHAFT, Skin Heads Against Fascist Tendencies. They looked ferocious as tigers ready to pounce. In a face-off, flanking the south side of the school steps were the other skinheads. Some were Dan's own WhiteSkins, and some were Denver ForeSkins whom he recognized, but most of them must have been strays from little towns around Boulder. Scott moved back and forth in the line, trying to find his place. Saffron sat on the lawn, with her baby in the hollow of her lap.

Dan spotted Laurel in the crowd. She was one of the few people standing voiceless, as if she were holding a silent vigil. She caught his eye, and quickly looked away. He would have missed her altogether except that she was next to her tall, redheaded brother. Patrick waved a neon-green banner with red and pink and blue and yellow letters that said STUDENTS ORGANIZED AGAINST RACISM SAY: LOOK AT ALL THE COLORS OF THE RAINBOW!!!

At least six mikes were thrust in Dan's face. Someone tried to clip a lavalier mike on him, bunching up half the National Front.

"Hey, watch the shirt," Dolby yelled. "It's valuable."

"How does it feel to have national notoriety all of a sudden?" one reporter asked. "Are you going to court with this?" "Tell us about your family." "Have you ever been in trouble?" "Are you outraged by this blatant violation of your First Amendment rights?"

Well, now, in truth Dan had never given five minutes' thought to the First Amendment or any of the five, ten, or twenty that followed. But suddenly his fame found voice. For the benefit of TV and radio stations in a five-state region, he said, "I have a right to free speech, just like the next guy. Some people burn flags, and that's all right. Some people say they want to get rid of all the bums in Washington, and that's all right. Hey, all I want to do is wear a shirt that expresses an idea."

"What's the idea?" one of the reporters shouted.

"That white people have rights, too. White Anglo-Saxon Protestants."

"What kind of rights do you want?" someone in the back of the crowd called out.

Dan stared at the throng of people; there was immense power in the anger all around him. Either it was the skinhead rage, or it was the rage of people who wanted to shut the skinheads up. "All I want," Dan said, and his voice sounded thin in his own ears, "all I want is a job."

Out of the corner of his eye, he saw the main door open, and Herrington slid out with two cops, one black, one white. They marched over to Dan as if he were Public Enemy Number One.

"This student is suspended," Mr. Herrington said. Each cop took one of his arms.

"Gestapo tactics!" someone yelled, and ironically, it was one of the neo-Nazi skinheads.

"Free speech is dead in this country!" shouted an old woman, who held a banner that looked like it might have been left over from the sixties. In worn letters it said SDS — STUDENTS FOR A DEMOCRATIC SOCIETY.

"Go limp!" Dolby shouted, and Dan let all his weight drop to his knees. The cops were dragging him, his knees scraping along the sidewalk. The jeans ripped. Already his knees were stinging.

"White rights! White rights! White rights!" The skinheads' chant could have worked as a football cheer. Waving their Confederate flags and Nazi flags, their arms outstretched like good Hitler youth, they roared, "The Final Solution Is White Revolution!"

A small band of Jewish students from the university wore shirts that spelled out the Hebrew words, *ANI V'ATAH M'SHANEH ET HAOLAM — YOU AND I WILL CHANGE THE WORLD*, and they chanted, "Never again . . . never again . . . never again."

TV 4 got Dan on camera as the cops forced him into the backseat of the police car. The on-the-spot reporter whispered into a microphone right next to Dan's ear, "The irony here, ladies and gentlemen, is that the constitutional rights that protect the symbolic hate speech of Daniel Penner and his kind are the very rights he would jettison if he and his Nazi hooligans were in charge of our democratic society."

"We shall o-ver-co-o-ome, we shall o-ver-co-o-ome," a cluster of black students sang, and one by one most of the crowd — except the two kinds of skinheads — began to link arms and join the magical incantation:

> Deep in my heart,
> I do believe,
> We shall overcome
> Some day.

Dolby and K.C. were waiting for Dan when the cops dropped him at home. "Looks like we got our rally after all," K.C. said, a big grin spreading across his face. "Too bad Zack Decatur didn't get here on time, but it was A-OK-first-class-rich-shit."

Dolby said, "Now we've got 'em where we want 'em, so we hafta do something really big time. Time to pick up the kid?"

"What kid?" Dan asked, still flushed with his new fame. "You talking about Saffron's baby?"

K.C. shook his head. "The time's not right yet, Dolby. I'll let you know."

Dan spotted Sudi rounding the corner, so he started herding K.C. and Dolby to the pickup.

"I'll tell you, this has been the greatest day of my life so far, how about you, Demon?"

"Yeah, yeah, K.C.," he agreed, but all he could think was, *get him out of here before Sudi spots him.*

CHAPTER TWENTY-SIX

Who could Laurel talk to about all this, about how she felt hoodwinked and betrayed? Her parents ruled the subject out of order, but she heard hushed conversation from their bedroom and was sure they were frantically discussing just how to deal with their poor heartbroken daughter who'd had the bad taste to fall for a Nazi who got himself on TV.

Patrick was into his own kind of craziness, a sort of cause-and-effect campaign where SOAR burst into action to respond to whatever Dan and the skins did, yet Laurel couldn't honestly see SOAR doing anything on its own. Nor could she join them.

She'd tried talking to Joy, but Joy wallowed in her own righteous indignation and was busy organizing the FemPower Coalition. "I swear, the real menace isn't racism, Laurel, it's sexism. Did you see any women in their battalions? No! They just view women as vessels that exist for the purpose of hatching pure white children. Excuse me, but I can't tolerate this kind of degradation of my sisters."

Everyone else seemed to be avoiding Laurel, as if she'd just been diagnosed with a terminal illness, or had a death in her family. Even Mike Gutierrez kept his distance, probably waiting for a signal from her. And the whole school was caught up in its variegated shades of animal rage.

Swine seemed to be the species of choice to describe Dan. In two days Laurel heard the guy who'd once given her red roses called lower than swine, a Nazi pig, a Fascist pig, a chauvinist pig, a publicity hog, and an animal with the manners of a boar. Joy thought "pig-headed idiot" probably covered the subject well.

Laurel's mind kept buzzing with the TV newsbreaks every hour, and the endless discussions in class, and the experts coming in to soothe and heal the Boulder High wounds, and the hum of demonstrators outside the school all day, and, of course, her own growing fury.

Yet when she crawled into bed — earlier and earlier each night, some nights before Kim even went to bed — loneliness poured through her and was only pushed out in a thin stream, like sugar through a funnel, by the growing calcification of her heart.

The books were nested, open page to spine, three and four deep. Dan wondered how much it would take for the rickety legs of their kitchen table to buckle under the weight of those leaden law books. The table groaned every time Saralyn yanked one book out from under its pile.

Mrs. Penner poured fresh coffee into their mugs and discreetly disappeared into the girls' bedroom, at least until Sudi came home.

"I haven't got a head for this," Dan said. His glasses were smudged with sweat. They'd been at it for hours, days, it seemed, and Saralyn gathered energy and enthusiasm the longer they pored over these books.

"Okay, there are just a few things you have to keep in mind. Danny! Pay attention."

"Tinker versus Des Moines Schools."

"Des Moines Independent Community School District, yes, what year?"

"I don't care what year."

"It was 1969. It was a landmark case, Dan. You've got to know this one if you want to give your own situation any credibility."

Dan gulped a mouthful of coffee and burned his throat. "Okay, some girl goes to school wearing a black armband. She's protesting the Vietnam War."

"Go on."

"I don't remember what happened."

Impatiently, Saralyn fired off the facts. "Her name's Mary Beth Tinker, she's thirteen. She and three other students are suspended for wearing the armbands. Does the school have the right to suspend them for this political statement? At issue is whether their symbolic speech 'materially disrupts classwork or involves substantial disorder or invasion of the rights of others.' The court decided it didn't and overruled the school authorities."

"How do you stand this stuff all day?"

"All right, now thinking about Tinker, tell me what you remember about Goss versus Lopez."

"Absolutely nothing." Dan got up and took a slug of orange juice from the cardboard carton. It turned to acid in his stomach.

"It's 1975, it's a test case on due process."

"More First Amendment stuff?"

"Fourteenth. Get a handle on your amendments, Danny."

"The only one I remember is the Seventh. 'Thou shalt not commit adultery.' " He straddled the chair, daring the pile of books to go up in smoke before his eyes. The phone rang again, and he lifted the receiver off its cradle and dropped it down again.

"The case came out of racial unrest in three Columbus, Ohio, schools. Kids were suspended for disrupting the educational process, or so the administration said. What they were really worried about was a riot breaking out. So, what the court upheld was the rights of public school students to oral or written notice of the charges, explanation of the evidence against them, and the chance to rebut the charges, before they could be suspended."

"So?" Dan asked wearily.

"Well, the point is clear, or would be if you'd shake the cobwebs out of your head. You were denied due process when you were suspended. We could maybe get them under the Fourth Amendment, too, if we could prove that suspension was cruel and unusual punishment."

"Hey, no, suspension's a free vacation."

"You are unbelievably smart-assed, Danny. I don't know why I bother with this."

"Because you eat this stuff up like pizza."

Saralyn tapped a book with her pencil. The phone rang again. "Just let it ring. Okay, next case. It's an all-black school in Mississippi, in the middle of the sixties civil rights movement. Do you get the scene in your mind?"

"Clearly."

"Now, three students come to school wearing buttons put out by SNCC, the Student Nonviolent Coordinating Committee, and the buttons say ONE MAN, ONE VOTE. Pretty radical idea in Mississippi at the time."

"Don't tell me, let me guess. The kids are suspended, right?"

"Right! Only, some of the parents refuse to roll over and play dead. They take the case to court to prevent the school from enforcing the suspension. The principal argues that the suspension's a reasonable exercise of school discipline, and the Federal District Court agrees. But the case is appealed, and the principal's argument is struck down."

"Students, one, principal, zip."

"Now, keep all that in mind, but here's the one you want to file at the front of your brain, where you can retrieve it easily. It's a 1988 mess that occurred in a little school near Raleigh, North Carolina."

"This is the Vice guy with the Confederate flag?"

"Right, Mark Vice, a ninth-grader. Out of the blue, he shows up at school wearing a Confederate flag sewn on the back of his jeans jacket. Just like in your case, the school principal tells him he can't come to school with this incendiary symbol on, because it's potentially disturbing to the 250 black kids in the school, so he's suspended. His parents have a fit that his free speech rights are being abridged, and they bring the North Carolina Civil Liberties Union into the hullabaloo."

It was too much, and Dan felt the anger rising as persistent as the tide.

"Now, listen closely. Here's the question we have to ask. Was Mark inciting violence? Did he have intention to harm students in the school?"

"That's two questions."

"Because the school and the courts and everyone could stop him flat if they could show that Mark's wearing the flag represented actual 'fighting words' designed to present a clear and present danger, like, for example, you can't shout FIRE! in a crowded theater."

"You know, I'm starting to hate Mark Vice, and he used to be such a nice guy. I'll bet he was an Eagle Scout."

"Yeah, a model citizen. But here's the thing, Danny. It doesn't go to court. Mark Vice's lawyer negotiates with the school, and they all agree to do some quality education instead."

"Wow! I can see the headline; I'm really into headlines these days: SCHOOL CHOOSES EDUCATION INSTEAD OF EXPENSIVE AND BORING COURT BATTLE."

"Refreshing choice, isn't it, but not as decisive as going to court, you understand. Anyway, the first thing they've got to do is to make sure all the kids in the school hear all the points of view — what Mark's First Amendment rights are, what the school's rights and responsibilities are, how the black students feel, and so forth. Then they have discussions in all the classes about whether hate speech ought to be protected under the Constitution, and over whether Mark's wearing this flag actually results in a disruption of the educational process. So what do they decide, Dan?"

"To send Mark Vice to the gas chamber? To burn down the school? No, no, wait, I've got it. They decide to send him to Hollywood to make a movie. They call it *Mark Vice Squad*, or maybe *Fascist Times at Ridgemont High*."

"Get serious, Dan, this is your life we're talking about. What the students decide is that wearing a symbol such as a Confederate flag" — she glared at him — "or a swastika doesn't represent fighting words and clear and present danger, and that free speech should apply to everybody, not just to the people whose ideas you agree with."

Dan slammed the top layers of books shut. "That's it. I'm going out."

"You can't," Saralyn said quietly. "You'll be mobbed out there."

The phone rang again, and Dan snatched it up, ready to swear at whoever was on the other end.

"This is Loc."

"Who? Oh."

"You gonna pick me up at school?"

"Not for a while."

"I don't understand what's going on."

"I don't either, Loc. But I've had a hundred calls, and I think yours is the only one so far that makes any sense."

Saralyn continued poring over the books and scribbling notes on her yellow legal pad. Dan took the phone off the hook and turned on the TV. The stubborn set refused to come into focus, but the audio was clear. A news conference was in progress. The picture faded in, and Dan saw a woman in her seventies, with her hair piled in red curls, and she was doing her best to seduce the press.

"Yes, I live next door to the Corner Store on Twenty-eighth and Arapahoe. I'm no busybody, but I just happened to be sitting in my window crocheting a baby bunting. My granddaughter's expecting, you know. So I saw two boys go into the store."

A reporter interrupted her. "Could you describe them?"

"Well, if you mean were they white or black, I can say for sure they were two young men of the white persuasion. Anyway, they must have parked in the back. My gold Buick was the only car in the lot. The Corner Store's my personal garage, you see, because it's always light there.

"Well, then, a neighborhood boy came down the street and went into the store. I must have finished about nine rows on my bunting, and nobody came out of the store. So I put a mackintosh on over my nightie, and I went over to see if that sweet boy who works there was okay. I said something like, 'Yoo hoo, anybody there?' "

This was getting to be more than a sound byte, and one of the reporters cut to the chase. "Why have you come to the authorities with your story after all this time, Mrs. Hennessy?"

"Well, because I know who the boy is, the last one who went into the store that night."

"Can you positively identify him?"

"Well I ought to be able to! He's on the news all the time. He's that Daniel Penner, the Nazi boy."

CHAPTER TWENTY-SEVEN

"I've got to get out of here."

Saralyn clutched his arm. "Danny, you're not going to run away, are you?"

"Watch me." He snatched up some gloves, a hat, a scarf, and his jacket from the front closet. "Tell Mom I'm okay."

"You're not."

"Lie, then."

"Laurel? Did you hear?" Joy's voice on the phone was exuberant, though she tried to cover it with dripping sympathy. "It's just so sad. Are you devastated?"

"I knew." Laurel whispered, so no one in the house would hear her. Her family was treating her like a grieving widow, smiling bravely, squeezing her hand, speaking in hushed, funeral parlor tones. But of course Laurel had known for days that Dan had lied about that night in the store. She'd known that he and his skinhead friends were responsible for leaving the Iranian kid blind in one eye.

"I'll come right over, do you want me to?"

"No, Joy. You just call everybody you know, especially all the people in your FemPower group, and tell them you were right all along about Dan."

"I never said — "

"You didn't have to." Laurel hung up on her ex-best friend.

K.C. was waiting for him at Dolby's. "Great time for a winter camping trip, hunh?" He stood in the middle of a heap of outback gear.

Dolby came out of the kitchen with two overflowing Safeway sacks. "Lucky break — it's my mom's grocery day."

They loaded the pickup and covered the stash with a canvas tarp. K.C. said, "Two of you are gonna have to freeze your asses off back here with the gear, because we've got to put the kid inside in case any cops get nosy."

The kid? Dan thought of Saffron's little coal-eyed baby again, but that made no sense. Then his stomach lurched as he thought they'd gotten to the Iranian again.

A minute later Scott came up from the basement, and he wasn't alone.

"Hey, Dan!" Loc said, stepping forward shyly. He still held his Vietnamese workbook.

K.C. said, "Chinaboy's our insurance policy."

Patrick did his best to bring some levity into a household that had grown too somber. At six-thirty he grabbed the car keys and said, "Don't bother

Laurel, Mom, I'll go pick up Loc." But Laurel couldn't stand hanging around the house another minute, so she went with Patrick.

A sappy Christmas song twanged along on the car radio. "I'm dreaming of a white Christmas . . ."

The last light went out on the third floor of Catholic Social Services.

". . . just like the ones I used to know."

Pretty soon, Mrs. Truong came out of the building, and Patrick honked for her.

She seemed flustered when she saw them. "Loc was the first one out of the class," Mrs. Truong said. "Before I dismissed."

Laurel's heart started racing — *oh no, oh no.*

"Maybe that American boy picked him up again."

The truck gasped and wheezed all the way up Canyon Boulevard into the Flatirons. "It's overheating," K.C. muttered. He pulled over to the side of the road, and Dolby immediately knocked on the window from the bed of the truck. They must have been freezing out there. K.C. stuck his head out the window. "I had to stop, couldn't help it." When he turned out the headlights, the huge shards of flat rock went black.

Loc was unnerved by the dark. "Where we going?"

"I told you," Dan said, "to this guy Steve's cabin." The word conjured up a cozy mountain retreat, with moose heads on the walls, and a great stone fireplace, and a sleeping loft. Dan had stayed in a place like that once, the time his father took him and the girls skiing.

Loc shivered; he had no fat to burn. "It's cold with the heat off."

"Shut the chink up," K.C. hissed.

After a while, the radiator cooled a bit, and they continued their climb. The city of Boulder was more than a mile high, and now they were probably a thousand feet above Boulder.

"There's sure not anyone up here," Dan observed.

"That's the point."

Loc's skinny body shifted around, and the more he wriggled, the more nervous Dan got. After all, this was a new experience, having half the cops in Colorado looking for you. And when they caught up with him, they'd get him for kidnapping, too. *If* they caught up with him. Maybe they'd all just conveniently freeze to death.

"I didn't get dinner," Loc said.

"I told you to shut him up."

Dan tapped Loc's shoulder as a warning. After another couple hundred feet of twists and turns, Loc said, "I'm gonna throw up."

K.C. slammed on the brakes and jumped out of the truck.

"What's his problem?" asked Loc. "I was just kidding."

"Not a good idea. K.C. doesn't have a great sense of humor, Loc."

Back in the driver's seat, K.C. hunched over the

wheel, looking for any landmarks in the dark sameness. The headlights revealed two big boards nailed together in an X, and painted on the top plank was the word DRAPERS. Dolby knocked on the window again as a signal, and K.C. turned into a path that was barely long enough or wide enough for the truck.

Ahead was the cabin. Dan's heart dropped. It was little more than a lean-to, with all the windows busted out, and a haphazard roof slung across the top. No chimney. So much for the blazing fire. So much for chili heated in a kettle over the open fire. No moose heads, either, and probably no plumbing.

Dan felt the truck shimmy as Dolby and Scott jumped out.

"Yeah, this is our Hilton Hotel," K.C. said, with great relief in his voice. "As soon as I get in, I'm ordering room service."

The first place Laurel and Patrick went was Dan's house. Mrs. Penner was the only one home.

She rubbed the sleep out of her eyes. "The phone kept ringing and ringing, until I went out like a light on Sudi's bed. Honestly, I thought Dan and Saralyn were still out here working." She glanced back, as though they might reappear in her next eyeblink. "I'm sorry. Danny hasn't been himself lately."

Back in the car, Laurel mulled over that comment. Who was Danny when he *was* himself? Did she ever know? Did *he* even know?

As soon as they broke the news at home, Mr. Grady called the police. They'd already been looking for Dan, and now they were looking for Dan and Loc together. "That would make him easier to find," the police officer assured Dad.

Laurel's parents argued over whose fault it all was. They blamed themselves, not each other, because that's the kind of marriage they had. Her mom had to restrain her dad from getting in the van and wildly driving all over Boulder County to find Loc. Meanwhile, Laurel slipped upstairs to call Dan's lawyer — if she could remember her name. It was some kind of bird, Laurel thought, a P bird. Pelican? Penguin? It couldn't be peregrine falcon. Falcon. Maybe it was an F bird. Finch? She turned to Attorneys in the *Yellow Pages* and ran her finger down the list, looking for any kind of bird.

The Coleman lamp shed light, but didn't much brighten the dreary shack. They'd have been better off without the light to show the piles of animal droppings, the spiderwebs, the shards of glass, the dead bugs frozen since fall. Dolby swept the hut out as well as he could with his boot, and they spread the sleeping bags on the floor as a carpet.

"The butler's getting dinner," K.C. said as Scott took out a loaf of Wonder Bread and a package of baloney. There was nothing to spread on the bread. Dolby tore into a big bag of Ruffles.

Loc thought it was a picnic. "The mother always makes potato salad for picnics."

"Yeah, well, the only mother we've got is Saffron, and she's looking for her old man in Cheyenne."

"That's okay," Loc said. "I don't like girls anyway." He stuffed half a baloney sandwich in his mouth.

"Go easy," Dolby warned. "That's all the food we've got. Who knows how long we'll be up here?"

"Maybe 'til the revolution starts?" Scott said.

After they ate, they just sank into their coldness. It was too dark to try to start a fire, and there wasn't a good movie on cable — or a TV, or even electricity, so K.C. told them all to go to sleep. "We'll make plans in the daylight, after we can get a fire going. Hey, it's got to be at least seven o'clock. You zonk out fast in this healthy mountain air."

Laurel's finger stopped at Phoenix, that was it, Aurelia Phoenix.

The lawyer answered the phone on the first ring. "Yeah?"

"This is Laurel Grady, a friend of Dan's." Once.

"Is he with you?"

"No," Laurel said, and for the first time she felt tears damming up behind her eyes. "But wherever he is, he's taken my brother with him. Loc, he's only eleven. Also Vietnamese."

"You realize your friend gets crazier by the day?"

"I know."

"Why did you call me, Laurel?"

"I didn't know who else to call. The police know, I guess you know that."

"Good news travels fast."

"I was hoping, well, I think maybe you're the only one who can help Dan."

The lawyer let out a deep sigh. "I'll do what I can."

They were short one sleeping bag. Dolby said Loc ought to go without, since he was the hostage. "The kid's lucky we're letting him sleep inside the cabin." Loc jerked his head toward Dan, but Dan tried to ignore him.

"Wait," Scott said. "I think Demon should give up his sleeping bag, because he didn't bring any gear of his own, and besides, he's the reason we're on the run."

Did Scott forget that his was the boot that landed on the Iranian's face? In the jungle, the animals have to declare their dominance, or they're breakfast. Dan said, "I'm taking a bag, and Loc's taking a bag, and Scott better take a bag, because he's too wimpy to survive the night without it. I guess that means you two handsome studs will just have to curl up together in one sleeping bag." That was enough to send homophobes like K.C. and Dolby into the shakes. Dan laughed, and Loc mimicked him, and Scott sort of looked back and forth trying to figure out what he'd missed.

Finally, K.C. and Dolby and Scott each got a sleeping bag, and Dan unzipped the bulkiest one and spread it across him and Loc. The floor was hard, cold, and crunchy with mysterious lumps. Loc was asleep in minutes, his head resting on his Vietnamese book, but Dan lay awake for hours, it seemed, listening to the deep breathing and snorty night sounds of the other guys, and the hooting of wild things outside. He refused to sleep, because he knew it would be the last night before he was caught. The next night he would sleep somewhere where he couldn't hear anything but his own breathing.

CHAPTER TWENTY-EIGHT

The Tropicana orange juice was slush, and they'd need a pickax for the milk. So they ate dry cornflakes, washed down with handfuls of snow. They turned the snow yellow around the back of the shack. Nobody ever warmed up enough to stop shaking. When the sun came out, they moved outside; even the wind was better than the bone-chill in the shack, because the wind was blessed with thin streaks of sunlight.

Scott gathered wood for a fire, most of the sticks green and wet. "If I could just get it going?" He poked and worried a few twigs that were too swollen with snow even to snap, and when there was the slightest spark, all the guys huddled to protect it from the wind.

Dolby's face was blue. "We could throw the kid in for kindling."

Loc looked to Dan for reassurance, and Dan said, "Why don't we burn your coat and jeans, Dolby? It would be a small sacrifice in the revolution for white supremacy. You could be a martyr."

Scott looked like he was actually considering this idea and might have leaped forward to snatch Dolby's coat, when a bolt of fire shot up. They all cheered like the cavemen must have when the first fire ignited and turned their faces crisp. Then Scott coaxed the fire and tended it like a shepherd.

K.C. debated about what to toast first, his hands or his feet, and finally he took off his boots and put his gray-black socks up close to the flame. Dan imagined how cold those nipple rings must be feeling about now against K.C.'s skin. He'd have to remember that. Reason #846 Not to Get Your Nipples Pierced: You might be stranded in the Andes, or the Flatirons, and ooh baby, that's cold.

K.C. called the meeting to order. There being no minutes from the previous freeze-out, he began telling them their business. "Okay, we're going to stay here another night, until Chinaboy's family is ready to sell their daughters into white slavery just to get the kid back."

Dan dropped his head, and Dolby sneered at him. "Watch it. Demon's hot and heavy with Chinaboy's sister."

Loc said, "She doesn't like him anymore."

K.C.'s foot shot out at Loc's hip. "Keep your mouth shut unless I tell you to talk."

Loc scurried right up against Dan and said boldly, "Anyway, I'm not Chinese, I'm Vietnamese."

K.C. generously ignored him and went on with

the battle plan. "Now, after a couple of days, they'll be ready to negotiate. What, Demon, you don't approve? What's the big deal? They're polluters. They've got about nine races all sitting down at the same table for dinner. You've got a sister, don't you, Chinaboy, who's not even pure of any race? I mean, it turns my stomach to think how *that* kid got made."

"Kim's okay," Loc said. He was starting to get fidgety, as though he might blow a fuse. Dan gave him an elbow jab, while K.C. went on.

"In case you haven't noticed, *amigos*, we're in major trouble."

"Big-time trouble," Scott agreed, "and you don't need to talk French to convince me."

"I'm not in trouble." Dolby scuttled to his feet. "I wasn't there that night in the store, and I wasn't in the barn when you guys cooked up that harebrained story about the black-dude crackheads." He thrust his palms up. "I'm clean."

"Sit down." K.C. waited a second. "Sit DOWN." Dolby decided to obey K.C. for the time being. K.C. got his temper under control and said, "We're all brothers, except for Chinaboy, of course. We're in this together. Don't let's forget our purpose here — to make the world a safer place for whites."

Dan thought about the hordes of people at the demonstration, and the threatening phone calls, and all the cops waking up to a fresh day of Dan-hunting. He looked at the gray slabs of ice and the new snow dotted by the beaks of starving birds, and the pink granite flat rocks that jutted out about sixteen hundred feet above Boulder, and at the red-orange spiked roofs of Boulder way below them. It sure didn't *feel* like a safer place for whites.

K.C. read his mind, as usual. "We're soldiers in this war, Demon. Soldiers don't have it easy."

Dolby interpreted. "So, you're saying we hang tight until Chinaboy's folks are ready to deal. And then we get 'em to promise we can get away safely, and they can have their kid back. You think they'd want him back?"

K.C. said, "Oh, probably. Maybe they think he's that reincarnated monk. Did you read about it in the papers? Some Tibetan Chinaman kid is supposed to be this Buddhist lama-priest-monk guy who died fifty years ago. There's probably good money in it for them, if they take him on the road."

"K.C., sometimes you amaze me," Dan said.

"Hey, sometimes I amaze myself," he replied with a grin.

Then Dolby asked, "So, how are we supposed to contact his folks?"

"Simple, Dolby. You're not involved, remember? No one's looking for you. So you take the pickup down the mountain tonight, and at the crack of dawn, you're their breakfast guest."

Scott asked, "What if he screws up?"

K.C. laughed. "Well, Scott, I think Dolby's going to do just great at the breakfast table with Chinaboy's wacko family. His AK-47 isn't exactly something you pull out of a box of Cheerios."

* * *

Laurel gave the police the names of anyone she could think of who'd ever had anything to do with Dan, even Tracy Maris from Limon.

On Friday night, Laurel and Patrick saw on TV that Mr. Herrington unlocked the school, and he and the police were poring over records and searching lockers. All bets were off on those constitutional niceties everybody had been harping on. Suddenly, when the life of an eleven-year-old child is in danger, no one worries about free speech, illegal search and seizure, probable cause, equal protection of the law, or due process.

TV 4 said, "It's the law of the jungle out there, and the only concern of the authorities is to force Daniel Penner, the neo-Nazi skinhead and alleged kidnapper, into the clearing where they can spot him and bring Loc Grady home to his frantic family."

And they *were* frantic. Laurel couldn't sleep Friday night. She huddled under her comforter, listening for a scratching at her window or a stone pelting it, in hopes that Dan would come in out of the cold as he had before. Suddenly, Kim bolted up in bed, screaming, as she apparently relived some horror from her earlier life. When she finally calmed down and was only trembling in Laurel's arms, she asked, "Where's Loc?"

"We'll have a better idea in the morning, Sweetie."

Her brown eyes were huge in the eerie nightlight. "Are they gonna come and take me, too?"

Laurel pulled her close and whispered into her

wooly hair, "No, Sweetie, we'd never let that happen."

But, of course, that was exactly what they worried about — that the insane skinheads would pluck off Laurel's sister and brothers, one by one. Look how easy it was for them to get Loc, and Kim was their most logical next target.

Dad had called a family conference right after the police left their house. If they hadn't already guessed how serious this was, they were convinced by the fact that he arranged them by age, like the children in *The Sound of Music*. This was to remind them that each of them was responsible for the next youngest child. There was a painful gap between Jonathan and Gary, where Loc should have been.

Their parents stood across from the rest of the family. Mrs. Grady's eyes were ringed with red. Her pocket bulged with used Kleenex tissues. Mr. Grady looked hunched over as he set down the ground rules. "No one is to leave this house until all this is settled. That means no one will go to church, to school, to work, to the grocery store, or anywhere. Is that clear?"

"Yes sir," they all said.

"This is an absolute no-exception rule, children."

Mrs. Grady backed him up. "Because we're safe here. No one can hurt us in our own home."

There wasn't much to do for kicks. They couldn't exactly go fishing in the little patches of meltwater that pooled in the worn rocks. Water skiing was out, for obvious reasons, as was synchronized swimming and any number of other Olympic events. But Dan knew that if they all spent the day, and the next, just begging some warmth from the fire, they'd get on each other's nerves pretty fast, and something ugly would happen. Already Dolby was saying, "K.C., you're famous for half-assed ideas. I don't really think Chinaboy's gonna be our ticket to ride."

And Scott added, "Hey, we're always talking about blood in the streets? About how the white revolution has to start by turning the streets red?" He leaned back, hung his head over a jutting rock. "It's a long way down from here, get what I mean?" Scott shoved Loc to the edge of the giant boulder. Dan grabbed Loc's arm before the kid lost his balance. Dan couldn't bear to see the terror in Loc's face. What he saw, though, wasn't fear at all, but hard eyes and lips set in defiance.

"Demon, Demon, this is war," K.C. reminded him. "You can't be so soft on the enemy."

"Jesus, K.C., he's an eleven-year-old kid."

"He's a living symbol," K.C. said gruffly.

"Of what? Of what bullies we are?"

"No, Demon," K.C. explained patiently. "He's a symbol of what we're losing. It's like the song says, 'Put up a fence/Close down the borders./They don't fit in/In our new order.' "

"Shut up — there's something out there." Dolby jumped to his feet. They heard the whine of a vehicle making its way up the mountain.

K.C. whispered, "Dan, take the kid back into the trees and keep him quiet. I mean QUIET. Scott, kill the fire. Me and Dolby are going to get into our sleeping bags and act like we're in dreamland. Scott, if anybody comes, you're just out there taking a leak. And all of you, keep your hats on."

A horn tooted as the driver signaled his arrival to any oncoming cars around the bend on the icy, narrow pass.

Dan pushed Loc ahead of him into the trees, which were too bare to provide much cover. "Lie down."

"In the snow?"

"Do what I say. If you make a sound, I swear, they'll kill you." Loc flattened himself in the snow. Dan lay beside him, with his arm flung over Loc to hold him down. He saw a Dodge Caravan appear like a mirage at the crest of the hill. A park ranger got out and walked across the road to the shack. The air was so thin, the mountains so still, and the canyon worked like an echo chamber, so Dan heard most of the exchange in the shack.

"What's going on here?"

Dan pictured K.C. lifting himself up on one elbow, faking surprise to see a stranger looming over him. He heard him say, "Morning, sir. Is there a problem?"

"I saw smoke. Kinda unusual this time of the year, up here."

"Yeah, well, me and a couple friends are having a winter campout. You must have seen what's left of our fire."

Dolby faked a sleepy voice, too. "I could use a little flame right now. Man, my feet are frozen." Dan imagined him fingering the AK-47 inside the sleeping bag. He'd have no problem blowing the ranger's head off.

K.C. said, "Things must be kind of slow for park rangers this time of year. Well, maybe not over on the ski mountains, but this one's all bald rocks."

"I keep busy," the ranger said. "Mind if I look around?"

"Naw, naw, not at all. Hey, where's what's-his-name? You'll probably find our other friend outside. He's, like, relieving himself."

"Only one guy? How come I see two other sleeping bags?"

Good old K.C. always could think fast. "We brought an extra in case something happened. You can't be too careful when you're camping in the mountains in the dead of winter. But it didn't seem fair to give it to any one of us last night, so we voted to just let it warm the floor. Hey, that's the kind of guys we are."

"Um-hmn."

Dan heard snow crunch under the ranger's boots as he went out to investigate around the shack. K.C. and Dolby apparently stayed inside so they wouldn't arouse suspicion. They sure didn't want a casual search to turn up Dolby's toy that didn't come from a Cheerios box.

Dan put his lips up to Loc's ear and whispered, "I've got to do something. One peep out of you, and you're dead meat. Kim, too." He grabbed a handful of hair and jerked Loc's head up. "Understand?" Loc nodded slightly under Dan's grip. Then Dan slipped away.

The ranger had found Scott and was checking him out at the front of the shack. Dan stole around the back, careful to step in silent places where boot-prints had already left tracks in the ice. At the clearing, he dropped to the ground. His jacket rode up as he began slithering across the road to the Caravan. Patches of ice soaked through his shirt; rocks tore at his belly. But he didn't dare stand up and draw fire.

To be safe, he continued his belly crawl around the back of the Caravan, to the passenger's side. The radio crackled with some message from the dispatcher — noise cover for Dan. He opened the door of the car, scared that the ranger would hear the dispatcher's voice get louder, but he pulled a small square from his jeans pocket and did what he had to do, fast.

Then he began the grueling journey back on his belly to Loc, reassured that the park ranger wouldn't even have the car in drive before he spotted the blue cover from Loc's Vietnamese book.

CHAPTER TWENTY-NINE

The first glimmer of hope came about eight o'clock Friday morning, when Laurel's dad was called to go down to the police station.

"I'm sorry, I can't leave my family," he told the officer on the phone. "We've made a pact to stay together. However, why don't you come out to the house?" When he hung up, the color drained from his face. "What if the policeman had said no, he wouldn't come?"

A few minutes later, the plainclothesman, who introduced himself as Detective Evan Coynes, sat in their living room, sipping Mrs. Grady's sassafras tea. He looked too large for the furniture.

Laurel and her parents waited nervously, their hands in their laps, like defendants watching for the jury to file back in. Finally, Detective Coynes hoisted his briefcase up onto his lap. The unsnapping sounded like prison locks. And then Laurel wondered if maybe he had very bad news for them. He slid a blue page sealed in plastic out of his briefcase, turning the I.D. tag so they couldn't read it. "Can you identify this?"

Laurel recognized it immediately. "It's from Loc's book. He translated the title for me once: *Old Land/New Land*."

"You found Loc? Is he all right?" Mrs. Grady's face was as pale as soap.

"All I can tell you is that his bookcover was placed on the car seat of a park ranger while he was out of the vehicle on a routine inspection."

Laurel's mother asked, "What does that mean, Detective?"

"I can't say any more without compromising the case."

At least it meant that *someone* knew where Loc was!

"There may be further communication from the perpetrator or perpetrators," the detective explained. "We'd like to send a technician over to monitor your phone. Meanwhile, we're continuing our investigation."

"Any sign of the young fellow, Daniel Penner?"

"I can't say, Mr. Grady. Stand by for further developments."

"You can be sure we will," Mrs. Grady said quietly.

K.C. ordered them into the shed.

"What about a fire?" Scott asked. They all looked longingly at the smoldering wood. Even the ashes seemed inviting.

"Can't afford to have a fire. We've got to stay

inside in case anyone else comes snooping around." Dolby balked, but K.C. said, "Listen, this is war. You think those soldiers over there in the Persian Gulf worried about air conditioning and ice cubes in their Cokes, while they snorted that desert sand up their noses? No. We've got to have military discipline, men."

"What an inspiring leader," Dan said.

"Why, thank you, Demon."

They sat on the floor, huddled close, to pool what little body warmth they had. Even a hot breath felt good, but smelled bad. Loc tucked his hands under each armpit and soon toppled over, asleep on Dan's arm. Dan waited, listened, his eye on the gun propped up by the door. Not that he'd know what to do with it, if he picked it up. But, still, if someone came back looking for them . . .

After a while, Dolby said, "Man, this is real boring. Anybody bring a deck of cards?"

"We could tell ghost stories?" Scott suggested.

K.C. slapped him on the back like a soldier buddy and said, "Yeah, we're regular Boy Scouts at Camp Run-A-Muck."

They fell into an itchy silence again, waiting — for what? In the daylight, Dan thought, the cabin/shack looked slightly more inviting. It was made of good cedar, but slapped together. One broken window still had a red-and-white-checked curtain hanging over it, turning the sun pink. The bare windowframe next to it allowed a slat of sunlight into the shack, and as it moved, they all moved their circle to capture the strip of warmth.

Anxiously scanning the room for some kind, any kind, of stimulation, Dan spotted the Vietnamese book on the floor to his left. Would anyone notice the missing cover? What if Loc woke up and said something about it? Dan reached out, as if he were taking a leisurely stretch. Loc clunked to his lap, and Dan was pinned in place. The book was just out of reach.

"Almost lunchtime?" Dolby asked.

"Yeah, if you eat lunch at eight-thirty in the morning," Dan said.

"Cold as we are, we could be our own Popsicles." Dolby ran his tongue across his dry lips.

With a bitter laugh, K.C. said, "At least we won't be Fudgsicles."

"We're still the pure white race," Scott said dreamily.

"And we're still sitting around in Siberia." K.C. got up and walked around the room; the circle closed in tighter.

They all heard the roar at the same time.

Someone's coming, Dan told himself. What was the plan? No plan. He was a pretty crummy strategic officer. How come the *Star Trek* crew always had a strategy? The plan was just not to get anyone killed, yes, that was the strategy. The noise grew louder until it seemed to be roaring from inside Dan's head.

K.C. opened the door.

"See anything?" asked Scott.

"Jesus, it's a goddam helicopter." K.C. jumped

back into the cabin, and Dolby crouched under a window, his gun ready.

"They'll never spot this shack in the trees," K.C. reassured them. "And if nobody's outside and nothing's moving, they'll fly right over and never know what they missed." K.C. darted from window to window. Again, Dan was reminded of how catlike K.C. could be — cunning, studying you with those heartless eyes, ready to spring.

The helicopter seemed to be spinning in a smaller circle now, hovering just over the trees. In a minute, they heard a garbled voice: "We know you're in there. Come out with your hands up." K.C. signaled them to stay still. The voice from the chopper was more insistent. "Come out with your hands in the air."

Dan jabbed Loc so he'd be awake, alert. This was *it*.

But K.C. had other plans. "We'll lay low 'til they move on."

The prop sputtered, and the voicc from the sky boomed again. "You might as well come out, because you're surrounded. Now, be good boys and don't make us act nasty."

K.C. confirmed the news. "There's half a dozen cars out there. You'd think this was the goddam David Koresh compound."

Must have been covered by the helicopter roar.

K.C. snapped his fingers, and Dolby jumped to his side. "Demon, you're going out for cover. Shove the kid in front of you."

Dan tried to reason with him. *Helicopter? Six cop cars? Come on.* "Give it up, K.C., this is stupid."

K.C. spun around, his eyes smoldering coals. "Don't EVER call Kevin Cabot stupid." He jerked Loc to his feet and shoved him toward the door. Snapping his fingers again, he motioned Dan into position right behind Loc, and Dolby behind Dan. K.C. stood flat against the wall. "Scott, throw the door open and drop to the floor."

Dan felt the blast of cold wind on his face as he thrust Loc ahead of him. *Cops everywhere, guns.* Fighting down sour juices, an untimely thought flickered through his mind: *If the guys in Limon could see me now.*

K.C.'s voice came from inside the shack. "Any one of you make a move and Dolby's gonna splatter the snow with Chinaboy's brains. Drop your guns."

The cop in charge nodded, and one by one they dropped their weapons.

Dan held Loc out in front of him, his wrist tight against Loc's throat. His knees buckled, his feet were numb. *Can't hold me up much longer.* If he went down, Loc would tumble with him, and Dolby would blow them both away. *Have to stay on my feet. Loc shaking. Puke in my throat. Lips cracked, bleeding. Who cares? Real blood's gonna flow.*

The cop yelled out, "Tell us what you want."

Go home. Warm. Go back a year. Before.

K.C. shouted, "We want you to clear out. We'll get off this mountain and leave the kid here. Nobody wants Chinaboy hurt."

The cop whispered something over his shoulder. *Dolby tense behind me*. The cop said, "Give us the kid first."

Then Dan heard Scott's voice: "You think we're that stupid?" There was a rocking thud, as Scott apparently fell to the floor under K.C.'s blow.

Loc moved his head around to make eye contact with Dan, so slowly that Dolby wouldn't even notice the movement. Dan read his face. *Has a plan. Alert. Follow lead.*

K.C. was saying, "Send the helicopter back, and all you guys get out of here. My friend's trigger finger's getting itchy."

No one moved. Suddenly, Loc threw his weight forward, in one of those moves Dan had taught him, and Dan crashed down on top of him. It was enough distraction for one cop to fling himself against Dolby and knock the weapon out of his arms. With a knee to Dolby's kidneys, the cop wrestled him to the ground, like a champion cattle wrangler.

Some place warm, but not home. No way home now.

A doctor dug flecks of gravel out of Dan's belly and bandaged him up. He spent the night in the county jail, with nothing to do but watch the swirls of ink on his thumbprint and feel the fire on his stomach. He had no roommate, maybe because he was too famous, or considered too dangerous, or maybe white supremacist kidnappers weren't the most popular guys in lockup.

The room wasn't so bad. It had a narrow bed with a brown wool government-issue blanket, and a bare metal desk and an empty bookcase. A few books and posters might have made it a livable dorm room for Sudi. But it had no windows, and the heavy metal door slammed shut automatically. Dan's teeth hurt as the lock slid into place with the sickening sound of a spoon scraping across a skillet.

He drifted off to sleep under the blanket, wondering when the warmth of the room would penetrate the thick layer of fear that kept him so cold inside.

The door burst open. Aurelia Phoenix slipped into the room and told the guard, "Fifteen minutes." The door locked behind her. Dan sat up, backed up to the cement wall that was the color of stale egg yolks. Aurelia Phoenix kicked off her shoes and sat on the end of the bed with her legs tucked under her. Her briefcase gaped open at Dan's feet.

"So." She handed him a stick of sugarless gum, which he greedily folded into his mouth. He couldn't remember when he'd eaten last, or what. The lawyer worked the gum in her own mouth and said, "Your mother's waiting out there, and your father's on his way."

"My father? He couldn't be."

"I'm getting you out of here and sending you back with him as soon as I can swing it."

Could it be that easy? Could he just walk out of this cell and get on a plane bound for Portland, Maine, and leave all this behind him?

Aurelia Phoenix gave him a look that made the newborn hope shrivel up inside him. "We're talking felony, Babe. And you're eighteen. They can try you as an adult. Hey, your show's folding in this town, either way. You're not exactly the Kiwanis Man of the Year. You better pray for a miracle up there with the gulls in Maine, Penner." She pulled a notepad out of her briefcase. "Let's get down to business, starting with the minute you walked into that Corner Store."

When the guard came back in fifteen minutes, Aurelia Phoenix waved him away. "This is gonna take a while," she said. "Don't call me, I'll call you."

Loc's frostbitten toes were treated in the emergency room, with police all around the Gradys. Mrs. Grady was given the name of a child psychologist at the university who agreed to see Loc after lunch. Laurel and Loc and their parents went to Tom's Tavern, on the Pearl Street Mall. It was so quiet on this December afternoon, although holiday shoppers slipped in and out of the shops. Generic winter music played — things like "Jingle Bells" and "Winter Wonderland," because Boulder city leaders would never allow anything so politically incorrect as actual *Christmas* music in the public mall.

The best thing on the menu at Tom's Tavern was its hamburgers, and Loc packed away two of them, an order of onion rings, and some chili. He held the bowl up to his chin and forgot all about his chopsticks. Mrs. Grady just let him shovel the chili into his mouth with a spoon. He didn't even notice that the rest of them could barely swallow.

After lunch Mr. Grady dropped them off on campus at the psychologist's building, and he went to park the car in Mrs. Grady's faculty spot across campus. Loc hobbled up the steps, Laurel and her mother each supporting an arm. Someone had scratched in the stone of the building, "Soon to be picturesque ruins."

"Won't we all be," Laurel's mother said with a nervous snicker.

While they waited at the top of the steps, Loc asked, "What's he gonna do to me in there?"

"He just has some questions, Darling."

"Well, I won't tell him anything."

"Why not?" Mrs. Grady asked calmly, but Laurel heard the underlying anxiety in her voice.

"Because they'll blame it all on Dan. It wasn't his fault. If it wasn't for Dan, I'd be dead."

Mrs. Grady glanced at Laurel, probably noticing how liquid her eyes were all of a sudden.

"That's what I'm telling the doctor in there. I'm telling him that Dan's still my best friend."

CHAPTER THIRTY

Laurel's parents were already in the courtroom. She had dropped them off and gone to find a parking place. It seemed like everyone in town was here for opening day of Dan's trial, and Laurel had to park three blocks away. A gentle spring wind was blowing dandelion fluff through the air as she walked up the steps of the courthouse.

"Friends?" Joy came up behind Laurel, her hands out, ready to reopen their friendship. "Isn't it time, finally?"

"I guess so." Laurel gave her a shallow hug, "Have you heard from Stanford yet?"

"I'm in," Joy said simply. "But I have sad news about Bella Donna Prozac. She had a tough winter. The FemPower Coalition buried her in my backyard with great pomp and ceremony. Her gravestone says, 'Here Lies a Boulder High Homecoming Queen.' "

"That should make the next owners of your house stop and think." Laurel responded automatically, but her mind wasn't on this sudden reconciliation. She stood before the nine-foot courtroom doors with their intricate fretwork. When those doors opened, she'd see Dan for the first time in four months.

"I just had to take the day off school to be with you today," Joy explained. "For our used-to-be's."

"Thanks. Go on in, Joy. Mom and Dad have a seat for me in the first row." Laurel needed a moment alone, had to take a deep breath, had to strike a careless pose before she summoned the nerve to go in.

When Joy opened the door, Laurel peeked into the courtroom, hoping to spot Dan before he saw her.

"Hello, Laurel." The voice behind her was familiar and sad, deeper than she remembered. She turned around, and there he was. His hair had grown back light brown and wasn't summer-blond yet. New glasses made him look about twenty, until he smiled. There was a new tooth where the ugly gap, the reminder, had been.

In Colorado, they were already picking daffodils, but spring was slower to come to Maine, where Dan was living with his father, and so his face seemed scrubbed and pale. "It must be gorgeous up in Maine." What a ridiculous comment, but then what else do you say to a person you once loved who's turned your life into a melodrama? She asked, "Is it okay living with your father?"

"We get along. How's Loc?"

"Great. Well, not great, but not as angry as he was then."

Dan seemed to understand the *then* and *now*, probably had his own set of thens and nows. In the months since it had all begun ending at the Mall Crawl, Laurel had found herself compartmentalizing time into BDC and ADC, Before Dan's Craziness and After Dan's Craziness, just as historians mark the time before and after the birth of Jesus. Before Dan's Craziness, Loc had been angry and hostile. After Dan's Craziness, Loc was just a wiry, watchful kid. Well, kidnap a boy, turn his toes to frostbite, hold a gun to his head, and it's amazing what it does to assimilate a kid who'd built a whole eleven-year career out of being an outsider.

Laurel spotted Dan's mother and sisters, hanging back from the conversation. They all wore gray suits and white blouses. Saralyn carried a briefcase. Laurel thought about the day Saralyn had spoken to her class, how she'd waved her glasses and gotten so worked up over freedom of speech; how she'd defended the skinheads' right to hold the rally.

Then Laurel heard the clickety-clack of heels echoing in the marble halls as Aurelia Phoenix, Dan's lawyer, made her grand entrance. She was out of breath and clutching her mid-section.

She slid right in between Dan and Laurel. "Show time, Penner. Here's where we work like little Trojans to keep your head off the guillotine. Pardon me, ladies, for my internationally mixed metaphors." She pointed toward the forbidding doors, but Dan said, "Go on, I'll be right in."

Aurelia Phoenix led the parade of Dan's women. *I used to be one of them*, Laurel thought with a pang. But that was last year, *then*. This is now.

Laurel followed Dan to a bench beside the courtroom doors, wondering what they could possibly say to one another. And, yet, something needed to be said, because there were two red roses rotting in a box on her closet shelf, and a third one, which was never delivered.

"Remember the Mall Crawl?" Dan began.

Laurel just nodded. Were they remembering the same things?

"Remember the two-headed aardvark? And Snow White and the Seven Dorks? And the fat Superman?"

"Vaguely."

"That night was so crazy. It was like a new beginning."

"Instead of the end." Laurel leaned against the cold marble wall. Voices echoed in the great hall. She could hear bursts of conversations, like instruments playing parts of a dozen symphonies at the same time.

Dan's voice stood out in the chorus. "It's not enough to say I'm sorry." He twisted a paper clip he'd pulled out of his suit coat. Probably the last time he'd worn it was for the arraignment in this courtroom, four months earlier. The paper clip snapped, and he tossed the two halves into a potted plant.

Laurel pulled her blazer tight around her. Body language. This means "I'm closed. You can check back tomorrow, but I may still be closed."

She watched Dan struggle with the words that

would not come. Finally, he said, "Whatever happens in there today, I just want you to know I'm really different now. K.C. and Dolby and all of them, I don't hang around with them anymore."

"That's because most of them are in jail."

"I wouldn't, even if they were out."

"Then it's because you live in Maine."

"What do you think, Laurel, there are no K.C.-types back east? One thing I've figured out since this all started, there's hatred wherever you look for it. I don't need it anymore. I'm learning to look away."

"This is good news, Dan."

His eyes pled with her and asked, *Is there a chance?* She wanted to lean over and squeeze his hand, wanted to say to him, "It's okay."

But it wasn't okay. Instead, she got up and pulled him to his feet. "You'd better straighten your tie," she said as she'd heard her mother tell her father a thousand times. And she walked away from him, into the courtroom.

In the front row, her mother scooted over to make room for Laurel next to her father. Just like old times, she thought, when it was only the three of them, before Patrick started the motley parade.

Laurel didn't need to turn around to recognize Dan's footsteps. He sat down at the table right in front of her, never glancing back. A panel in the polished wall opened, and the judge appeared. Laurel heard just the faintest intake of breath in the audience, which had not expected that particular judge.

The bailiff called out, "All rise."

Dan stood up and pushed up the knot of his tie. During the shuffle of feet, Aurelia Phoenix bent toward Dan, and Laurel heard her say, "I'm telling you, Penner, every inch of you better be the repentent sinner. Every bone, every corpuscle, every nerve ending, and every follicle of hair on your head better be oozing regret and remorse."

The judge's eyes glared at Dan. "Be seated."

Again there was a shuffling of feet and chairs, and Aurelia Phoenix's dramatic whisper: "Because, believe me, Penner, Judge Nabuki Yamato doesn't just look at a guy skin deep."

ABOUT THE AUTHOR

Lois Ruby, a former Young Adult librarian, is the author of several novels and short story collections, including *Arriving at a Place You've Never Left,* which was an ALA Best Book for Young Adults, as was her most recent novel for Scholastic, *Miriam's Well.*

Ms. Ruby was born in San Francisco, California, and now lives in Wichita, Kansas, with her husband, who is a psychologist. Their three sons are scattered in interesting cities across the country.